For Susan—
Wishing you much
success.
Roz Lee
AAP '14

Inside Heat

Roz Lee

ISBN: 1470147238
ISBN-13: 978-1470147235

DEDICATION

For Terrell.
Thanks for believing.

ACKNOWLEDGMENTS

Whoever said a writer leads a solitary life didn't know what they were talking about. Sure, I spend hours a day in front of a computer, but many more are spent conversing in person or virtually with the people who encourage, collaborate, consult, cheer, critique and otherwise keep me sane while I translate the stories in my head into words on a page. This book would not have been possible without my friends from the Los Angeles Romance Writers. Much of this book was written during the monthly SPEW weeks (Stop Procrastinating- Everyone Write) led by our head cheerleader – Sarah Vance.

I have to thank my critique partners – Robyn, Carly, and Chellesie for telling me like it is, even when I don't want to hear it.

Many thanks to Mr. W. who not only tried to teach me World History in high school, but lent me his name for one of my characters in this book.

I can't begin to thank my family enough. My dear husband supports my writing career more than I could have ever hoped. After thirty-three years, he's still my best friend, and that's a treasure beyond words. My thanks to our daughters who proudly tell everyone their mother is an author, even if my covers have naked people on them! I'm truly blessed to be loved and supported by such wonderful people.

CHAPTER ONE

Megan leaned over the railing. She stretched her arm out toward the tall guy with the crooked smile and waved the program at him. *Please. Please. Please. Pick me. Come on.* She repeated the mantra in her head, all the while feeling perfectly ridiculous standing in a crowd of pre-adolescents begging for an autograph. To top it off, she wasn't even sure she was waving her program at the right guy. She'd studied Christopher's baseball card, knew the face she needed to find, but unless she missed her guess, the guy had a twin brother, and they both played on the same team. Just her luck.

There wasn't anything she could do about it now. She continued to wave the program at the one closest to her, and prayed he was the pitcher – Christopher's idol. In retrospect, it had been foolish to promise the kid she'd get the autograph for him, but she'd made the promise, and she was going to honor it – somehow.

An endless supply of excited youngsters replaced the ones who had gotten an autograph and left. Megan held her ground amidst jostling bodies and annoyed looks from the other autograph seekers. So what if she was an adult? It wasn't like she wanted the autograph for herself – even if the guy was hot. Seriously hot. She'd thought he was good looking when Christopher handed her the baseball card he kept with him twenty-four/seven. But the card didn't come close to capturing the real Jeff Holder, or was it his brother?

"Hey Jeff!" the kid beside her yelled. The man on the field turned toward her. So this one was the one she sought. Good thing because the other one had his own admirers at the rail. No way would she be able to fight her way through the crowd to get to him in time. Now that she knew she'd had the right guy all along, she renewed her bid for his autograph, waving the program with new enthusiasm. The kid next to her elbowed her in the stomach, accidentally she was sure, and despite being half her size, shoved her hard. Megan made a grab for the seat behind her to keep from falling.

She straightened and turned back to the railing, coming eye to eye with Jeff Holder. Holy cow! The man was gorgeous. Sinfully gorgeous. Cream her panties gorgeous. It had been a long time since she'd had that kind of reaction. Hell, if she were being truthful with herself, she'd never felt that jolt of awareness before. It was as if her body recognized his, and responded.

"Are you all right?" he asked with genuine concern in his deep, testosterone-laden voice.

God, he had beautiful blue eyes, surrounded by dark lashes that contrasted with his blond hair. His eyes focused on hers with pinpoint accuracy while taking in the broader picture all at once. It was more than a little unnerving – and arousing. Megan shoved the thought out of her head as quickly as it had come. She didn't have time in her life for a relationship – not that one was possible with someone like Jeff Holder. A girl could fantasize though.

"Uhm…yes. I think so." She grabbed the rail with her free hand to steady herself.

"Good." He smiled and held out his hand. Megan stared at his even white teeth and his full lips she instinctively knew would feel wonderful on hers. "Did you want an autograph?"

"Uhh…what?"

"Autograph. Do you want one?" He tugged on the program in her hand, and she snapped out of her lustful stupor.

"Oh! Yes, please." She studied his face as he bent his head to scribble his name on her program. *Get a grip.* Megan chastised herself. She wasn't here to ogle the man. She was here to get an autograph for Christopher.

He thrust the program toward her. His gaze raked over her again, as if sizing up an all you can eat smorgasbord. She swallowed hard and pressed the program over her fluttering heart with both hands. "Th...thanks," she stammered. And then he winked at her. *Winked.* She blinked in surprise as he turned his attention to the new crop of autograph seekers.

She hadn't planned to hang around for the game, but that wink must have scrambled her brains because here she was holding onto the railing with a white knuckled grip as she made her way to her seat. Who knew you needed mountain climbing gear at a baseball stadium? One wrong move, a slip of the foot, and she'd tumble all the way down to the field. Yeesh! She dropped into her seat and closed her eyes to stay a wave of dizziness. Megan counted ten deep breaths and concentrated on bringing her heart rate down to an acceptable level before opening her eyes. Below her, *waaaay* below her, the playing field sparkled like an emerald, accented with red-orange and white. It was a spectacular view, as was usually the case from a mountaintop, even if the players were nothing more than ants on a beautiful picnic blanket.

She took in the spectacle. Families filled the seats around her. Kids with hot dogs and mustard stains on their clothes, parents passing napkins and juggling soft drinks brought a smile to her face. This was what baseball was about – fresh air and fun. She waved a hot dog vendor over and decided to forget the mountain of laundry waiting at home, and the fact that her cabinets were empty. If she hurried after the game, she could still get the grocery shopping done and do enough laundry to get her through the next few days. It seemed the one day a week she managed to get off work amounted to nothing but more work – without pay. It wouldn't hurt to spend an afternoon at the ball game.

Megan reasoned herself into staying, and to consuming at least one of every treat offered by the stadium hawkers. How long had it been since she'd eaten a hot dog, or cotton candy? Years, it seemed. She refused to feel guilty about the extra calories or the dent in her wallet. Between the ticket, parking and gluttony, she probably could have taken a weekend cruise. None of that mattered. The sky was too blue, the grass impossibly green, and…she had Jeff Holder's autograph in her bag.

Thoughts of Christopher slowly wasting away in his hospital bed brought a tear to her eye. Here she was, surrounded by happy, healthy children enjoying one of life's simple pleasures with their families, and reminded Megan of the good she and others did for critically ill children. She loved being a nurse, and her usually upbeat manner made her a favorite among the kids in the special wards. It wasn't easy keeping a smile on her face, even harder to keep the tears from showing when she looked into the hopeful eyes of a sick child, or the worried eyes of a parent, and knew there wasn't a thing modern medicine could do to help them. Her work was gut wrenching at times but then there were the success stories. Those were the ones that kept her going, kept her doing whatever she could to give a child a fighting chance against the injustice of sickness.

She pulled the program out and wiped away the sudden rush of tears before they could ruin the autograph. If Jeff Holder's signature could bring a smile to Christopher's little face, Megan would give up every one of her precious days off to make it happen.

Megan tried to focus on the signature through blurry eyes. She fished a tissue from her purse and dabbed at the corners of her eyes until she could see clearly again. She blinked. Then she blinked again.

"No!" she shouted. Everyone around turned and glared at her. Megan apologized for her outburst, and tried to explain it away by saying she'd spilled something on her program. She received a few sympathetic comments before everyone returned their attention to the game.

Her heart sank as she read what Jeff Holder had written. She couldn't give this to Christopher! Fresh tears threatened to spill over as she curled the program into a glossy weapon.

Of all the…

How could he?

What was he thinking?

What am I going to do now?

Disappointment roiled around in her stomach along with hurt and anger until she thought she might be sick. Or it could have been all the stuff she'd eaten. Either way, she'd wasted an entire day in pursuit of an autograph. And what did she have to show for it? A pick-up line. That's what. Did he really think she was going to show up at the restaurant he'd indicated, at the time he'd indicated? Who did he think he was anyway? God's gift to women?

The crowd surged to their feet and a deafening roar pushed her budding headache over into full-fledged pain. She stuffed the now useless program into her bag and stood to see what was going on. Absolutely nothing. Except for the one guy throwing pitches to the catcher, everyone else was standing around in groups of two or three, chatting.

She bent and yelled at the kid next to her so he could hear her over the clapping and cheering. "What's going on?" He looked to be about Christopher's age, ten or eleven. He'd hardly taken his eyes off the field the entire game, so it was a safe bet he knew what was happening.

"Are you kidding? The Terminator just came in to pitch. All we need is three outs to win." His enthusiasm allowed his voice to carry above the din. If he'd been at home, his mother would be scolding him to use his indoor voice.

"Who's the Terminator?"

"Jeff Holder. He's the best in baseball!"

Megan looked closer at the guy on the pitching mound. From this distance it was impossible to tell if he was the same man who'd made her heart flutter, then crushed her dreams, and Christopher's, with a few pen strokes.

"Why is everyone standing?" she asked. The entire stadium was on their feet, clapping and cheering.

"Because it's the Terminator!" he yelled, as if that made perfect sense. Then he turned back to the game, dismissing Megan as only a kid could do.

Her head pounded in rhythm to the clapping, and the foot stomping that rocked the upper deck. With every pitch, every strike, every out, the crowd grew impossibly louder, and Megan grew increasingly angrier. What was she going to do? She'd promised Christopher, and she couldn't bear to see his face when she told him she'd failed. He'd be crushed, and the last thing the little guy needed was more disappointment in his life.

Before the Terminator threw the last pitch, she pushed her way to the aisle and picked her way down the almost vertical steps with as much grace as a mountain goat that just discovered a patch of locoweed. If she beat the crowd, she might get home in enough time to change clothes and meet Jeff Holder at the restaurant he'd written on her program. She had one last chance to get the autograph for Christopher. She'd meet Jeff Holder, get the autograph, and then she'd tell him what a despicable low-life he was.

❧

He would pick a place where parking was nearly impossible. Megan's headache hadn't completely gone away, and thoughts of her wasted day didn't do anything to help. Now, here she was playing musical parking spaces, instead of buying groceries to get her through the week. One more thing to heap on Jeff Holder's head.

She expected a restaurant filled with players and fans what she found was a cozy place with oilcloth- covered tables and dripping candles jammed into empty Chianti bottles. The wood paneling was dark with a combination of age and garlic fumes, and there wasn't a Texas Mustangs T-shirt in sight. Megan spotted Jeff at a table against the back wall, and she felt a jab to her gut, only this time there wasn't anyone else around. How could he do that to her? He looked right at her and motioned for her to join him. She sucked in a deep breath and tried to remember why she'd come. Christopher. She'd come for an autograph, and as soon as she got it, she'd leave.

He stood as she approached. "I was afraid you wouldn't come."

Megan sat and he signaled for the waiter. He ordered a bottle of wine as if he knew exactly what he wanted. Megan interrupted. "Please. Don't. I can't stay."

Jeff placed the order anyway and rested his crossed forearms on the table. "Why did you come?"

For a split second, looking into his extraordinarily blue eyes, she couldn't remember why she'd come. A slow burn started somewhere near her heart and melted everything from there to her core. "I...I need your autograph," she blurted out.

He leaned back and studied her. "I signed your program."

The waiter returned with Jeff's wine, two glasses and a basket heaped with fragrant bread. Jeff took the bottle and filled his glass. Megan covered hers with her hand.

"One glass. It won't hurt to have one glass while you tell me why you're angry with me."

She moved her hand and watched the ruby liquid swirl into her glass. Just because he'd filled her glass didn't mean she had to drink it. The interruption allowed her to wrestle some control over her wayward body, enough to find the program he'd signed and slide it to his side of the table. "I'll tell you why I'm angry. How dare you? What kind of man does something like this? All I wanted was your autograph, and instead, I get a pick-up line. The only reason I came here tonight was to get your autograph, and only your autograph."

Jeff picked up the program and looked it over while he sipped his wine. Megan could almost hear her wristwatch ticking in the silence that hung between them. Eventually, he tossed the program across the table at her. "So?"

"So?" Anger boiled her blood. "So? That's all you have to say? I used my day off to go to the game just to get your autograph, and this is what I got?" She stabbed the cover with her index finger. "Now, here I am, still trying to get the autograph of a man I can't stand the sight of, when I should be doing all the things I put off so I could go to the game."

He set his glass on the table and for once, she thought she might have his full attention. "Why is my autograph so important? I'm pretty sure you don't want it for yourself."

"Darn right I don't. I don't know you from Adam, but I know someone who thinks you are the best thing since sliced bread. I can't take him this." She flicked the program toward him again. "What would I tell him?" She shook her head. "As it is, I don't know how I can act like you're still a hero when he's spouting off about you, without hurling. Anyway, I promised I'd bring him your autograph, and I'm going to do it." There. She'd said what was on her mind. Maybe it wasn't eloquent – who said hurling anymore anyway? Judging from the furrow between his eyebrows, and the way he'd narrowed those magnificent eyes at her, she'd gotten her point across.

"Hurling? I can't believe you said that. Who are you? And why don't you tell me who your friend is, and why he sent you to get my autograph. Why didn't he come himself?"

"My name is Megan Long. I'm a Pediatric Nurse at Southwest General. Christopher is one of my patients. I can't go into specifics, but I can tell you he isn't well enough to come to a game, but he watches you on TV. He has your baseball card, and he keeps it with him twenty-four/seven." As she spoke, Jeff sat up and listened intently. Perhaps she was going to get that autograph after all.

"Do you have something you want me to sign?"

"Uhh. No." Damn. Why hadn't she thought of that? "I didn't think that far ahead." She knew there wasn't anything in her purse she'd cleaned it out before she went to the ballpark. She glanced around the restaurant – nothing. Absolutely nothing.

"Okay. I'll make a deal with you. I'm hungry. Stay while I eat – I'll even buy you dinner. When we're done, there's a sporting goods store down the street. I know the owner. We'll go there, get something suitable, and I'll sign it for Christopher."

Something in his tone of voice calmed her. Maybe he wasn't as bad as she thought. "You'd do that?"

"Sure. Why wouldn't I? Look, Megan, I'm sorry about the program. If I'd known, I wouldn't have done that. In my defense, I don't get all that many beautiful women trying to get my autograph." His smile was a ray of sunshine in the dim restaurant, and Megan's insides turned to liquid. "Not that I mind signing for kids. I like kids. But a beautiful woman? It was a calculated risk, but one I'm glad I took."

"Well...I guess I understand, but I'm not entirely sure I believe you." She picked up her wine glass and took a sip, glad her hand was steadier on the outside than she was on the inside. "So, what's for dinner?"

Jeff signaled the waiter again, and a short time later they were served an authentic Italian dinner the likes of which Megan had never tasted. "This is wonderful. Do you come here often?"

He urged her to take another slab of garlic bread from the basket in the center of the table. "Once a week, when we're in town. If I ate like this all the time, I'd be as big as a barn."

Megan closed her eyes and savored the burst of rich flavor. She swallowed, licked her lips to get every delicious drop, then opened her eyes. Jeff sat frozen, his fork halfway to his mouth. His eyes smoldered with unmistakable desire. Every female cell in her body reacted to the barrage of pheromones coming from across the table. She reminded herself she didn't really know this guy, and he'd lured her here, admittedly for his own reasons. It took some doing, but she wrestled her hormones under control. "I'm not sleeping with you."

"You sure about that?" He popped the morsel on his fork into his mouth and chewed, all the while watching her watch him. "I think you're as attracted to me as I am to you. But that can wait. Tell me something about yourself."

"You know everything you need to know. I'm a nurse. I work with sick kids."

He was persistent she'd give him that. It was one thing to be evasive, another to be downright rude, so when he began to ask specific questions, she answered – as vaguely as possible. Still he managed to find out more about her than he had a right, or need, to know.

"Your job must be difficult. How do you do it?"

"I like kids. I like being a nurse. The two go together."

He sat back from his empty plate and sipped his wine while the waiter cleared the table. "It's more than that. I think it takes a special person to do what you do. I'm sure Christopher has plenty of nurses who take care of him. None of them took their day off to hunt up an autograph for him."

He was right about that, but that didn't mean the other nurses were any less caring. They all put in long hours and gave up personal time in one way or another. "No, they didn't. But they care about him every bit as much as I do."

"I'm sure they care about his physical self, but the autograph won't make him well."

"There's more to getting well than just medicine. A smile can heal too."

Jeff signed the check and stood. "Let's go. You held up your end of the bargain. Now it's my turn."

CHAPTER TWO

Jeff escorted Megan to the small sporting goods store a few blocks away. Everything that made him a man urged him to touch the woman beside him. He tucked his hands in his pockets in an effort to keep them under control. He'd known from the moment he first saw her standing at the rail that he wanted to get to know her. There was something about the way she held herself that demanded his attention, and when that kid elbowed her, she brushed off the incident without a word of reprimand to the little monster. Not many people would have been so magnanimous, especially since he'd done it on purpose. That's why his program now said, "Always treat a lady with respect," just above Jeff's signature. It wasn't exactly a reprimand, but he was pretty sure the kid would understand. If he lost a fan over it, so be it.

Her strides were long and purposeful – a woman on a mission. He could imagine her in her nurses' scrubs, covering the pediatric ward with the same enthusiasm. Jeff slowed his pace, hoping she'd notice and slow too. He wasn't ready to let her out of his sight. She adjusted her stride to match his, but not before she let out an exasperated breath.

"How far is this place?"

"A couple of blocks."

"It's getting late. Will they still be open?"

He pulled out his cell phone and punched in a number. Alec would be there, stocking shelves and reordering inventory until much later than this. Or at least he was supposed to be. If he weren't, he'd have a few things to explain to the owner. Alec answered on the second ring, a good sign, and assured Jeff he'd let them in. "No problem. We'll get in."

"You can do that? Call up a store and they'll let you in after hours?"

"Only with this one. I own it."

"Seriously?"

"Well, Jason owns half, but yeah, seriously. What do you think Christopher would like? A hat, a jersey? How about a glove?"

"I don't know. He's ten. What do ten-year-old boys like?"

"Ten, huh? I guess that rules out the beer logo clock and the shot glasses. Just about everything else is in the realm of possibility."

"I suppose you have a lot of Mustangs stuff in the store?"

"Yeah. The hard part will be picking out the right thing."

Alec met them at the door, locking it behind them. Jeff introduced Megan to the store manager and pulled him aside after sending Megan off to pick out anything she wanted.

"Do you have a digital camera around here?"

"I have one in the back. Why?"

"Get it. Anything Megan wants, put it on my tab. Then I want a whole bag of stuff for a ten-year-old boy. Mustangs stuff. A stadium throw, a glove, hat, posters, jersey. You know what a kid would like, but this one is real sick, so not a lot of active stuff. Bag it for me and I'll be in to pick it up in the morning."

Alec went in search of the camera, and Jeff caught up to Megan. "Find anything yet?" She turned her velvet brown eyes on him, and he almost forgot his own name. Earlier, when he'd gotten close enough to the rail to see details, her eyes had captivated him. In the past, it had always been the overall package that captured his interest rather than the details of a woman's body. Not that Megan didn't have a killer body and he'd have to be blind not to notice, but her eyes were her best feature. They were windows to her soul, and from what she'd let him see, her soul was Grade A. Megan was the kind of woman you took home to meet your mother, and those were harder to come by than World Series wins.

"There's so much to choose from, but it needs to be something he can keep in the hospital with him."

"He spends a lot of time there?"

"You could say that."

Even if the sadness in her voice hadn't given her away, her eyes would have. She knew much more than she was saying, but he understood the patient confidentiality thing. The fact that she had gone to as much trouble as she had to get his autograph, told him the kid was really ill. No health care worker would go to this much trouble on their day off for a kid with good prospects.

"Then, why don't we go with a glove? It's small enough, but soft. He can hang on to it, sort of like a stuffed animal, in a grown up sort of way."

They moved to the wall covered with gloves from ceiling to floor and Jeff pulled one down. "This is like the one I use. I can autograph it for him."

She smiled at him. The first genuine smile he'd seen from her, and blood rushed to places it had no business being.

"Really? You can autograph something like this?"

"Sure. Come on. I bet Alec has a pen up front."

They made their way to the front of the store where Alec was waiting for them, pen and camera in hand. Jeff pulled Megan close while he signed the glove. Alec snapped photos as Jeff signed, then he took one of the two of them holding the glove so the signature could easily be seen. "If you give Alec your email address, he can send you the photos. You can print them for Christopher. I bet he'll get a kick out of seeing his favorite nurse with his favorite player."

"Thanks," she said. Alec pushed a business card across the counter and she wrote her email address on it. "You've both been more than kind. I can't thank you enough."

"No thanks needed. I'm sorry you had to go to this much trouble. If I'd known…"

"You couldn't have…"

"I know, but still." He thanked Alec and ushered Megan out the door, back toward her car. "I can't say I'm sorry to have met you."

"Thanks for dinner, and the glove. I can't wait to see the look on his face when he sees this."

"I wish I could see it too. Hey! Why don't I come by the hospital tomorrow and we can give it to him together? Do you think he'd like that?"

Megan's eyes twinkled with moisture and her jaw dropped. "You'd do that?"

"Sure. What time would be good?"

"Morning? Around ten, maybe?"

"Ten it is. We have a game tomorrow afternoon, so I can't stay long."

He watched her drive off, then headed back to the store to thank Alec, and get Megan's email address. Just in case, he told himself. Besides, now that he was going to see her again, he could take the photos to her himself.

❧❧

Megan glared at the man standing next to the nurses' station. She should have known Jeff wouldn't show. It was a good thing she hadn't said anything to Christopher. Building his hope up, then having to tell him his hero wasn't coming might be too much for a kid in his condition.

"Where is he?" she demanded.

"Who?" the man asked.

"Your brother, that's who. Did he send you, thinking a look-alike would do?"

He smiled at her, his crooked smile a mirror image of his brothers. "You can tell us apart?"

She resisted the urge to roll her eyes. Of course she could tell them apart. The two men shared the same DNA, but this one was…well, he wasn't Jeff. Not that he wasn't sexy as hell too. Even

14

though her head told her this wasn't Jeff, her body didn't seem to notice. Every physical reaction she'd had to Jeff came back in a rush, a very inappropriate, unwelcome rush. Megan squashed the feeling, wondering how she could react so strongly to two different men at the same time. Since she couldn't exactly pinpoint what it was that had told her from the other end of the hallway that this man wasn't the one she was expecting, she fell back on her original question. "Where is Jeff?"

"He'll be here in a minute. He had to park the car. We were running a little late, so he sent me up so you wouldn't think he flaked. I'm his brother, Jason." He offered her his hand and Megan reached out to shake it but stopped short when the elevator door swooshed open and Jeff Holder stepped out. He stopped for a split second to get his bearings, then headed straight for them. Oh lord. She tried to convince herself her reaction yesterday had been a fluke, but watching him walk toward her with that easy gait of his – his eyes locked on her as if she were the only person on the planet – and she knew she was already lost.

"Sorry I'm late. I had to stop and pick up some stuff." He lifted a bag from the sporting goods store he'd taken her to the previous evening. "Is this a good time?"

"As good as any. Christopher's mother is here. Why don't you wait here? I'll go get her so she can talk to you before you see Christopher. They've been through so much, I hate to spring something like this on her without fair warning."

A few minutes later, Jeff and Christopher's mother took the elevator down to the cafeteria, leaving Megan alone with Jason. "What was that all about?" she asked.

"Jeff always does that. He'll be back in a few minutes, then we'll go see Christopher. In the meantime, why don't you show me around?"

"You want to see the hospital?"

"Not all of it, just the part you work in. Are there any more baseball fans here?"

No wonder Jeff couldn't stop talking about this woman. She was sexy as hell, and he'd never seen a pair of scrubs filled out so enticingly. He followed her down the corridor, watching her sweet round ass sway from side to side. She pointed out various treatment rooms, and Jason made appropriate comments. This wasn't his thing, the treatment rooms brought back too many memories, none of them good. He preferred the one-on-one with the kids. Megan paused in the next open door and swept her arm wide.

"This is the day room." Jason peered around the doorjamb. A small group of kids, some in wheelchairs, others sitting on beanbags, were gathered around a television set. He recognized the animated movie.

"Would they mind if I interrupted their movie?" The first genuine smile he'd seen changed her face from pretty to devastating. Jason's heart stalled and he almost missed her response.

"No. I don't think so. Wait here for a second. I'll pause the movie and introduce you." She started to move into the room, but Jason stopped her.

"Let me." His fingertips tingled where he touched her. Her skin was soft, and warm, and he had no business thinking the things he was thinking about her. Jeff had seen her first, and he hadn't given any indication he was interested in sharing her. "Go see if Jeff is back. He's got some publicity stills in his bag of stuff."

"Okay," she said. Her eyes hadn't left his since he touched her. The heat in them didn't do anything to dispel his interest. "I'll...you'll..."

"I'll just talk with them for a while until you get back." He pulled a felt-tipped pen from his shirt pocket. "I can sign hands or IV bags, if I have to." She glanced into the room again, then back at him. "I won't hurt them, I promise." He gave her his most innocent smile. It didn't win her over completely, but she hustled down the hall in the direction of the nurses' station. Jason took a couple of deep breaths to steady his heartbeat before he stepped into the room.

Oh, lord. Megan inhaled deeply and let it out slowly. This was so wrong. Yeah, they looked alike; identical twins did that, but they were two different people. She shouldn't be attracted to both of them. It wasn't right. She turned the corner and stopped, pressing her back against the wall for support. Her heart was racing faster than a doped thoroughbred, and all Jason had done was lightly touch her arm with his fingertips.

She pushed away from the wall and peeked back around the corner. Jason was nowhere in sight. It should have eased her mind to know he'd done as he said he would, but it had the opposite effect. Her heart swelled and her stomach flipped. What were the chances he was the genuine article – a good-looking guy with a heart?

Megan hurried to the nurses' station, hoping to catch Jeff before he went to Christopher's room. Too late, the volunteer informed her, holding up a picture of Jeff and Jason together in uniform. Jeff's signature graced the bottom left corner. "He's in Christopher's room. He said to send you down."

The hospital had strict visiting hours, but on this wing, they were more like suggestions than actual rules. Megan stopped to speak with half-dozen parents and patients as she made her way down the hall to Christopher's room at the end. She'd never understand how a person could work with these kids every day and not get attached. It wasn't possible. And the attachment went both ways. No matter the outcome of the child's illness, the parents often kept in touch with the doctors and nurses. Many had become friends and were a great resource for parents new to the process. Sometimes it took hearing it from someone who'd been on your side of the fence to make it sink in.

Christopher's mother was one of those special parents. She knew as much about the hospital, its staff, and the procedures as anyone, and she was always willing to help less experienced parents. She was a good listener too. In the early days of an illness, having someone listen was a gift beyond measure.

Megan wasn't surprised to see Roxanne standing inside her son's door, her arms crossed over her midsection as she lounged against the wall. Some parents clung to their kids, whether to reassure themselves, or to comfort the child. It didn't matter which. Roxanne understood Christopher's need to be a normal kid, and that meant letting him have what little space she could give him, under the circumstances. When he needed her to hold him, give him a hug, or just be present for him; she was there, but this wasn't one of those times. Christopher was face-to-face with his idol, and he didn't need his mother hovering as if he were fragile.

Christopher's smile said it all. Normally pale, his cheeks were tinged with pink and his blue eyes were saucers as he hung on Jeff's every word. Roxanne acknowledged Megan's entrance with a subdued smile. The gleam in her eye told Megan how much Roxanne appreciated this brief moment of happiness in her son's otherwise bleak life.

Jeff was good. His attention never wavered from Christopher when Megan entered the room. The two were deep in a discussion of the Mustangs playoff prospects, and their chances of making it to the World Series. They came to some sort of agreement, and Christopher finally took his eyes off Jeff for a moment.

"Nurse Megan," Christopher cried out. "Come see! It's Jeff Holder!"

Megan stepped closer. "I see. How wonderful for you that he came by today."

"Nurse Megan," Jeff said. "I was just telling Christopher about the trick I played on you when you came to get my autograph for him." He winked at Christopher, which set the child into a fit of giggles. "He said I owe you more than a dinner for such bad behavior."

"Oh, no," she protested. "Dinner was more than enough, and you coming here…well, that's more than I ever imagined. No, you don't owe me a thing."

"He brought you tickets, Nurse Megan! He said they're right over the Mustangs' dugout – where all the girlfriends and wives sit!"

"I…"

"You can't say no, Nurse Megan," Jeff pleaded. "I promised Christopher a set too, when he gets sprung from this joint." He shared a guy look with Christopher that made Megan's heart flip. Damn, did the man not have any flaws? If wanting to get well was a miracle drug, Christopher would be out of here tomorrow.

"But I don't know anything about baseball," she argued.

"I can tell you all you need to know," Christopher said. "We can go together."

God, she hoped that was true. She'd sit through every game the Mustangs played for the next year, if it would make Christopher well. The kid loved baseball, and he deserved a chance to go to a game, or better yet, to play. "Then why don't we plan on that?" She exchanged glances with Jeff. "We'll go together sometime, and you can teach me about the game."

"It's a deal!" Christopher looked at Jeff. "If that's okay with you, Mr. Holder?"

"That's fine, Christopher." His smile turned to a frown. "Hey, what's with the Mister stuff? We're friends now, so call me Jeff."

Megan didn't think Christopher could be any happier. If he hadn't been anchored to the bed by monitors and an IV, he'd be floating on the ceiling. He practically bounced with excitement. As wonderful as it was to see, she had to get what she came in for and get back. No telling what kind of trouble Jason had gotten into while she was gone.

"I hate to interrupt, but your brother said you had some publicity stills?"

"Where is Jason? I told Christopher he could meet the best catcher in baseball, and the National League homerun leader."

"You brought someone else with you?"

Christopher and Jeff looked at each other and rolled their eyes. "Geez, she really doesn't know anything, does she?" Christopher said to Jeff.

"I'm sure she knows lots of stuff, just not baseball stuff," he said, his gaze shifting from Christopher to Megan. "Jason is the best catcher in baseball, and he currently leads the National League in homeruns," he explained.

"Oh, well…this paragon of baseball is in the day room with some other patients. He sent me to get the photos from you."

Jeff dug a stack of photos from the bag at his feet and handed them over. "Just make sure he comes by here when he's done, and if the kids aren't tired of baseball stories, I can stop in to see them too."

"That would be great. I'll go see how he's doing, and I'll send him this way when he's done."

Megan heard Jason's deep voice a few steps before she reached the day room. She glanced around the doorframe and had to fight back tears for the second time in less than an hour. The television was off, and Jason Holder sat on a large beanbag chair, surrounded by adoring kids, reading to them. She recognized the book. The kids all loved the popular kid wizard, and there were several copies of the series in the hospital library. She stood for a moment, listening to the timbre of his voice, noticing the way he gave personality to the individual characters.

As distractions went, this was the best kind for the kids. There was nothing more important than being treated as if there was not a thing wrong with them, and Jason was doing an excellent job. She waited until he reached a stopping point before she interrupted. The chorus of groans subsided when she produced the publicity photos and explained that Jeff Holder had offered to visit with them too. Jason signed photos and autographed a few IV bags before he excused himself to go see Christopher, promising to send his brother back to see them.

"You were great in there."

"What?" Jason feigned shock and disbelief. "You thought I wasn't up to the task?"

"Honestly, no. We get a lot of celebrities through here, but they usually bring along a photographer, take a few pictures with the doctors, and leave. Taking the time to do something as simple as reading to the kids means a lot. You get points for that."

"I wasn't looking for points," he said, a touch of real anger lacing his words. "I did it because one of the kids asked me to."

"I'm sorry. I didn't mean to offend you, it's just…"

"Just that you don't know me."

"I guess that's it. I don't know you, but if what I just saw was any indication, you're a good man, Jason Holder."

"I try. It's tough to see these kids, but I know what it's like to be stuck in one of these places."

"Hey!" It was Megan's turn to be offended.

"I didn't mean it like that. This is a great facility, and if all the staff is as concerned as you are, then these kids are getting the best care possible. I was referring to the confinement, the uncertainty, the fear. It's hard for a kid, no matter how great the hospital is."

"You sound like you have some experience."

"You could say that. I spent a lot of my childhood in a hospital bed."

Megan stopped, dumbstruck by Jason's admission. They'd reached Christopher's room, and Jason didn't spare her a backward glance, but she noticed he squared his shoulders and put on a big smile as he stepped into the room.

CHAPTER THREE

She really didn't know why she had agreed to meet Jeff and Jason after the game. She was dead on her feet, and she had to work the early shift tomorrow. The only place she should be going was to bed. Hers. Alone. Instead, she was waiting in a restaurant for two men she hardly knew. They'd been so good with the kids this morning that when they insisted she meet them after their late afternoon game, she'd have sounded rude and unappreciative to have turned them down.

They were great with the kids, and it would be wonderful if they became regular visitors. Besides, she wanted to ask Jason about the comment he'd made about spending a lot of his childhood in hospital beds. Nothing in his online bio referenced anything about a childhood illness. But if it were true, and he'd overcome it to be the star player he was now, his story could be an inspiration to critically ill children everywhere. It seemed impossible that the media hadn't picked up on the story and exploited it already. According to her research, the Holder brothers had been in the upper echelons of the baseball world for several years.

A gust of hot, humid air lifted the edge of her skirt as the outer door opened. Megan smoothed her hem down and stood when she recognized the two men entering. They were in a good mood, laughing together at something. Jeff and Jason stopped when they noticed her standing in the small entryway. She'd seen interest on men's faces before, but these two looked at her like she was the last slice of cherry pie, and they were starving. The look they gave her was enough to make her blood pressure skyrocket, and her insides melt. If she hadn't been tongue-tied by the sight of the best-looking man she'd ever seen in her life, times two, she might have scolded them for it. Jeff moved first, stepping up to place a friendly kiss on her cheek.

"Thanks for coming," he said, stepping back to let Jason have a turn. "You look great."

"She looks like a million dollars," Jason said. "Glad you could make it. I hope we haven't kept you waiting too long."

"No. I just got here. I didn't leave my apartment until the game was over." The hostess waved them to a table in the back. Megan followed, hyper-aware of the two testosterone towers a step behind her. It was late, and the restaurant wasn't crowded, but heads turned as they wove through the tables. Jeff held a chair for her before he and Jason took the ones on either side.

"You saw the game then?" Jason asked. Megan almost wished she had. Jason's enthusiasm was so real it was contagious.

"I'm sorry. I didn't get home in time to see the whole thing, but I did see the last few minutes."

"Then you saw Jeff's save."

"I saw him throw a few pitches. Is that what you mean?"

"Leave her alone, Jase. She's not a baseball fan. Not yet anyway." The waiter brought a bottle of wine and Jeff poured for all of them.

"Do you eat out a lot?"

"Yeah. Neither one of us cooks, so in order to stay alive, we eat out," Jeff explained.

"You live together?" *Cute.*

"We always have," Jason said. "When we first started out in the Minors we couldn't afford two places, but now it's become a habit."

Bit by bit, Megan relaxed in their company. They had a way of telling stories that was amusing to watch. One would start, and by some secret cue, the other would continue. It was as if their brains were sync'd by an invisible cord. Prepared to find something to dislike, she chastised herself for categorizing them before she knew them.

Jeff insisted on dessert, and they lingered over the mountainous chocolate cake and another bottle of wine. They were nearly through when Jason spoke. "Why don't we take some chocolate cake home. Then we can smear it all over each other and lick it off – real slow."

Megan wasn't used to drinking more than an occasional glass, and at first, she attributed what she'd heard to the three glasses she'd consumed tonight.

"What?" She closed her eyes and forced her brain to focus. Surely, she'd misheard Jason's comment. She was long past trying to deny her attraction to the pair, but conjuring up propositions went way beyond fantasizing. It bordered on drunkenness and possibly, insanity. "Would you repeat that, please?"

Megan mentally congratulated herself for sounding rational when she was working with seriously compromised judgment.

Jeff touched her lightly on the arm and she turned her now pounding head in his direction. "Jason can be a bit crude sometimes. I apologize for his behavior." He shot his brother a look that said, "Way to go, asshole," then turned his attention back to Megan. "What he meant to say, was, we'd like for you to come out to our house this weekend. We want to get to know you better, and give you a chance to get to know us."

That sounded more rational. Megan tore her gaze away from Jeff, and risked a glance at Jason. His smile made her insides warm, or maybe it was the wine. Jeff's fingers still rested lightly on her forearm, not demanding, but conveying a message all the same. She jerked her arm off the table and twisted her hands in the cloth napkin in her lap.

"No pressure," Jeff said. His voice vibrated along her nerve endings. "We like you, a lot. And we think you like us. We want to explore that further, to see if perhaps you might like a lot more from us."

"I think I've had too much to drink. What exactly are we talking about here?"

"This isn't the place to go into details, but I think you know. We want you, Megan. Both of us. We'd like to find out if it's something you'd be interested in. We don't expect you to answer right away. That's why we want you to come out to our place. You can see the way we live. We can discuss the details then, if it's something you think you might want."

She didn't know what to say. It seemed she had heard Jason correctly. He'd asked her to go to bed with them, tonight. More specifically, he'd suggested licking her body – all over – and allowing her to do the same. It hadn't been her overactive imagination, spurred on by too much wine. As appealing as that sounded, and she wouldn't lie to herself, it did sound appealing; she wasn't into that kind of thing. At least she didn't think she was. She didn't do no-strings-attached-kinky-ménage sex.

"I've got to go." She jerked her purse off the back of the chair as she stood. Her head swam, and this time, she knew it wasn't entirely the fault of the alcohol. She was off balance, but she couldn't blame it on drinking – not entirely. She made it as far as the front door, and turned to ask the maitre d' to call a cab. Two towering males blocked her way.

"We have a car waiting. We'll take you home." Jeff slipped an arm around her waist while Jason signaled to a car parked down the street. The sleek black town car pulled to the curb, and a moment later Megan was in the backseat, flanked by the two sexiest men she'd ever seen. Jason asked for her address, relayed it to the driver, then closed the partition, sealing them off from the world.

One hot hand skimmed her thigh, sneaking under the hem of her dress to stroke dangerously close to her throbbing parts. Another slipped around her neck, long fingers massaging her nape as the thumb stroked her jaw, gently turning her face in the opposite direction from where the other hand had come from. She found herself looking up into Jeff Holder's eyes. Before she could form a protest, he bent his head and took her lips in a kiss that loosened every muscle in her body, and did serious damage to her moral fiber. The hand on her thigh tugged, and her legs slid open. Fingers stroked a path to her core, and she groaned against Jeff's lips as another set of fingers joined the fray. Her thighs spread wider in silent invitation.

She fell under their sensual spell. A strobe of traffic and streetlights flashed against her closed eyelids as the car glided through the near empty streets. Jeff's lips coaxed and promised. Together, their skilled hands opened, explored and pleasured her beyond anything she'd ever felt before. Soft words of encouragement whispered across her consciousness, urging her on toward the peak of pleasure. When at last she found it, Jeff swallowed her scream, then gently laid her head back against the seat.

Her skin flamed, and goose bumps formed where it was exposed to the cold air of the air-conditioned car. She fought her way back to the real world, slowly realizing how thoroughly she'd given herself to them. Megan slid first one leg, then the other off the masculine thigh it had been resting on. How her legs had come to be draped over their thighs, she had no idea. Their hands slid from beneath her skirt as she squirmed back into an upright position. She used the minutes before the car stopped in front of her apartment to smooth her skirt down, perhaps a few hundred times more than necessary. Neither man spoke, and she couldn't bring herself to look at them.

She had to admit, they argued a good case in favor of a relationship based on physical gratification. She'd had little enough of that in the last few years. But hadn't she told herself she wasn't going to settle for less than what she wanted in life? And what they were offering was a whole lot less than love, a home and a family.

Against her protests, both men accompanied her to the door. Jeff took her keys from her hand and unlocked it. Before she could step inside, Jason pulled her tightly against him and kissed her. It wasn't a goodnight kiss. No simple I-had-a-nice-time kiss. It was carnal, seductive, and left her knees trembling. Jason released her, smiled as if he was going to eat her up, then turned her around. His hands rested on the curve of her hips and brought her hard against his front. She couldn't mistake the ridge at her back, or the one at her front as Jeff pressed himself against her, sandwiching her between them. Befuddled, seduced, and aching, she didn't protest as Jeff took her mouth in a kiss every bit as carnal as his brother's.

❧❧

"Do you think she'll come?" Jason asked as the car sped along the interstate toward the home he shared with Jeff outside of Dallas.

"I don't know. I hope so. Are you as interested as I am?"

"Yeah, I am. Damn. Did you feel her come? She was like a volcano erupting, all hot and wet and…shit, she's a screamer."

"I noticed," Jeff grinned at the memory. "I was afraid Carl would hear her and drive us to the police station instead of her apartment."

Jason chuckled. "Did we push her too hard for the first time?"

"Maybe. But she wasn't exactly saying no. She could have stopped us at anytime with just a word."

"True." Silence filled the compartment. At last, Jason spoke. "I want her to come next weekend. I want to show her the house, show her what it would be like."

"Me too. She's smart, and compassionate, and beautiful, inside and out. I hope we didn't scare her away. We're a lot to handle, especially for one woman."

"We can do this. I know we can, but you saw her first. If you want me to back off, I will."

"No. I did see her first, but I wasn't ever thinking of her for me alone. We work together, you and me. We're a team. We always have been."

"Yeah, well it's damned hard to find a woman who's a team player too," Jason said.

"I'm not ready to throw in the towel. Are you?"

"I guess not. At least Megan was screaming good things. She wasn't screaming for help."

Jeff smiled. "Yeah, that's a good sign."

27

"Okay then. Maybe we should send her some flowers or something, let her know we're thinking about her while we're gone."

∽◊∾

Megan admired the giant bouquet at the nurses' station. They didn't often get flowers for patients on this wing, and when they did, they were usually accompanied by balloons and teddy bears. This one was filled with yellow roses and several other exotic flowers Megan couldn't name, but she knew they didn't come cheap. Just as she decided the arrangement had been delivered to the wrong floor, one of the volunteers came around the corner.

"Someone has an admirer," she said.

"Who are they for?"

"You." She pointed to the small envelope held in the grasp of a plastic pick. "You're the only Megan on this floor."

"There must be a mistake," she said as she reached for the card. "I'm not the only Megan in the hospital." It took both hands to slip the card from the holder without toppling the arrangement. Her heart rate kicked up a notch as she pulled the card from the envelope and saw the neat masculine scrawl. The message was short, and signed by both Jeff and Jason.

"Well, who's it from?"

Megan's fingers trembled as she slipped the card into the envelope and tucked the whole thing into her pocket. "A friend."

"Must be a very good friend," she said with a wink.

Megan responded with a weak, "Yes," and picked up the chart she'd come to get. She had no idea how good a friend either Jeff or Jason were, but if what they'd said and done last night in the back of the town car was any indication, they wanted to be very, very good friends. The big question was, did she want the same thing? She was still a little shocked by the proposition. And that's what it was, a bold proposition. After they guided her inside her door last night, told her to lock up, and then called goodnight when she slid thrown the deadbolt, she sank into the first chair she'd come to. Dazed and confused, she ran the entire evening over in her mind, and came to the unmistakable conclusion that Jeff and Jason Holder had propositioned her. By morning, she'd convinced herself it had all been a joke, but the flowers, and their accompanying note, said otherwise.

Thanks to Christopher, she knew the Mustangs were on a road trip and wouldn't be back until the end of the week. They had Friday night off, a night game on Saturday and an afternoon game on Sunday. Not much time for a relationship, she mused. Her schedule wasn't much better, not that she was even considering their proposal. All they wanted from her – with her – was sex. Not that it would necessarily be a bad thing. On the contrary, that little sample on the ride home was evidence that it would be very, very, good sex. Probably the best she'd ever had. But was that enough for her? Could she sleep with them? Do the wicked things she'd imagined ever since that car ride and not lose her heart to them? And if she did lose her heart – what then? There was no guarantee they would love her back. Besides, she couldn't marry two people anyway. One was the legal limit in Texas and every other state in the union. No. She'd be better off to stay far away from Jeff and Jason Holder.

She heard nothing more from them until Thursday when another bouquet arrived. This one was delivered to her apartment, along with a note, and directions to their house. She read the missive, handwritten by Jason this time, telling her they would understand if she didn't want to explore the chemistry between them; but if she did, they would give her all the time she needed to decide. He ended with an invitation to spend the day with them at their home.

Megan reread the note until her eyes blurred. It was ridiculous. Who did things like that? And as she went through her daily routines, the proposition wasn't far from her mind. Memories of the ride home in the back seat of their hired car crept into every still moment, making her wonder if she weren't as depraved as Jeff and Jason Holder. Could she do it? Could she give herself to both men, at the same time?

She wasn't any closer to an answer when she got home, than she had been when she left. After showering, she turned on the television, surfing the channels for anything that would take her mind off Jeff and Jason, and the way their hands felt on her, in her. She couldn't be certain, but she thought at one time, they both had a finger, or two, inside her. She'd been too far gone to pay close attention. What else would they want to do at the same time?And how would she feel about that? She shifted, pulling her legs up on the sofa and curling her feet under the soft throw she kept folded over the back. She paused in her channel surfing on the Mustangs' game. The score was 2-1, in favor of the Mustangs. The score box in the corner of the screen said it was the bottom of the ninth. Christopher had made it his job to educate her on the basics, so she knew the game was almost over. This was Terminator Time, according to Christopher. Sure enough, the man who entered the field via a door in the outfield fence, was Jeff Holder – The Terminator.

Megan watched as he strode confidently across the field, not too slow, but in no hurry either. The announcers gave him his due, confident in their assessment that the game was all but over now that The Terminator was in to pitch. They went on and on about inside heat. It took Megan a moment, but she figured out they were talking about a type of pitch – one Jeff apparently threw exceptionally well. She had a lot to learn if she was going to...

No. She wouldn't go there. Not tonight.

The catcher strode out to the pitching mound. She would have known it was Jason, even if he hadn't carried his helmet in his hand. Jason walked with the same stride as his brother, despite the protective gear he wore. They spoke, shielding their lips from the prying eyes of the television cameras with their gloves. The conversation lasted no more than thirty seconds, then Jason dropped the baseball in Jeff's glove and returned to his place behind home plate.

Megan dropped the remote and settled in to watch. Jeff made it look so easy, but if you looked closely, you could see the strong muscles in his arms and legs as he wound up and threw the pitch. It didn't take a genius to know that kind of speed and pinpoint precision took skill and strength. Between pitches, the camera always returned to Jeff for a close-up. He never gave anything away. His face was a blank mask, but when he leaned in to take the pitch call from his brother, Megan could almost see the calculations going through his head. How to hold the ball, fingers here, adjust the grip, coil the muscles to the exact degree necessary to power the ball at a specific speed, and control. Control every muscle so that the end result would be a perfect pitch.

The Terminator threw perfect pitch, after perfect pitch. He wiped sweat from his forehead with a shrug of a shoulder, replacing his cap with all the concentration of a surgeon. And that's what he was, Megan realized. She'd seen enough steady hands in the hospital to know the absorption and command of body it took to wield a scalpel with skill, to deliver a perfect slice. What Jeff did wasn't life or death, but it took as much physical control, and a lot more stamina.

Jeff systematically removed the first two batters as efficiently as any surgeon. Megan couldn't look away. His body fascinated her. His legs had to be all muscle beneath his snug-fitting uniform. The short-sleeved shirt revealed the long, corded muscles in his forearms. Her breath caught in her lungs as the camera focused in on the ball in his hand. Leaning toward home plate, he twirled the ball between long fingers, feeling for the grip he wanted. Strong fingers, fingers that could find the perfect spot without looking, fingers that had found her perfect spot in the darkness of a backseat, unhampered by her skirt and panties.

The announcers expected no less from the Terminator. They praised his success and speculated on whether he would break records in his career. As the batters came and went, the cameras also captured the other half of the action, the man behind the plate. The man calling the pitches. The man cloaked behind pads and a mask. Jason might not have the pitching skill his brother did, but his contribution to Jeff's success was obvious. Megan marveled at the amount of detail Jason must have memorized. He'd have to know every batter's strength, as well as his weakness, and know what his brother was capable of throwing at that point in time.

No doubt Jason could memorize an entire encyclopedia, but the rest probably had to do with their twin connection. Jason knew Jeff's body as well as he knew his own.

The third batter swung and missed the first two pitches. The hometown crowd was on their feet, willing their batter to hit the ball and give their team one more chance to tie the score. The camera focused on Jason. Fingers flashed between his legs in a code that only Jeff would understand. Megan's skin flushed at the memory of those fingers on her. In her. He shifted, raised his glove…the camera shot changed. Jeff straightened. He lifted his left leg, fell forward as he brought his right hand up and over, releasing the ball as his left foot landed hard. The camera shot shifted again. The batter swung, the ball crashed into Jason's glove hard enough to rock him back on his heels. The umpire behind him did an elaborate dance and yelled, "Strike three!"

Jason stood, yanked his helmet off, and trotted toward the mound. Jeff met him halfway and the brothers shared a guy hug. Their identical faces wore matching smiles as the rest of the team joined in the celebration. Jeff and Jason walked off the field side-by-side, swallowed up by a flood of teammates from the dugout, and a tidal wave of reporters.

Megan watched as the on-field reporter made his way through the crowd to Jeff and Jason. The brothers stood together, conquering warriors, accepting good-natured back slaps and handshakes from their teammates. Her heart skipped as they turned those disarming identical smiles to the camera. A few nights ago, they'd smiled at her like that, and she hadn't been immune to it. She still wasn't.

The reporter praised Jeff's accomplishment, but before he could go too far, Jeff stopped him. "Hey, I only played one inning. The real praise goes to the guys who were out there for the other eight innings," he clamped a hand on Jason's shoulder, "guys like Jason who put the runs on the board. If Stewart and Harding hadn't done such a great job on the mound, I never would have come out of the bullpen."

The reporter tried his best to put Jeff back in the limelight, but the Terminator wouldn't have it. Every chance he got, he turned the praise back on his teammates. Sincerity was in every line of his face, and evident in his tone. He believed what he was saying. The reporter eventually gave up, and turned his questions to Jason. His modesty was less, but he couldn't very well deny it was his homerun, with a runner on base that had given the Mustangs the two runs they needed to win.

Megan turned the coverage off after Jeff and Jason moved on to field questions from one of the throng of other reporters waiting to interview them. They'd be coming home from the road trip tonight, and they'd already invited her to their house tomorrow. She still hadn't made up her mind, but staring at the flickering screen where a mediocre sit-com couldn't command her attention, all she could think about was Jeff and Jason Holder.

They wanted sex. With her. It seemed ridiculous to deny the prospect appealed to her. Who wouldn't want to roll around in the sheets with two great looking guys? She knew firsthand how entertaining they could be, and how skilled they were at seduction. She'd parted her legs like a wanton – *in the backseat of a car* – for crying out loud. What would she do for them in the comfort and privacy of a bedroom?

She grabbed a throw pillow and hugged it tight against her chest. The real question was, what would they do for her? To her? She'd read a few erotic novels about ménages, but they'd seemed like fantasy to her. People didn't really do that. Did they? And if they did…could she?

She was still pondering the question when she slipped between the sheets that night. The smooth cotton was cold against her skin, reminding her how long it had been since she'd had a hot-blooded male to warm her bed. Her crazy schedule, nights one week, days the next, kept her perpetually short on sleep, and even when she wasn't tired, she was often exhausted from the emotional stress of her job. That didn't leave much time or energy for dating – even if she had someone to date.

Just because she didn't have time for a relationship didn't mean some hot sex now and then wouldn't be welcome. That's what Jeff and Jason were offering – sex. Nothing more. Men like them weren't candidates for a relationship. If she could look at the arrangement from the same perspective – not get emotionally involved – maybe it would work out. Maybe she could enjoy what they were offering – if the three of them could find the time.

Three of them. Suddenly, she felt too warm under the covers. She tossed off the comforter, leaving the light sheet to caress her heated skin. She wiggled until the hem of her Cowboys sleep shirt rode high on her hips. Her fingers snuck low to brush across the hidden bud of nerve endings, sending a wave of longing through her system. It was no use. Touching herself wasn't anywhere near the same as having long, callused fingers do the touching. Fingers that knew how to make her body sing, knew how to make her forget everything, and want more.

Megan sat up and flipped on the lamp next to her bed. She picked up the novel she'd begun on her lunch break and slid the card out she'd used to mark her place. The directions to their home were simple enough, just a few turns, and if she weren't mistaken, more than a few miles of nothing. Unless something had changed, there wasn't much out where they lived. That didn't sound like what she expected from big-time athletes, but so far, nothing she'd learned about Jeff and Jason was what she'd expected.

She slid the card back into the book and turned the light off. This time, she closed her eyes and sleep came easily. She'd made up her mind. In the morning, she'd drive out to Jeff and Jason's house and see exactly what they had in mind. What could it hurt? She knew enough about them to feel certain that if she said no, they wouldn't be angry. Heck, they probably did this all the time. She was probably one of dozens who'd been invited to their lair for some kinky sex, then shown the door when the twins tired of the conquest.

CHAPTER FOUR

Jeff paced the large eat-in kitchen like a caged mountain lion. "She isn't coming," he groused at his brother. Jason sat calmly on a stool at the raised bar, using an apple as if it were a baseball, tossing it as high as he could and catching it. The apple was long past edible having hit the floor hard more than once, a testament to his lack of concentration.

"She'll be here," he stated with confidence he didn't have. "It's early."

"Not that early. She'd be here by now if she were coming."

Jason straightened from picking up the apple yet again. A low, familiar hum had his heart racing. Jeff was at the window before Jason could toss the apple back into the bowl. The house faced the main road, and the curved driveway swept under a portico off the kitchen. The house was barely visible from the road, just the way the brothers liked it, but you could see anyone approaching from this vantage point. "See? I told you she'd be here."

"Shut up. How many times did you drop that apple?"

"Okay, you don't have to rub it in." Sometimes having a twin who knew you so well was a pain in the ass. "Should we greet her or something?"

"Yeah," Jeff said, heading to the leaded glass door that led to the portico, "we should."

Jason followed his brother. He'd never seen Jeff so worked up about a woman. Not that he could blame him. It was easy to see Megan was special. She was smart, and kind, and had a tender heart — she'd have to with the kind of work she did. And, she was drop-dead gorgeous. That she didn't recognize her beauty only added to her appeal. She might have faults, but vanity wasn't one of them.

She exited her practical little sedan with the grace of a queen, but Jason noted she fumbled with the straps of her purse. Nerves, maybe? He instantly felt better about asking her to come out to the house. If she were nervous, then this wasn't something she did every day. He never thought she did. She wasn't the type to hop into bed with men she hardly knew, despite the way she'd given herself to them in the back of the town car. Even then, he sensed her reserve, but they'd given her little choice. He was determined that today, the choice would be hers.

Jason hung back as Jeff welcomed their guest. Over the years, he'd become good at observing players and using the knowledge he gained to find their weakness. His talent extended to the world outside baseball too, so he was glad for the time to watch Megan. She was definitely nervous, but she tried hard to hide it as Jeff steered her toward the kitchen door.

"Hi. Glad you could come," Jason said when she stopped in front of him.

"Thanks for the invitation." Her eyes met his, strong and unwavering even though her hand trembled when their palms touched. He tugged her hand gently and pulled her closer, pressing a soft kiss to her cheek.

They settled at the big, scarred kitchen table. Jeff filled tall glasses with iced tea and brought them to the table. "Thanks," she said, wrapping her fingers around her glass as if searching for something solid to hang onto.

"There's no need to be nervous, Megan. Nothing will happen unless you want it to," Jason assured her.

"I don't even know what, exactly, we're talking about here," she said. "I…well – "

"Megan," Jeff interrupted, "we invited you out to see our home, see the way we live. Jason and I are both attracted to you. You're smart, you're caring, and kind. You're beautiful, and sexy, and we want to get to know you better, and we'd like for you to get to know us too."

Jeff's compliments made her blush and she became more nervous than before, if that was possible. She wasn't used to being told she was beautiful. Jason silently vowed to change that. "Don't let Jeff scare you. We don't want to pressure you into anything. Let's sit here and talk. Maybe later you'll let us show you the house, and the property. "

"Look, I don't have much time. I have to work later today, and I know you have a game, so can you just tell me what you have in mind?"

Jason glanced at Jeff, noted the approving smile, then turned back to Megan. "Okay. We'd like you to stay with us for a while. A week for starters – longer if you like the arrangement."

"Stay with you?" She waggled a finger between them. "You don't mean as your housekeeper, do you?"

"No," Jeff replied. "We want you in our bed. We want to have sex with you every way two men and a woman can have it, that is, without the men…you know."

Megan clutched her tea glass in a white-knuckled grip, but she didn't get up and run. "After the way you responded to us the other night, well, we thought you might be interested," Jason added. Two red blotches dotted her cheekbones and the rest of her face turned a dark crimson. Jason shifted in his seat, wondering if her skin turned that shade when she came. It had been too dark in the car the other night to see clearly. Next time, they'd have the lights on.

"Would it be both of you, together?"

"Usually, but not always. It might be one on one sometimes, or maybe one would just watch. It depends. The decision would be yours, but we've always worked well as a team, and we'd like to stay that way," Jason said. "If you're home alone with one of us, then there isn't any reason you can't go one on one."

"You've done this before."

"Some," Jeff said. "But we've never had a long-term relationship, and that's what we're looking for. With you."

"Long-term," she repeated. "How long is long?"

"Until you, or by mutual agreement we, decide it's over. That could be a week, a month, or years," Jason said. "It's mostly your decision. We won't pressure you to stay if you don't want to."

She took a deep breath and let it out, then brought the glass to her lips. Throughout the discussion, she'd kept her eyes glued on the tea glass in her hands, but something they said had made her feel braver, and she glanced from one brother to the other as she drank. Jason could almost feel the tension easing between them, but it was too much to hope for, too soon to hope for anything at all. She set the glass on the table and for the first time, her fingers slipped from it. Her hands drifted to her lap, but her shoulders were still sharp points of tension. The room was silent except for the ticking of the clock on the wall above Jeff's head. The simple rooster print clock seemed too ordinary to be an observer of such a strange conversation.

Megan tried to relax, but the conversation was only going to get more bizarre. She couldn't believe she was even considering their proposition. It was every bit as inappropriate as she'd expected. The two worked like a tag-team, bouncing from one to the other, trying to convince her to accept. Jeff had been amazingly blunt about what they expected, but if she were going to seriously consider this, he was going to have to be even more so. She didn't want any surprises.

"Tell me exactly what kind of sexual things you want to do, and what you expect from me," she asked Jeff. "Please be specific. I'm a nurse, I know the big words so you may use them." To his credit, Jeff didn't even blush as he described the various orifices they intended to make use of. He went into graphic detail as to the male organs and other items they might use to bring her to orgasm.

"Jason and I don't touch each other – ever. We'll see to your pleasure first before taking our own."

"If you have specific fantasies you'd like to pursue," Jason jumped in, "then let us know. We'll do whatever we can to fulfill them. We won't invite anyone else into the bed, and we expect you to abide by that rule as well. We'll be exclusive to the relationship, and again, we expect the same in return."

"And we would do this here?" she asked.

"Always," Jason confirmed. "We aren't hounded by reporters away from the field – usually, but we can't take the chance of going to your place too often. That wouldn't be good for you, or for us."

"I would be your dirty little secret."

"No, not a secret exactly," Jeff said. "You'll have game tickets in the family section, and you can go to any team functions you want to, but there aren't that many. When we're in public, you'll be our guest, and if necessary, we can designate one of us to be your official date whenever we're out. That way, there shouldn't be any question as to whom you are with."

"Like Jeff said – you wouldn't be a secret, but our private lives are just that – private. We'd like to keep it that way. It's in everyone's best interest – especially yours."

"That's why we live out here." Jeff swung his arm wide toward the big kitchen window. "The house can't be seen from the road, and our nearest neighbor is over a mile away. The security gate was open today because we knew – well, we hoped you would come. Otherwise, it's locked. The entire property is fenced, and we have state-of-the-art security on the grounds. You'll be safe here, and what we do inside these walls is no one's business but ours."

Up until Jeff had pointed out their need for security, Megan had been too busy trying to make sense of their proposition to consider whom, exactly, these men were. She took a mental step back. Not only was she actually considering having an affair, or a relationship, or whatever, with two brothers, but they were celebrities. They were well known in the area, and they might get by unrecognized alone, but when they were together, that would be impossible.

They had state-of-the-art security for a reason. She thought of the single deadbolt on her apartment door and realized how different their lives were. What was she thinking? She couldn't do this. She pushed back from the table and stood. "I've got to go." Jeff and Jason were on their feet before she took a step.

"Please," Jeff extended his hand, palm out. "Stay a little longer. Let us show you the rest of the house, at least."

"Really, I should go." She took a step. "This…won't…can't work."

"Megan, don't go," Jason said. "You don't have to decide anything today. Just let us show you the whole house before you go. We'll give you all the time you need to decide, but don't say no because you're scared."

"We won't let anyone hurt you," Jeff said. He moved closer while he spoke, close enough that Megan could feel the heat radiating off his body. She took a step back. Before she knew it, she was sandwiched between them. They towered over her by a foot, making her feel small. A moment of panic flitted through her mind. She really didn't know them very well. She took a deep, calming breath. They smelled like sunshine and red-blooded male. Combined with the heat from their bodies, it made her knees go weak.

"I don't know…"

"You don't have to know, not right now." Jason slid an arm around her waist and pulled her back against his hard chest. His erection pressed into the small of her back. His breath fanned over her ear as he spoke. "Let us show you the house. If you decide you'd like to stay a while longer, that's okay; but if you need to go, you can. We won't stop you."

It sounded so reasonable, spoken in that low, masculine voice that it sent shivers down her spine and made her hips move against his. *What would it hurt to see the house?* her inner vixen argued while her rational side kept silent – probably struck dumb by the feel of Jason's erection pinned between them. God, he felt good – another reminder that sex with these two would likely shake the earth. The fact that she was still here, listening, testified to her susceptibility around them.

"This is the kitchen," Jeff said just before his hands found her breasts and his lips brushed the pulse in her neck. She shivered and pressed her breasts against his palms. "We eat in here. I can't wait to feast on you."

Then they touched her, everywhere. Like a well-orchestrated symphony, their hands moved over her body, never going beneath her clothing, but her skin didn't care. She broke out in a full-body blush and when two sets of lips nibbled on her earlobes, she closed her eyes and let her head fall back against Jason's chest. When had her head become so heavy? And her brain so useless? A protest formed somewhere in the deep recesses of her mind, but never made it to her lips.

"We'll stretch you out on the counter and taste every inch of you," Jason said between nibbles.

Blood rushed to her lady parts and an embarrassing dampness heated the spot between her legs as her oxygen-deprived brain created an image to go with Jason's words.

"I could bend you over the table right now and fuck you," Jeff said right before he covered her mouth with his. His lips were soft, but insistent. She opened under him, allowing his tongue to sweep in and steal what was left of her brains.

"But that can wait," Jason said, stepping away, leaving her backside cold and bereft. She would have fallen if Jeff hadn't had a firm grip on her waist. She clung to him, relying on his strength to guide her for the next few minutes.

She glanced at the remaining rooms downstairs, vaguely registering the enormous size of the house. There was a formal living room, dining room, and a front door that led to somewhere. There was an indoor pool and a den that resembled the man-caves she'd seen on television. In each room, the brothers went into great detail about what they wanted to do to her in them. They pointed out the various surfaces they would take her on, under, against, and in some cases went so far as to position her just so. She felt like a ragdoll, being bent and shaped to their will, then one would pull her close and hold her as if she were a cherished toy.

Was that all she would be? A toy? Something to play with until they tired of her, or found someone else?

The entire upstairs was one great master suite, complete with three bedrooms connected like the spokes of a wheel by a sitting room in the center. There were two enormous bathrooms, one on either side of the rooms the brothers occupied. The third bedroom had its own bathroom and a closet roughly the size of Megan's entire apartment.

"This would be your room. We haven't decorated it, so you could design it however you want it," Jeff said.

"Why don't you try the bed?" Jason said. "It's the biggest of the bunch. We had it specially made to accommodate three people."

The enormous four-poster bed would have dwarfed any other room, but this one was big enough to hold it, and then some. Standing in the room, flanked by Jeff and Jason, it suddenly hit Megan. This was real. They actually wanted to do this, had planned to do this. It was too much to wrap her head around. Why her? Why now? Had someone else occupied this room previously? As if she'd voiced her innermost thoughts, Jeff answered.

"We had the house built when we first came to play for the Mustangs. This room has been empty the entire time. You're the first person to see it, other than the housekeeper. She keeps it dusted. We'll have to buy some stuff for the bathroom too."

"Why?" she asked, turning to face them. She preferred to look at them rather than the giant bed. "Why me? Why now?"

They shrugged matching broad shoulders like two kids, and then they answered in unison. "Because we want you."

Megan laughed at their response, and the absurdity of the situation. "I can't believe this. I don't know what to say." She half turned to look at the bedroom again, then turned back to the matched set watching her. It was absurd, but she missed their touch now that they were back to discussing the situation as if it was a business deal. "I have a life, a good life. I have a job. I can't move in here and become...what? Your sex slave?" She cursed her fair skin, knowing it was now an unbecoming shade of crimson.

"No, that isn't what we want," Jason said. "We aren't asking you to give up your life or your job."

"Megan," Jeff said, drawing her attention. "When's your next day off?"

"Tomorrow. Why?"

"We have a game tonight, and another tomorrow afternoon. Let us send a car for you tonight when you get off work. Come spend the night with us."

"We won't pressure you into our bed," Jason added. "But don't walk away from the possibility that this could be something special. Jeff and I," he glanced at his brother, then back to her, "we haven't felt this instant attraction for the same woman in a long time. And we think you feel it too. It's hard to explain, but we've waited to find the right person, and we think you're the one."

"We don't want a slave, Megan," Jeff said. "We want a partner, a lover. And not for just one night. Though, if you give yourself to us for one night and decide it doesn't work for you, we'll understand."

It was crazy. Or maybe she was crazy because she was beginning to consider…well, consider getting to know them, at least. She couldn't deny the way her body reacted to their touch. Since she'd arrived, they'd touched her many times and she'd been putty in their hands.

"Come back tonight. We'll spend the morning together, then you can go to the game or stay here until we get home. You'll be back in your apartment in time to go to work on Monday," Jason reasoned.

"But…I don't get off work until eleven."

"No problem. We won't be home until after eleven. Then we have to be at the field at noon tomorrow," Jeff said. "It's not much time together, but we want to spend it with you."

All the way home, Megan mentally kicked herself for agreeing to spend the next two nights at their home. She'd always thought of herself as levelheaded. Ever since high school, she'd known exactly where she was going, and she'd plotted her way there, never once wavering from her predetermined path. She'd studied Pre-Med in college, earned her degree and enrolled in the best nursing program in Texas. Her college friends said she was nuts not to go on to medical school, but she knew that wasn't for her, however, she did want to have the science classes as a base for further studies.

She loved helping people, especially the kids. Their vulnerability touched her. She knew what it was to feel powerless, to live in fear. Growing up, shuttled from one distant relative to the next, she had no control over her life, and lived in constant fear of being turned out completely. It wasn't any way for a child to grow up, but she'd found strength within herself and survived until her maternal grandparents found her and took her in. She was a ragtag teenager by then, with no direction in life.

The youth group at her grandmother's church was going to the local Children's Hospital to celebrate Halloween with the kids, and she'd signed Megan up to go. Money was tight, but her grandmother had come up with an old-fashioned white nurse's uniform for her costume. It was her first Halloween costume ever, and she loved it. She was only fourteen at the time, but the youngest kids must have thought she was older, and mistook her for a real nurse. When the church group was ready to leave, they found her playing a card game with a group of kids.

From that day on, Megan knew what she wanted to do with her life. She hadn't had time for boys in high school, although she had dated some in college – enough to lose her virginity to another Pre-Med student. After nursing school, she dedicated her life to her work, with the idea in the back of her head that one day she'd fall in love with Mr. Right and have a houseful of kids. Not that she had much hope of finding Mr. Right when she spent so much time at work. It had never seemed like a sacrifice until now. Now she wondered if she hadn't been missing something in her life.

CHAPTER FIVE

Now, all she could think about was the two men who wanted her. *Her.* And, she wanted them more than she had ever wanted any man. They had an insane life – on the road for a week or more at a time – games almost every day. Finding time to be with them would be almost impossible.

Since the Holder brothers' visit to the ward, many of the children had become baseball fans. Christopher was doing better, but he still wasn't well enough to join the group gathered in the day room to watch the game. So Megan made a point to stop in as often as possible to catch a few minutes of the game with him. If he'd been a fan before Jeff's visit, he was a worshiper now. His favorite baseball card, now autographed, sat on his tray table surrounded by what Megan thought of as a shrine.

Christopher improved daily, and everyone noticed his renewed enthusiasm for life. A positive outlook and a real desire to get well could work wonders for any patient, but especially children. Megan smiled at the exuberant boy clutching his Mustangs stadium blanket in one hand, while his new baseball glove dwarfed his other hand. Jeff had given him the items, and as he autographed the glove, told Christopher not to give up his dream of being a professional baseball player. If dreams and wishes could make it so, then one day she'd be watching Christopher on television too.

"Hi, kid. How's the game going?" she asked.

"Not so good. The Mustangs are behind, but it's only the fifth inning."

"There are nine innings, right?"

"Right." He rolled his eyes at her scant baseball knowledge. "Everyone knows that."

"Hey, give me a break," she teased. "I'm new to this, but I'm learning." Out of habit, she checked the monitors hooked up to Christopher. Assured all was as well as could be expected, she turned her attention to the ballgame. "Who's pitching now?"

"That's Renner. He's good, but he doesn't throw anywhere near as hard as Jeff does."

Renner threw a pitch for a strike. "Looks pretty hard to me."

"Yeah, well what do you know?"

"Not much, apparently." The camera shifted to the catcher, and every one of her woman parts jolted to attention. The camera shot was straight on, providing a close-up of Jason Holder's face. The mask hid everything but his eyes which were trained on the pitcher in absolute concentration. It was the same look she'd seen on Jeff's face when he was pitching. She couldn't help but wonder if they'd apply that much focus to making love, and if they did, how wonderful it would feel to be the recipient of that concentration. Maybe she'd find out tonight.

She missed Christopher's next comment as the realization set in. She was going to do it – at least for tonight. She'd made up her mind. One night. She'd give herself this one night to see if what they described was something she could live with.

❧⹇❧

The house was dark, except for the warm glow coming from the west end. As the hired car pulled into the portico, Megan went over what she knew of the house. If she weren't mistaken, the single illuminated room housed the swimming pool. The driver opened the door for her, set her overnight bag on the porch, and pulled away, leaving her standing all alone on Jeff and Jason Holder's doorstep. Were they even home yet?

As promised, the door was unlocked so she let herself in. A small light beneath the kitchen cabinets provided enough illumination to see her way through the kitchen. She tripped over a pair of shoes, catching herself before she crashed into the furniture in the living room. Her eyes adjusted to the dim light, and she noticed the trail of discarded clothes leading toward the pool. She followed, stepping carefully around the small heaps.

She heard them before she saw them in the brightly lit pool. Two sets of broad shoulders and arms split the surface, followed by two firm, flexing, lily-white asses. She smiled and stepped to the edge of the deep end to better admire the view. They made the turn at the far end, and in perfect synchronization stroked their way toward her.

They were equally matched it seemed, kicking and stroking, breathing almost as one. She'd planned to come here, spend some time getting to know them before she decided if she wanted to carry their acquaintance any further. But seeing all those muscles flexing, she suddenly couldn't wait to get her hands on them. I'm going to be sensible about this. *I'm not going to dive into a sexual relationship with two men just because they're drop-dead gorgeous and built like Adonis.*

Then they came to a stop in front of her. Two identical heads broke the surface, and their eyes instantly lit with recognition. Two perfectly crooked smiles told her they were happy to see her.

"Hi, Jeff," she nodded at the one on her left. "Hi, Jason," she nodded at the twin on her right.

"You can tell us apart that easily?" Jeff asked.

"Did I get it right?"

"You did," Jason confirmed. "Not many people can do that, especially with so little to go on."

"If I saw more, do you think it would be easier?"

"Oh yeah," Jason said. One eye closed in a mischievous wink, and all her good intentions flew right out of her brain. "Jeff's dick is tiny," he said. Jeff clocked his brother on the back of the head, splashing water onto the pool deck and Megan's feet.

"Jackass," Jeff said. "If my dick is tiny, so is yours." He folded his arms on the edge of the pool, dismissing Jason. "Don't mind him. We're identical, as far as nature goes. It's the unnatural part that makes him different."

"Shut up, Jeff," Jason warned. "She'll see for herself soon enough." He joined Jeff, hanging from the edge. "Why don't you lose all those clothes and join us? We'll show you how identical we are."

Oh God! She really was losing her mind because she wanted to touch them, to test those muscles beneath her fingertips, to have them touch her. Somehow, she knew Jeff and Jason would make her feel very good. She tried one last time to force some reason into the situation. "I didn't bring a swimsuit."

"So?" they said in unison. Megan smiled. They were so much like little boys, but all her lady parts were telling her these were full grown men. Men she wanted to be with, no matter how insane it was to want it. She kicked her shoes off, and followed them with the sundress she'd put on when she got off work. She should have been self-conscious standing in nothing but her bra and panties in front of two men, but the way they looked at her made her feel something entirely different. She felt empowered, and bolder than ever before. She reached behind her and opened the clasp on her bra. Her breasts sprang free. Her nipples, already puckered with need, grew tighter in the cool air.

Jason uttered a curse and sank beneath the water. Jeff remained where he was, staring at her. "The panties," his voice was harsh, ragged. "Take the panties off. I want to see you."

She did as he asked and Jason's head broke the water again. Sliding her thumbs beneath the band, she slid the scrap of lace past her hips, kicking them off with the toe of one foot when they pooled at her ankles.

"Holy, mother of God," Jason said. "Come here, sweet thing. Let us touch you."

The few times she'd been naked with a man, they'd been in a dark bedroom and she'd been glad they couldn't see her. But standing there in the bright lights of the pool enclosure, naked as the day she was born, she felt like a goddess. The pure masculine appreciation in their eyes sizzled through her, making her bold and daring. She stepped forward, then launched herself over their heads.

She surfaced in the middle of the pool and before she could brush the water from her eyes, two warm bodies sandwiched her between them. Blinded by chlorinated water sluicing down her face, she knew without a doubt that Jeff was in front of her, and Jason was at her back. When she cleared her eyes, she saw she was right. It was uncanny how easily she could tell them apart, and she'd been able to do it almost from the beginning.

"I'm going to kiss you," Jeff said. Then his lips were on hers, hard, demanding, coaxing. Hands roamed her body, making her weak with need. Jason lifted the curtain of wet hair to one side and placed a hot kiss to her nape. A groan slipped from her gut to her lips and vibrated there, trapped by Jeff's mouth. "God, you taste good," he said. Then he was turning her in the water. "Jase, you have to taste her. My God, man, she tastes like heaven."

She spun like a top and came face to face with Jason. Her hands came to rest on his chest a half-second before he crushed her lips beneath his. Behind her, Jeff's hands and lips roamed every inch of her body. She couldn't wait to know their bodies as thoroughly as they were learning hers. Her fingers trailed along Jason's chest, over his pecs, brushing the flat discs of his nipples. She followed the contour of his muscles to his breastbone and stopped.

Jason released her lips, his eyes searching hers. "That's the unnatural part," he said.

"What happened?" she asked, even though she knew only one thing could produce such a scar.

"Open heart surgery when I was nine."

"Oh my God." She half-turned so she could see Jeff. "You too?"

"No, just Wonder Boy."

She ran a hand down his chest, feeling for an identical scar and found none.

"But…"

"We're identical, but Jason was born with a defective heart. They repaired it and said he'd be okay. So far, they've been right. Except for the brain damage, they couldn't fix that."

She was having a hard time wrapping her head around what Jeff was saying, then he added the part about brain damage, and she knew he was making a joke at his brother's expense. She laughed as Jason reached around her and slapped Jeff upside the head in a not so loving brotherly fashion.

"Hey!" she cried. "Naked woman here. Cut it out."

Instantly, their attention returned to her. "I want to know all about it, Jason. But not right now." Her hand skimmed lower, stopping on the softer skin of his abdomen. His rigid cock bobbed against the back of her hand. "Right now, I want to do other things." Her fingers closed around his shaft, and his head dropped back on his shoulders with a groan. Feminine power rushed through her veins, cleansing her of any doubt about what she was doing.

"Jesus, " Jeff said. "Let's get out, and we'll let you do anything you want." He lifted her in his arms and they followed Jason out of the pool.

A large chaise occupied one corner of the room, surrounded by lush tropical plants that created an almost private oasis. Jason sprawled on his side, waiting for them, his turgid cock cradled in the palm of his right hand. He was all hard planes and angles, and simply magnificent in his nudity. He hadn't taken the time to towel off, and water droplets slid in sparkling rivulets along the valleys of his musculature. She shivered with the realization that soon, that body, and another identical one would be hers to touch. Jeff cradled her closer.

"We'll warm you up," he whispered against her ear.

With each step, his cock brushed the small of her back like a matchstick striking, ready to ignite. Another shiver racked her body. There was no need to warm her up. Her insides were molten lava already, her sex, swollen and aching for their touch. If she got any hotter, she might spontaneously combust.

Jeff laid her next to Jason, then stretched out on her other side. Hands found her breasts, kneading, playing. She closed her eyes and reveled in the sensations. Their hands were strong, but gentle. They were rough and callused from years of playing baseball, and so masculine, it took her breath away. When they took both her breasts into their mouths, sucking greedily, desire shot through her like lightning, and she arched her back to give them better access. She wrapped her arms around them, cradling the backs of their heads in her palms and holding them there.

While her upper body strained for more, her lower half went lax. In the remote recesses of her mind, she recognized her behavior for the primitive instinct it was, but the way her hips lifted and her legs splayed in invitation was beyond her control. "Please," she begged, still holding fast to their heads. Two hands skimmed down her body, found her swollen center and she writhed to get closer, to have more.

One firm hand settled on her abdomen, while another – Jason's – delved between her folds and coated her outer lips and clit with her own juices. "Relax, sweetheart. Let us love you," Jeff crooned against her ear as his hand pinioned her hips against the cushion. She opened her eyes and looked straight into Jeff's face, hovering inches above hers. Their gazes locked. Something transpired between them in that moment. Something she didn't understand, but something she wanted to reach for with her whole being. He looked away, and whatever it was, vanished. Had he felt it too?

Strong hands skimmed her inner thighs and pressed them up and out, exposing her most private parts, banishing whatever thoughts she had. A tongue swept over her aching flesh from anus to clit. Jeff's hand on her abdomen held her still as Jason fit his mouth to her and began an assault on her senses she'd never thought possible.

Jeff's tongue swept past her lips, stroked along the inside of her bottom lip, before thrusting deep. She needed oxygen, and tore her mouth away to suck in a long breath.

"Hang on, sweetheart. That feels good, doesn't it?" Jeff's gaze remained focused on her face, while his hand continued to control her lower body. She wanted to close her thighs around the face between her legs, but Jason's shoulders held her spread wide. He stroked his tongue over her repeatedly, then closed his lips over her clit and sucked. Megan shut her eyes and bit her bottom lip to hold in her cries.

"Don't hold it in, darlin'. Let us hear you. We want to know what you're feeling." Jeff's words released her from her self-imposed modesty, and when Jason's tongue delved into her vagina at the same time Jeff lowered his head and sucked her nipple into his mouth, she flew right out of the atmosphere. Her scream echoed off every hard surface in the room.

She had no idea how long she drifted in space. It might have been seconds, or hours. It didn't matter, for when she became aware of her surroundings once again, the warmth that had caressed one side of her body was gone, but replaced by a similar one on the other side. She opened her eyes to find Jason hovering over her. "You taste like honey," he said. Moisture glistened on his full lips and chin. "Here, let me show you." Fingers framed her jaw, turning her face to his. He dipped his head, covering her lips with his. She groaned at the taste of herself on his lips and tongue. It was wicked and arousing. She thrust her tongue into his mouth, searching for the unique taste of Jason combined with her own flavor.

God, he tasted like the finest wine, and she was well on her way to being intoxicated when a hot, wet tongue swept the sated flesh between her legs. Jason trapped her cry with his mouth while one strong hand pressed against her abdomen, holding her in place for his brother, just as Jeff had done for him.

"Relax," he whispered against her ear as he held her close to his chest. "Let Jeff take you there too." Like she had a choice, surrounded by two hard male bodies – one, half cradling her upper torso against his, the other between her legs, his arms wrapped securely around her thighs, and his mouth fused to her secret flesh. She'd just had the most powerful orgasm of her life, and didn't think she could achieve anything close for a long time, but Jeff was as skilled as his brother, and soon she found the desire mounting again.

He took his time, stroking, sucking, thrusting his tongue into her. He played her clit like a fine instrument, flicking his tongue lightly over it, then sucking it into his mouth until she thought she might die from the pleasure. His teeth nipped at the swollen nub and stars burst behind her eyelids at the sharp pain. "No!" She cried out, and bucked against Jason's restraining hand. Jeff released her clit, bathing the tender tissue with his tongue before capturing it between his lips and gently rolling. "Oh God," she sighed at the exquisite pleasure accentuated by the brief bite of pain.

She was still reeling from the taste of pleasure/pain when Jeff shifted, lifting her hips off the cushion. He thrust a finger deep inside her. Jason cradled her closer. She felt more than heard his soothing words vibrating through his chest. Then another finger filled her. Her breath came in short, insufficient pants as Jeff worked her pussy, finding the spot inside that promised heaven. She whimpered when his fingers left her.

He drew a slick line south to her other hole and she tried to clench against his exploration. Jason's hand on her abdomen stroked and soothed as he crooned unintelligible words to her. No one had ever touched her there. Her brain said no, but her body heated as Jeff continued his gentle exploration. His hands stroked her ass cheeks, soothing and reassuring before his fingers returned to find more lubrication. She forgot to breathe as he probed the tight little hole.

Jason relaxed his hold on her and she sighed in relief. "Breathe, Megan. Jeff won't hurt you." He stroked her hair with his free hand. "This is your first time?"

She knew what he meant, her first time to… She nodded her head, embarrassed to look at Jeff there, between her legs, and afraid her voice would falter if she tried to speak.

"He's only going to try one finger tonight," Jason explained. "One of these days, we hope to both have you at the same time." She remained silent as Jason explained and Jeff continued to lubricate her with her own juices. "Nod if you understand." She nodded. "Good.

Nod again if you want to try this tonight." She nodded again and as she did, Jeff pressed one finger past her tight barrier.

Her heart stopped, and every muscle in her body turned to mush. She'd never felt so weak, so vulnerable in her life. Jason crooned something else before he bent and sucked a nipple into his mouth. Jeff's finger took up a rhythmic pumping, then his mouth closed over her clit and it was as if she'd been launched into space on the back of a missile – without benefit of oxygen. Her world exploded as her body soared through the maelstrom – straight into heaven.

CHAPTER SIX

She woke alone and naked in the giant bed. Used to late nights followed by early mornings, she wasn't surprised to find the sun was just a blush on the horizon. After giving her the most amazing night of her life, Jeff and Jason walked her to her room, saw her tucked into bed, and left. She'd gone to sleep almost as soon as her head hit the pillow. Now, in the deep purple pre-dawn haze, she let the night replay in her mind. They'd seen to her needs, created some she didn't know she had, and left her exhausted and weak. Her body still sang with the memory of recent use, but she couldn't remember ever feeling so...

She searched for the right word. Loved? No, but close. Jeff and Jason didn't love her, but the way they'd handled her, like she was special, cherished. That was it, cherished. They hadn't really asked to do the things they did to her, but they'd given her every opportunity to stop them. And now that she thought about it, neither one of them had...

No, there had been no intercourse. She was sure of that. Everything that happened last night had been for her. Not that they hadn't enjoyed giving her pleasure. She wasn't foolish enough to believe men didn't gain satisfaction from mastering a woman's body, but doing so without reaching climax themselves wasn't the norm. You didn't have to be overly experienced sexually to know that.

By the time they'd walked her to her room, she would have taken them to her bed without a second thought, but they hadn't asked. They hadn't even acted as if they expected it. What was with that?

She spied her overnight bag sitting inside the door and remembered Jason carrying it up the stairs for her while Jeff held her steady. She pulled one of the extra pillows over her face and groaned into it. No way would she have made it up the stairs without Jeff's support. Her knees – no, all her joints had been lifeless when they were done with her. Even now her body felt euphoric, and well used. It was a feeling she could get used to, very quickly.

Someone had stocked the bathroom with towels and some toiletries that bore the logo of an expensive hotel chain. No doubt the tiny bottles had been snatched by one of the brothers on a road trip with the team, but as she lathered her hair in the shower she was grateful for their thoughtfulness. The shower was luxurious and like the bed, built to accommodate either one giant, or three humans of reasonable proportions. Water sluiced down her back as she raised her face to the spray and rinsed the conditioner from her hair. Saying Jeff and Jason were built in reasonable proportions might be understating things. She hadn't had much time to examine their bodies, but what she'd seen, and touched, had her rethinking her estimate. She'd managed to wrap her hands around them for a brief time, but it hadn't lasted long. They'd both allowed her to play for a minute, no more, before they'd lifted her hand and started in on making her lose her mind again.

She dressed in the jeans and T-shirt she'd brought for the day, towel-dried her hair and pulled it into a high ponytail. Her hosts had thought of the basics, but apparently, that didn't include a hair dryer. She hastily dabbed on some mascara, and patted some balm on her lips, still tender from the previous night's workout. Her reflection in the gilt-framed mirror gave her pause. What was she doing here? She straightened and looked around the custom-built bathroom. A chill swept through her, and she had to clutch the counter to keep from falling.

They'd planned to have a relationship with a woman. One woman. Even though they'd said as much, it really hadn't sunk in. Until now. They'd had the house built with this in mind. Megan made her way to the door and leaned against the doorjamb, studying the bedroom as if she'd never seen it before. The custom bed, the dimensions of the room all made sense now, and the chill shivering through her body turned to a cold, hard lump of apprehension.

What were they looking for, really? Had they brought her here hoping the house, their wealth, the luxurious lifestyle would seduce her into becoming… What? Being kept as someone's sex toy wasn't anything she'd ever dreamed of.

Sure, she'd hoped one day to find the right man, someone who respected her, someone who would applaud her accomplishments, and love her. That part was essential – the love part.

But this wasn't about love. This was about sex. And she was virtually their prisoner here. Apprehension gave way to anger, at herself for not insisting on driving herself, and then for agreeing to come in the first place. This wasn't her. She didn't let men run her life, and she wasn't desperate enough for sex, no matter how good it was, to give up everything she'd worked for to be someone's live in plaything.

She grabbed her overnight bag and opened the door. The sun had risen enough to illuminate the sitting room through the skylights. The doors to Jeff and Jason's rooms were closed with no telltale sliver of light showing beneath them. They'd be up soon, or so they'd said. They had a one o'clock game, which meant they had to be at the stadium in a few hours. Since her only choices were to steal a car, or wait for them to get up and arrange for her transportation home, she banked her anger and headed for the kitchen. Coffee would go a long way toward calming her nerves.

She'd barely noticed the kitchen the day before. Now, she took the time to admire it. Someone who knew what they were doing had designed it. Acres of granite-topped counters and custom cabinets flanked restaurant-quality appliances. They might not do much cooking, but it wasn't because they lacked the facilities. Any gourmet chef would be happy to call this kitchen home.

Megan opened a few cabinets before she found a box of tiny, foil-covered plastic cups that said they were coffee. More searching produced a fancy coffee maker designed for their use. It took some experimentation and a few false starts before she figured out how to use the machine, but once she had a cup in her hands, and caffeine surging through her system, she began to calm.

She would just tell them she wanted to go home, and that would be that. They wouldn't hold her to staying any longer, especially after she told them she wasn't going to be their plaything. She wasn't into playing house with them, or anyone else.

The same pantry where she'd found the coffee also yielded a box of cereal, but the refrigerator cleverly disguised as a cabinet held a case of beer and half a twelve pack of sodas – not diet, she noticed, and no milk. She popped another coffee disc in the machine and settled on a barstool with the remains of her first cup of coffee and the box of cereal. Ordinarily, she would have poured the cereal into a bowl, even if she wasn't going to pour milk over it, but she doubted the guys would care if she ate it straight from the box.

She was still there, munching handfuls of dry cereal and washing it down with coffee when Jeff and Jason came downstairs. Bare-chested, but wearing cartoon character boxers, they looked like overgrown boys with their sleepy, unshaven faces.

"Good morning," they said in unison, stopping to place a kiss on her cheek as they went past her. In a better mood since the infusion of legal stimulants – caffeine and sugar – Megan watched as the pair shuffled around the kitchen in silence, opening cabinets and staring at the empty shelves as if they expected an elf had stocked them overnight. Jeff snatched a coffee packet and fumbled with the coffee maker while Jason grabbed a soda from the refrigerator and joined her at the bar. He grabbed the box of cereal and helped himself to a handful. They both watched Jeff. After a few grumbled curses aimed at technological advances, he finally managed to coax a cup of java from the machine and joined them at the bar.

Maybe it was the coffee, or the crunchy sugar-coated cereal, but something inside her softened. If this were seduction, or even an attempt to convince her to make the relationship permanent, then she'd eat the cereal, box and all. Obviously, they weren't morning people. Their hair stood out at odd angles, and up close she could see creases on Jeff's face from his pillow. Jason yawned, scratched the scar on his chest and farted. Megan smiled, even as she scooted her barstool further away.

"Hey, we've got company," Jeff scolded.

"Sorry," Jason grunted before he repeated the cereal, soda routine.

"Don't mind me," Megan said, reaching for the cereal box. "Do you always live like this?"

"Like what?" Jeff asked.

"Like you don't live here? How do you exist without any food?"

"I told you. We eat out. Jase can't cook for shit, and I'm not much better."

"Why don't you hire someone to cook for you?"

"Tried that," Jason said. A big belch followed, then he continued. "She thought we should keep regular hours, and when we explained we didn't have any control over the game times, or which ones were out of town, she quit. Said it was too much trouble."

"We only have Danni now. She keeps the laundry done, and the house clean."

"Look, guys," she waited until she had their attention. "I don't know what you want from me, but I'm not interested." They needed a keeper, someone to look after them. As touching as this was, she wasn't going to become their keeper any more than she was going to be their plaything. "I need to go home. Can you call a car for me?"

Two sets of identical blue eyes stared at her and she fought the urge to pat her head to see if her hair looked as bad as theirs did. Slowly, sleep left their faces and she knew she had their full attention.

"You have a game today, and I need to get home. I have stuff to do," she lied.

"We thought you were going to stay until tomorrow," Jason said.

"Why do you want to go?" Jeff asked.

"Look, I don't know what you expect from me. It's clear you've given a lot of thought to sharing…a woman. You have the room set up, and everything, but I don't think I'm the woman you want."

"Why do you think that?" Jeff asked. His coffee sat forgotten in front of him now.

"I can't do this." She waved her hands around to indicate…something. "I'm not going to give up my career to be your plaything, or to be your keeper. I'm sorry if I gave you the impression I was interested in that kind of arrangement."

Silence rang through the kitchen like a death knell. Jeff and Jason didn't move, didn't take their eyes off her. This wasn't going well. Not at all. The coffee maker beeped and she almost jumped out of her skin. Finally, Jeff spoke.

"It was never our intention for you to be either. If we wanted those things, we can afford to buy them." Megan flinched as the barb struck home. Wasn't that what she really objected to, the thought that they were trying to buy her…services? Jeff motioned to a row of keys hanging on the wall next to a short hallway. "Pick any car you like. The keys are labeled. We'll send someone to pick it up later."

Oh boy. She'd struck a nerve, and Jeff had struck back with enough hurt in his voice to make her wish she'd never come in the first place. His dismissal should have made wings grow on her feet, but instead, her heart sank like a lump of lead, anchoring her to the spot.

"Wait," Jason said. "Don't go."

He punched Jeff in the arm. "Apologize, dickhead. Unless you're trying to make her go, and I know you don't want that anymore than I do."

Why wasn't she halfway down the driveway now? Everything reasonable inside her said she should grab a set of keys and get the hell out, but another part of her wouldn't let her leave. Not like this anyway. "Why don't you tell me what, exactly, you want from me?"

"I sure as hell don't want you to be our keeper." Jeff said the last word with enough scorn to make it clear he'd objected to her use of the word. "We do fine by ourselves. We don't pay for sex, and we don't bring women here. If we wanted a *keeper*, we'd advertise for one. What we want is you. I said it before. We want to get to know you, and not just in bed. We like you, and we respect your job. We'd never ask you to give it up to cook and spread your legs for us. Frankly, I'm insulted you think that's what we asked you out here for."

"Megan, if you choose to be with us, we'll hire a cook — or at least buy some groceries. Honestly, we aren't home enough to even notice we don't have any. When it's just us, it's easier to eat out. Stay today. You're welcome to use one of our cars while we're gone. Or better yet, come to the ballpark. We'll talk after the game. Promise." He held his hand up in a Scout pledge, but he didn't look like any scout she'd ever seen. Scouts didn't look dangerous, and Jason Holder was dangerous. All her woman parts new it.

"You said we'd talk last night, and I don't remember a lot of that going on."

"Don't take your clothes off tonight," Jeff said.

"Okay, I guess I'm as much to blame for the lack of conversation as anyone, but there's one thing I'm curious about."

"And what would that be?" Jeff asked.

"Last night...why didn't you...I mean...why didn't we..."

"Fuck? Are you wondering why we didn't fuck you?"

A heated flush crept up from her neck to her hairline. Jeff was being deliberately crude. "Yes, that's what I'm asking."

"We didn't have any condoms," Jason said. "We're going to be busy this afternoon, but if you go out, stop and pick some up, will you?"

"You really weren't expecting to have sex last night, were you?"

"No. We thought you were coming here to talk about a possible relationship with us, one that would include sex, when you were ready for it. Not before."

His comments took the starch out of her indignation, and her shoulders sagged. She'd been wrong. She'd jumped to conclusions based on…nothing. She had absolutely nothing on which to conjure her wild imaginings but her own insecurities. "I'm sorry. I've never been in a situation like this. I misunderstood."

Jeff's voice lost the edge it had before. "We should apologize. We gave you the wrong impression last night. We shouldn't have taken advantage of you the way we did. We teased you, never expecting you to actually take your clothes off." He shrugged his shoulders. "We're only human. You have a great body, and we were dying to touch you, to taste you." He turned to his brother. "Hey, Jase. We've got to get going or we'll be late."

Megan stood when they did. "What time will you be home?"

"We should be back by six, unless the game goes extra innings. Earlier if there aren't a lot of base runners," Jason said.

"How about I fix dinner for you then?"

"Okay. But only if you want to. We could pick up something on our way home, if you would rather," Jeff offered.

"No. I'd like to cook for you. I'll have to see what you have, and go pick some things up, but it's the least I can do for jumping to conclusions the way I did."

As they were leaving, dressed in suits and clean-shaven, Jeff stopped and pulled out his wallet. "Just so you know, we want to be with you, but we won't act on that without protection, and we aren't going to buy any." He handed her two one hundred dollar bills. "This should cover dinner, and condoms, if you think you might be ready to take that step. If not, we'll wait until you are."

Megan sat for a long time sipping coffee and listening to the silence of the big, empty house. Everything they'd said and done played over in her mind, and the more she remembered the more clear her situation became. She wanted to believe them, but really? What kind of testosterone fueled, single athletes didn't have condoms stashed? It was unheard of. But, if it were true, she bargained with herself, then she did owe them the home-cooked meal she'd promised.

A search of their bedrooms and bathrooms revealed a few things she hadn't previously known. Jeff was a neat freak, and Jason was only a slob around Jeff. She'd been certain it had been Jeff who'd collected her clothes from the previous evening, folded them neatly and stacked them on the dresser in her bedroom. But now she wasn't so certain. Jason's closet and personal space was every bit as neat as Jeff's. She had to conclude Jason's slovenly ways outside his bedroom were nothing more than a way to annoy his brother, or perhaps it was his personal rebellion against having a clone.

After snooping into their nightstands, medicine cabinets and every other place she could think of to stash condoms, she concluded they had told the truth. They really didn't have any in the house.

She unloaded the groceries, enough for dinner and breakfast, hid the box of condoms in her overnight bag, and took it back to her room, along with full size bottles of her favorite bath products. Somewhere between the produce aisle and the pharmacy section, she'd made up her mind to stay the night. She'd purchased the condoms, but still hadn't decided if she wanted to use them. She wasn't stupid. It was better to have them and not need them, than the other way around. She knew in her heart that if they kissed her the way they had last night, then asked to join her in bed, she wouldn't be able to say no.

She turned the game on in the den and curled into the corner of the big, overstuffed sofa to watch. It was an easy game to follow, but she knew there was more to it. The announcers talked about pitch strategies, about right-handed batters versus left-handed pitchers and the depth of both teams' bullpens. Megan listened carefully, trying to learn as much as she could about the game. If she were going to spend time with Jeff and Jason, she needed to understand what they did for a living. The Mustangs were ahead by one run in the eighth when Megan headed to the kitchen to begin dinner preparations.

Later, with the chicken ready to put on the indoor grill and the peach cobbler in the oven, she returned to the game. Reporters stalked the opposing team as they celebrated their victory. Her heart sank as she watched the replay of the final inning. Jeff had given up a run, then the next batter had hit a homerun. He struck out the next batter for the third out and stalked off the field.

CHAPTER SEVEN

Jeff slammed the door shut behind him and stormed through the kitchen as if the hounds of hell were on his heels. Megan followed his progress with her eyes, unsure if she should follow or not. Then Jason came in, shutting the door with a soft click. Weariness lined his face and added weight to his shoulders. He settled onto a barstool and sighed.

"What's wrong with him?"

"Blown save," Jason said. "Give him a few minutes. He forgets he's not the only one on the team sometimes."

"Where's he going?"

"To the pool. He'll swim a few laps, then he'll remember that I struck out in the fifth with the bases loaded, and he'll be mad at *me* for a while. By morning, he'll put it behind him and focus on the next game."

"Is he always like this when the Mustangs lose?"

"No. Only when he gives up the winning runs. Fortunately, that doesn't happen very often." Jason looked around, sniffing the air. "What's that smell? It smells like food."

Megan laughed at his enthusiasm. "We're having grilled chicken and veggies. We have peach cobbler for dessert." She pulled a plate of cut-up vegetables from the refrigerator and set it on the counter in front of Jason. "This is ranch dip. I thought you might want something to snack on until the chicken is done."

Jason scooped up a handful of baby carrots and ate them like potato chips. "These are good. When's the chicken going to be ready?"

"Soon. Should we wait for Jeff?"

"No need to wait," Jeff said from the door. Megan gaped. He was stark naked and dripping wet, standing in the doorway he'd stormed through a few minutes earlier. He caught her look and shrugged. "We're out of towels in the pool room. We must have used them all last night."

Megan rolled her eyes. "The chicken isn't done yet. Go get some clothes on."

Ignoring her, Jeff grabbed a fistful of celery sticks and dragged them through the bowl of dip. He left, cradling the dripping vegetables in one hand while he stuffed one stick in his mouth. "I'll be right back."

Jason continued to pop carrots in his mouth, unconcerned about his brother's nudity, or his juvenile behavior. Megan turned back to the chicken cooking on the built-in grill. She flipped the pieces over blindly. All she could see was Jeff's limp package as he stood in the doorway and his tight ass as he disappeared in the direction of the stairs. They were supposed to talk tonight, but she wasn't going to do much talking with her tongue stuck to the roof of her mouth.

She reached for the glass of wine she'd poured earlier and left sitting on the counter. Perhaps alcohol wasn't the best idea right now, given the state of her resolve, but the smooth spirits did a passable job of ungluing her tongue. After a few sips, she set the glass aside before she did something stupid like run upstairs and dig the box of condoms out of her bag. She was determined to give herself time to know these men before she let their relationship go any further.

Not that it was going anywhere tonight. Jeff returned, dressed in jeans and a Mustangs T-shirt. Jason's suit coat hung over the back of the barstool. Megan grabbed his tie off the counter and folded it before setting it out of harm's way. She transferred the meal to serving dishes and handed them each a plate. They helped themselves at the bar, then at Megan's insistence took seats at the table in the breakfast nook. She poured them each a glass of wine and topped her own off before joining them at the table.

"This is good. Really good," Jeff said as he lifted another forkful of mashed potatoes. "Thanks."

"You're welcome." She ate silently, watching the brothers for some clue as to their mood. Even though Jeff had been polite since returning fully clothed, Megan couldn't help but think they were sitting on a powder keg that could explode at any minute. She soon found she wasn't wrong.

"Why couldn't you have just hit the fucking ball?" Jason cut his eyes to Megan at Jeff's outburst. His wink and half-smile reminded her this was what he'd told her would happen.

"I didn't hit it because it broke before it got to the plate. If you could throw a breaking ball, you'd know what I'm talking about, and maybe you wouldn't have given up a fucking homerun to the number nine batter on a roster full of number nine batters."

Megan listened as the brothers exchanged insults over the dinner she'd worked so hard to prepare. As they threw verbal arrows at each other, she was glad they hadn't gone out to eat after all. When they finally pushed their plates away, they seemed to have exhausted their insulting vocabulary. She dared to ask what was on her mind.

"What would you have done if you'd had to eat out tonight? Would you have had this same…conversation…in a restaurant?"

"No. We probably would have called the pizza dude," Jason said. "It's the way we blow off steam. Jeff does this every time he blows a save. He blames himself first, then he blames me, then he comes to the truth – it was the whole team's fault. Any number of plays in the course of nine innings could have changed the outcome of the game. It's unreasonable to blame it on the last few pitches."

"That still doesn't change the fact that I gave up hits to the two worst batters in the major leagues," Jeff said. "I couldn't focus."

"Focus is a big thing?" Megan asked.

"It's everything," he answered. "Truth?"

Megan nodded, afraid to hear what he was going to say.

"I was afraid you would change your mind, and you wouldn't be here when we got back. All I could think about was you. Getting home to you, holding you, making love to you."

Her woman parts, already loosened up by the wine, softened more at his admission. Then, as his words sunk in, she was horrified. "Oh no! You aren't blaming me for this. I didn't have anything to do with the game."

"Whoa," Jason said. His hand on her arm stilled her. "That's not what he's saying. No one blames you. The game is about mental discipline as much as it is about physical ability. Jeff was distracted tonight. He knows better, but he could have found the focus somewhere, if he'd wanted to."

"Jase is right. I fucked up. I let my guard down because the team we were playing is the worst in the league. I let my mind wander, and I shouldn't have. It was my mistake. However, we should have beaten the Anglers by a dozen runs. We certainly had the base runners to do it, but we couldn't come up with the hits when we needed them. Apparently, I wasn't the only one on the team who didn't think they had to bring their brain to the field today. The entire roster is at fault, starting with the manager and all the way down to the bullpen. Probably the only person who didn't have his head up his ass today was the ball boy."

"Amen," Jason added.

"Well, just so you know – I'm not taking the blame for your screw-ups," Megan said.

"Never," Jeff said. He rose and took his plate and glass to the sink. "Why don't you go get comfortable in the den? Jase and I will clean up in here."

She was half-asleep on the sofa when they joined her. They brought bowls of warm peach cobbler, and they'd found the exorbitantly expensive ice cream she bought to top it with. They ate in silence, Jeff and Jason sprawled in the two big recliners, her on the sofa with her legs folded beneath her. The men made satisfied noises as they finished off their servings, which she noted were twice as big as hers. She smiled. Leftovers wouldn't be a problem with these two around.

"What's so funny?" Jason asked as he sat his empty bowl on the table next to his chair. He had to shove a few things around to find a level spot first.

"Nothing. I was just thinking that I'd have to cook bigger meals if there were going to be any leftovers around here."

"Then you're thinking about staying?" Jeff asked. He had no trouble finding a spot to set his bowl down. Everything on his side of the room was military neat.

"I guess I am. At least a little. I'm not ready to move in, but I would like to spend more time with the two of you. I'd like to see if there's enough between us…"

"We've told you what we want from you," Jeff said. "Why don't you tell us what you'd like from us."

And there it was. The big question. The one she'd been struggling with since the night she'd allowed them to seduce her in the back seat of a town car. The one she still didn't know the answer to. "I don't know," she answered. "I'd be lying if I said I wasn't interested in the sex." Her skin heated and the box of condoms stashed in her bag flashed in her mind. "So far, what I've experienced with you has been spectacular, but I don't know if being a part of a threesome is something I want. It's exciting to think about it, to fantasize about it, but in reality?" She shook her head. "I don't know if I'm up to it, or if I could…uhm…handle two men at the same time…all the time."

"We wouldn't always ask you to be with both of us at the same time. There will be times when we'll want you separately, or perhaps one will be with you while the other watches," Jason said.

"Or we could come to you alone. One-on-one. We'd try not to do that to you on the same night, but it could happen." Jeff grinned. "Right now, I don't see a time when I wouldn't want you."

"Oh," she said. Calculations ran through her mind. How many times a night? A week? A month?... "That's a lot of intercourse."

"It is, but we promise your pleasure will come before ours. Of course, you're free to decline at anytime. We understand that you might not be up to fucking, but there are other things we can do."

That damned heat was creeping up her neck again at the thought of "other things".

"What, 'other things' are you talking about?"

"Oral sex comes to mind," Jason said, grinning ear-to-ear. Oh God. Why did she have to ask that question?

Megan gave herself extra points when she arrived home on Monday via the town car Jeff had called for her, and the box of condoms remained unopened in her overnight bag. It had been a close thing, more than once, but she stuck by her decision not to take the relationship any further until she knew them better. And since Jeff and Jason were leaving on a week-long road trip today, getting to know them was going to take a while.

She unpacked, and stepped into the shower. It had perhaps been unwise to linger this morning, but waking up in the same bed with two of the most gorgeous men she'd ever seen in her life was a moment to savor, if ever there was one. She had to give them credit for creativity. She'd asked about the other things they could do instead of intercourse, and they'd spent most of the night showing her.

Megan slumped against the shower wall, closed her eyes and let the hot water steam around her. Memories and images played through her mind in an endless loop. She soaped her washcloth and ran it over her tender nipples. Her breath caught in her lungs as she remembered all the ways Jeff and Jason had touched her, and the promises they'd made while doing it.

"Your nipples will be sore tomorrow," Jason promised as he sucked one between his lips and pulled it hard against the roof of his mouth.

"Every time your bra shifts, you'll think of this, of us," Jeff promised as he pinched an areola between his callused fingers, then clamped the protruding nipple hard with his teeth. She'd writhed beneath them, desperate for more, but they'd promised nothing more than touching until she asked for it, and provided the protection.

Her nipples still stood at attention, and sore didn't even begin to cover it. The skin was chafed, leaving the nerve endings raw. She covered one breast with the hot soapy washcloth, and the other with the palm of her hand. The heat felt good on her tender skin, but it did little to ease the ache. It was useless to deny she missed them, missed their hands on her. But this was the way it would be if she took them up on their offer. They'd do all manner of wicked things to her body, and then they'd be gone for days, weeks on the road, and she'd be left standing in the shower alone, trying to ease the ache with a washcloth.

Her legs wobbled beneath her and she pressed her empty hand to the wall to steady herself. With the other, she moved the slick washcloth lower until she cupped her sex. They'd been gentle with her here, but even still, there was only so much the delicate tissues could take. Her heart tripped as she remembered lying in the vee of Jason's legs, supported against his chest, her legs held wide open by his giant hands and strong arms.

Her knees gave out, and she sank to the shower floor, spreading her legs as far as she could in the confines of the stall. Would she ever forget the sight of Jeff between her thighs? Or the promises he'd made while he explored her most intimate parts?

"You taste so good," he said between gentle laps of his tongue over her pussy. "You'll remember this when we're away. You'll remember how it feels to have my tongue inside you."

Her head banged hard against the shower wall as she dipped her terrycloth-covered finger inside, feeling the rasp of Jeff's tongue as she did.

"We're going to take you here, too." His tongue flicked against her back door and she'd gasped and struggled to get free. Jason held her for Jeff's explorations. His words did little to ease her concerns, and everything to make her long for what they were promising.

"Let him touch you, sweetheart. We want to take you there as well, but we won't until you're ready." She'd cried out when Jeff thrust his finger deep inside her. "Shh," Jason crooned. "Relax. Concentrate. The hurt will ease in a second."

"You're so damned tight," Jeff said between her legs, looking up to meet her eyes. Hunger and need blazed through her, and she relaxed in Jason's embrace. "That's it," Jeff crooned, "let me in." Another finger joined the first one and Megan tensed again.

"Tomorrow, think of us. Imagine how it will feel to take both of us inside you at the same time," Jason said as Jeff inserted another finger and began to work her tight muscles. "I can't wait to fuck your ass, and your pussy. I want all of you. We want all of you," Jason said as Jeff took her clit between his teeth and tugged.

When she'd floated down from the heavens, she noticed the fullness where Jeff's fingers had been. "Wear this tonight," he said. He flicked the knob protruding from her ass and her pussy creamed as the sensation vibrated through her. "We'll take it out and put it back in several times throughout the night so you get used to wearing it." He produced an array of plugs in sizes varying from the small one she wore to a big one she was sure would injure her if they tried to insert it. "They'll get bigger and bigger until you think you've had enough."

They'd done it too. All through the night, they used her body in tender ways, bringing her to climax over and over again. Sometimes she came with one of the butt plugs in, sometimes without. Each plug became progressively larger and heavier, and by morning, she had taken the largest into her with ease. It was this one she'd brought home with her.

"Wear it while we're gone, and think of us, think of how much better it will be to have a cock there," Jason had said.

The water grew cold, and Megan reached up to turn it off, remaining on the tile floor until she thought her legs could hold her.

That day, her shift at the hospital seemed as if it would never end. Her leg muscles ached, her nipples screamed like fire and her pussy and anus throbbed with remembered pleasure, and pleasure denied. Two days later, she took her dinner break in Christopher's room and watched part of the Mustangs game with him. She'd bought a book, *Baseball for Dummies*, and studied it whenever something happened she didn't understand, and that was more often than she cared to admit.

After four days, she gave in and inserted the butt plug after she'd showered and curled up in bed to read. They called her on the fifth night. The team had a day off in Seattle, and they said they wanted to hear her voice. Their conversation had been like she imagined lovers of long standing would carry on. They said they missed her, they wanted only her, and then they asked about her work, and Christopher, specifically. She told them what she could without giving away confidential information, then they asked about what she did in her free time. She told them about the baseball book she'd bought, and they laughed good-naturedly at her attempt to learn the game.

They told her stories about their travel experiences, and spoke of the games as if they were boring business meetings. She almost told them about the butt plug, that she was now wearing it at night, but something held her back. They promised to call again when they could, and as she hung up, she choked back the words she longed to say.

She missed them so damned much. She filled her free time studying every book about baseball she could find, and watching whatever game was being televised.

They called again two days later. Their road trip was ending, and they'd be home in another two days. She wished she'd asked them to Skype her so she could see their faces when she answered their unspoken question. Would she be there when they got home?

The question had hung over their time apart like the blade of a guillotine. If she said no, the relationship would be severed. Jeff and Jason would not push her to do something she didnot want to do, but if she said yes…her life would change beyond anything she'd ever imagined.

They'd exhausted all the usual areas of conversation, and a dark silence sounded over the phone line. Megan knew they were waiting for her to answer the question.

"What time does your plane get in?" she asked. It wasn't exactly an answer, but it was answer enough. She smiled at the audible sighs on the other end of the line. They'd been afraid she would say no. Her heart clenched and she wiped tears from her cheeks. They'd only known each other a few weeks, but she couldn't imagine her life without them now. And everything they'd promised to do to her body, things she'd never thought possible, she craved now with every fiber of her being.

"Six o'clock," Jason said. "There's a key under the mat."

CHAPTER EIGHT

Megan put away the groceries she'd brought. If she were going to spend any time at all with Jeff and Jason, she wasn't going to starve. Number one on her list was laying down some ground rules, the least of which was, she wasn't going to be their housekeeper, cook or – heaven forbid – their mother. She was pretty sure they weren't thinking in those terms, but these days it was acceptable for a woman to voice her expectations up front, and that's exactly what she intended to do.

"Wow. What's all this?" Jeff asked as he and Jason dragged their suitcases through the kitchen.

"It's food," Megan said, transferring a steaming casserole from the oven to the island. "Don't get used to it."

Jason parked his suitcase near the door and hopped onto a barstool. Jeff wasn't far behind. "This is the second time you've cooked for us," Jason said as he looked appreciatively at the food. "It would be real easy to get used to it."

Megan brought another dish to the island and her gaze locked with Jeff's. Unlike his brother, Jeff wasn't focused on the food, he was focused on her. "You look good enough to eat," he said.

"Thank you." Megan felt a flush creep over her face that had nothing to do with the heat from cooking and everything to do with the way Jeff made her feel every time he looked at her. "I enjoy cooking, but as I said, don't get used to it." She poured glasses of homemade lemonade for each of them before taking a seat at the far end of the bar so she could see them both. "I made dinner tonight because I wanted to talk to you, and I thought the best way to get you to listen was to fill your mouths with food."

She scooped the casserole onto plates and passed them to Jeff and Jason before filling her own plate. Once they were settled with full plates in front of them, she resumed. "I've given this arrangement a lot of thought." Two identical sets of eyes turned to her. "Go ahead. You can eat while we talk." She waited until they had their mouths full before she continued. "I know you said all you wanted was sex, and I think I've come to terms with that, but I want to make my expectations clear."

Jeff swallowed, then washed it down with half a glass of lemonade. "Okay. We're listening."

"Good. I won't be the cook or the maid. I won't pick up after you, and I won't do your laundry. I'm not your servant or your mother. If you want those things, I'm not the woman to give them to you."

"We aren't looking for any of those things, especially the mother part." Jason shuddered at he said the last part. "Did we do anything to give you that impression?"

"No. No you didn't," she admitted. "I just wanted to make sure we're on the same page here before...well, before we..."

"Fuck?" Jason said.

"I was going to say, get intimate, but I guess it's a bit late for that."

"We understood what you meant, didn't we?" Jeff elbowed Jason in the ribs.

"Yeah, we understood."

"Second, I'm not going to move in with you." They both sat up straighter and looked at her.

"Why the hell not?" Jason asked.

"Because, I'm not ready for that. I have a life. A job. An apartment. And I don't know what I would do with myself when the two of you are gone. For now, I'll spend time with you here when I can, but that's all I'm willing to do. For now," she added.

Jeff and Jason looked at each other, then back at her. "Okay," Jeff said. "But we want you to know you can change your mind at any time."

Megan inclined her head in acknowledgment. "Understood." She took a sip of lemonade to calm her nerves and allow herself another second or two before she said the rest. "I know you both said you were looking for a long-term relationship, but I'm under the impression you mean a strictly sexual relationship – nothing more. Am I correct?"

"More or less," Jeff confirmed. "I'd like to think we're friends, and that we can become better friends."

"Friends." She let the idea roll around in her head for a moment. "Yes, I think we're already friends, of a sort. I just don't know if it's possible for me to have the kind of sexual relationship you want without becoming more emotionally involved. I don't have any experience with this kind of arrangement."

"What, exactly, are you saying?" Jason asked.

"I don't know, exactly. I've never been in a strictly sexual relationship. I guess I'm wondering what happens if it becomes something more...serious."

"It's already serious," Jeff said. "If you think it isn't, then we haven't conveyed the right message. We never would have invited you to join us if all we wanted was physical gratification. That's a part of it, for sure, but we could get that with anyone. We want more from you, Megan. We want you to be a part of our lives. How much you're willing to give is up to you. We're hoping it will be a lot more than just your body, lovely as it is."

Suddenly, her stomach felt like a rock and she couldn't eat another bite. Did Jeff mean they might develop feelings for her over time? Did they hope she would reciprocate? It was crazy the way she yearned for it to be true, and the absurd thought that perhaps it already was true, at least on her part.

"Well then…I'll need tests. I won't sleep with you until you've been tested. I took the liberty of bringing my test results. We have to be tested every six months – hospital regulations."

"Not a problem. We both got tested a few weeks ago. You're welcome to look over the results," Jason said.

"Oh. Well." She was stammering. She really hadn't expected them to have been tested…unless…. "Was there a particular reason you had the tests done?"

"No particular reason," Jeff said. "We have annual physicals as part of our contract with the Mustangs. There is always the option to be tested and we took advantage of it. You know…better safe than sorry. We have the test results for the last five years, if you're interested."

"That's good. The latest results will be enough."

"I'll get 'em," Jason said. He slid off the barstool and before Megan could organize her thoughts, he was back, sliding two sheets of paper at her. She perused them with a critical eye, found what she wanted – and a few more things she didn't have the right to know.

"You both need to seriously work on your cholesterol levels," she said with a grin.

"Thanks, Nurse Megan," Jeff said. "What do you suggest?"

"A healthy diet, and plenty of exercise?" she quipped.

"And what kind of exercise do you have in mind?" Jeff's voice had lost all humor. It was now or never. She'd opened the door to more, and if she backed out now, she'd lose more than great sex – she'd lose two friends.

"I have some ideas, but first I want to get to know you better." They both opened their mouths to protest, but Megan continued before they could get the words out. "That didn't come out right. What I mean is, I want to get to know your bodies better. You're very much alike, but there are subtle differences. So, this is what I have in mind…"

A few minutes later, Megan watched as Jeff and Jason removed their clothing. Jason tossed his impatiently aside, while Jeff took the time to fold and stack his. Her mouth watered as acres of smooth skin came into view, one section at a time. It was almost too much to take in all at once, but she'd asked for this, and she wasn't going to back down now.

"Those too," she wiggled her finger to indicate the last stitches of clothing – well filled out briefs. It wasn't as if she hadn't seen them before, but this was different.

"Okay, but how long is this going to take?" Jason groused. "I'm already hurting here."

"Not long, I promise. I just want to familiarize myself with your bodies. I'm sure there are differences."

"He has a big-assed scar on his chest," Jeff pointed out as he folded the last garment and added it to the stack he'd made on the dresser.

"I know that, but there has to be more. How else can you explain how I knew you apart that day you came to the hospital?"

Broad shoulders shrugged as they considered the inexplicable truth. She had been able to tell them apart even when they weren't side by side, and now she had the chance to examine them closely with the goal of being able to distinguish between them with her eyes closed. She'd yet to let them in on that part, but she would soon enough.

"Go ahead then," Jeff said.

She stood back as far as the confines of her bedroom would allow. At first glance, they were indeed identical, but as a nurse, she was trained to observe carefully. She studied the outlines of their bodies, noting the subtle difference in the curve of their shoulders and thighs. Moving closer, she noted how Jeff's right shoulder was somewhat stronger than his left. His pitching arm. It made sense. She stepped closer and placed her hands on his shoulders. His skin burned beneath her palms.

❧

Her hands on him were the purest form of torture. Jeff craved her touch, but at the same time refraining from grabbing her and returning the favor took more control than facing any batter in the league.

"This shoulder is larger than the other," she observed. "Let me see your arms." He held his arms out and she ran her hands along the corded muscles from shoulder to wrist. "So strong, but the muscles of your right arm are more defined than your left." Wrapping her fingers around his wrists, she turned his hands palm up. She examined the left one first, then the right. "Just as I thought, the fingers of your right hand are more callused than your left." She took her time studying his right hand, learning every callus with first her fingertips, then her lips. Jeff jerked to attention as she sucked his index finger into her mouth.

"Christ, Megan," he hissed.

"Shh," she whispered. "You said I could look all I want. That's what I'm doing."

"What about me?" Jason said.

"You're next. Don't worry. I'll give you all my attention in a few minutes." She dropped Jeff's right hand back to his side and continued her leisurely inspection. He groaned as she traced his pectorals with her index finger, stopping to tease and lick the flat copper discs there. His dick leapt to attention, straining for her to taste it as well.

"No touching yourself," she scolded when Jason took his cock in hand. "Tonight is my night. I'll do all the touching."

Jeff understood his brother's torment. It was all he could do to remain still, and if his cock got any harder he could use it as a battering ram.

"Then come on woman," Jason urged. "Touch me."

"Soon, I promise."

Jeff had been through dozens of physicals, but nothing compared to this slow, torturous exploration. Megan's deft fingers found every nerve ending, touching, stroking until his skin was on fire and his dick throbbed with his rapid heartbeat. She pushed his legs apart so his balls hung free while she trailed her hands over his back. He locked his knees to remain upright when she slid a finger between his ass cheeks, then lower. His balls drew tight as she explored him from behind.

"You're going to have to stop – unless you want to see me come," he warned with the last bit of sanity he had.

Her hands left him and he forced his muscles to relax. Too bad his dick wasn't paying attention. It was still bobbing like an eager puppy begging for scraps. She'd touched everything but his cock, and that part of his anatomy was none too happy about it.

⟡

Jason didn't know which was going to explode first, his head or his dick. Watching Megan's hands covering every inch of his brother was killing him, imagining how it would feel when she got to him. And when she did, her hands were silk, fluttering over his skin, igniting fires wherever she touched.

He couldn't care less that his shoulders were equal in musculature or that his forearms were thicker than Jeff's. She ignored the scar on his chest, instead, flicking her tongue over his nipples as she had with Jeff. He thought she made some comment afterwards, but her tongue on him short-circuited his auditory system. He couldn't hear, couldn't think, couldn't breathe. But he could feel, and that was enough to drive him insane. He had to have her. Had to spend as much time learning her body as she was his. It was only fair.

"Megan." He forced her name through clenched teeth.

"Almost through here," she said from behind him. He couldn't help but squirm when she explored his ass, then his balls. Thank God, she was a nurse because he was going to have a heart attack if she didn't stop the torture soon.

⟡

Megan smiled to herself as she fondled Jason's balls. Telling the twins apart wasn't going to be easy, but if she kept her wits about her, she should be able to do it. There were enough subtle physical differences to distinguish one from the other – under the right circumstances. The real test would be telling them apart without benefit of sight. If this relationship were going to work, she couldn't think of them as one, she had to learn what made them individuals and respond to them accordingly. As alike as they were, they were two different people, two different men who would be touching her.

Her trained eye noted their rapid breathing and the flush of their skin. She had to give them credit for the control they exhibited while she learned their bodies. Other than the one time Jason had twitched, they had remained statue still, but it was time for that to come to an end.

"I saved these for last," she said as she wrapped a fist around each velvet-encased cock. The groans and identical strings of curses her actions coaxed from Jeff and Jason sent a bolt of desire through her. She still wasn't sure she wanted to have them both at the same time – the idea was as frightening as it was arousing, but she was ready to feel them inside her in the traditional way.

"You're large – both of you." Her comment earned another string of curses interlaced with a few promises she was all too eager to take them up on. She released them and received yet another creative exclamation from each of them. Ignoring their protests, she crossed to the neat stack of Jeff's clothing and picked up the item she wanted.

Megan held up the necktie she'd taken from Jeff's things. "Would one of you use this to blindfold me, please?"

"It's my tie. I'll do it," Jeff said, reaching for the length of navy silk. Megan turned slightly so he had access to the back of her head.

"What's the blindfold for?" Jason asked.

"It's a test, sort of. For me. I want the two of you to make love to me – slowly. Don't tell me what you're going to do next, or who's doing it. I want to see if I can tell you apart using my other senses."

Jeff completed the knot and turned her. "How's that? Not too tight?"

"No. It's perfect. I can't see a thing."

"Now what?" Jason asked.

"Now, I need you to touch me – both of you. I'll tell you when to stop."

Jeff signaled Jason to change places with him, then they began to peel Megan out of her clothes. He wasn't sure why it mattered for her to tell them apart, but if she wanted them to test her, he was all for it. Like all twins, they'd done their share of trading places as kids. As adults, the challenge hadn't seemed like much fun – until now.

She allowed them to remove her blouse and slacks so she stood there in nothing but two wickedly small scraps of black lace. Thankfully, he and Jason didn't need spoken language to communicate. One glance at his brother and the two reached a silent agreement. Megan Long wasn't going to know who was touching her, and if they did it right – she wouldn't care.

Megan gasped as the brothers touched her. She'd expected them to get into the spirit of the game, softly touching, caressing her, allowing her to guess whose hand was where. Instead, they launched an all out assault on her senses. One minute she was shivering in anticipation of that first touch, and the next her brain was scrambling to make sense of all the incoming stimuli.

Hands and lips, and hard bodies were everywhere. One of them crushed her back to his front, slipping a long-fingered hand past the elastic band of her panties while the other pushed her bra up, freeing her breasts. Hands swept beneath her breasts, crushing them together a fraction of a second before he sucked one aching nipple into the hot cavern of his mouth. Megan searched her memory bank trying to distinguish between her lovers. Which one was at her back? Which one had her breast in his mouth while the other stroked her folds? She tried to focus on their touch. If she could isolate the details, she would know which hand belonged to which brother. Was that a left hand, or a right? Jeff's left hand was smoother than his right.

Before she could distinguish any difference, she was flat on her back and her panties and bra were gone, slipped from her faster than wrapping paper on Christmas morning. Hands stroked her most intimate places. Lips and tongues feasted. Legs twined with hers, twisting her this way and that as they manipulated her body like a tactile tornado. She'd never felt so much at once. Her brain lit up like a Las Vegas marquee as every nerve ending fired simultaneously.

She cried out as one of them buried his face between her legs, tonguing her clit, then dipping lower to taste her pussy. Cradled in strong arms, callused fingers stroked her cheek, while whispered words brushed across her ear.

"Shh, darling. You're ours now," he crooned. "Let yourself go, then we'll show you how to fly."

Megan whimpered as the warm mouth left her. The strong arms that had been holding her on one side slid away, replaced by a set on the other side. As if hearing in stereo, a rough voice whispered in her other ear. "Relax, sweetheart. You're ready for us." Then a solid male weight pressed her into the mattress and no sooner had she felt the pressure between her legs, than a cock slid inside her, hard and hot and big. She gasped as her body stretched to take him all in. Which one was it? Jeff or Jason? "God, that's beautiful." The words met her ear as a heated palm stroked her hip and along her splayed thigh. "A few strokes, then we'll have all of you."

She tried to wrap her mind around the cryptic remark, but couldn't think for the exquisite sensation of the cock sliding out, then back in with such tender talent. Dear God, he felt wonderful. Her hips rose and fell with his, driving him deeper each time. The heavy male body on top of her felt like heaven, molding her breasts to his hard chest while his brother pressed close to her side.

CHAPTER NINE

"She's fucking amazing."

Megan thought the same thing about the man inside her, but couldn't form a coherent word to say so.

"Let me see."

They switched places in the span of a heartbeat, one rolling off her to lie on her opposite side while the other settled atop her and sank into her pussy with one strong thrust. Her heart stilled and behind the blindfold, she had a sudden insight. This was different. Sure, the size and shape was the same, but this brother was different. Her body knew this one. As he seated himself fully inside her he stilled – almost as if he felt it too. Megan had to remind herself to breath as a darkness that had nothing to do with the blindfold threatened to overtake her. She sucked oxygen into her lungs as he slid almost out of her and drove back in.

"Christ almighty!" The words seemed wrenched from his heart as he began to fuck her in earnest. She met him thrust for thrust as if her life depended on having him inside her. Maybe if he thrust hard enough, she could absorb him into her. This was how it felt to be one with another. This was what everyone made such a fuss about – that connection. The instant that you knew your life wouldn't ever be the same without this person in it.

Suddenly, she knew who it was. Her fingers couldn't tell the difference, but her heart could. This was Jeff. She tried his name on her lips. "Jeff."

"Yes, sweetheart." His lips covered hers in a kiss that spoke of possession, and she knew he felt the same thing she did. "Hold on, we're going to make you ours."

Then she was on her side. Jeff remained inside her, throbbing, moving slowly as he held her crushed to his chest. He claimed her mouth again as Jason pressed against her forbidden entrance. Her breath caught in her lungs at the imminent intrusion.

Jason's arm snaked around her waist and his hips rocked against her ass.

"Relax, Megan. It's going to be good." Jeff's words acted as a balm and she went limp in his arms. Taking advantage of her acquiescence, Jason breached her barrier. He groaned from behind her as Jeff crooned in her ear, "That's it, sweetheart. Let us love you."

After the initial pain of Jason's entrance faded, she concentrated on the fullness and the incredible feeling of safety she felt cradled between these two men. Behind her, Jason set a slow rhythm that Jeff soon matched. Megan buried her face against Jeff's chest and counted his heartbeats beneath her cheek. Slow and steady, just like the way they claimed her, one tandem stroke at a time. She felt boneless, dependent on their strength to support her.

She'd worried unnecessarily about taking both of them at the same time. They'd been right about the butt plug, and she was glad she'd worn it while they were away. But as great as Jason had felt inside her pussy, and now inside her ass, it was nothing compared to what she felt when Jeff entered her. How could they be so different? And how was it she could tell them apart when her brain couldn't function well enough to tell a right hand from a left, much less register calluses or the lack thereof?

They kept up a litany of praise as they took her. She barely registered their words as her nerve endings sent frantic messages to her brain from every part of her body. As she lay like a limp doll between Jeff and Jason, their hands and lips made sure no part of her lacked for attention. It was like a drug, this overdose of pleasure. Could one die from too much pleasure? As her body coiled tightly around her center, she knew she was willing to die right here, right now, if only she could reach the pinnacle that was so close.

"Jesus, God, I can feel her. She's almost there." Jason.

"You're safe with us. We're going to fill your ass and your pussy, sweetheart. We're going to give ourselves, just like you've given yourself." Jeff. Sweet, Jeff. His words wrapped her heart in the golden gauze of love and tears slid over the bridge of her nose and dampened the silk tie. Then Jeff's lips were on hers, and her whole body convulsed.

They held her in their male cocoon while contractions shuddered through her. She might have heard words of encouragement, she wasn't sure – couldn't comprehend anything but that she was dying in their arms, with these two tender men inside her body, and she couldn't have been happier.

She drifted back to reality – minutes or hours later – she had no idea. Two walls of maleness supported her, and filled her.

"Are you okay?" Jeff again. Caring for her, loving her. She nodded her head, unable to form the words to tell him she'd never been better in her entire life.

"Hang onto me then. We're going to finish making you ours."

They pulled from her, then filled her again. Over and over. Hard, tandem thrusts, and then they turned to stone, crushing her between them, hips grinding uncontrollably against her, back and front. They poured their life into her, and her body responded, clamping rhythmically around their shafts, coaxing every heated drop from them.

Megan couldn't stem the tears anymore than she could stem the love she felt for these two men. She'd never dreamed it could be this way, or that she could feel so much, so soon for not one, but two men.

Behind her, Jason loosened the knot on the tie and slipped it from her eyes. She blinked at the harsh light, suddenly self-conscious lying there with two cocks still inside her. Softer now, she noticed, but not limp.

"You could tell us apart." Jeff said, a smile on his face and in his voice.

"Yes."

"No one has ever been able to do that before," Jason said.

Megan shrugged her shoulders as best she could surrounded by so much hard male muscle. "I didn't have to think about it. I just knew. I can't explain it."

"I can," Jeff said. "It means you were meant for us."

Meant for you, she thought, but said, "I think you might be right." Now wasn't the time to tell Jeff Holder she thought she was in love with him. It was an insane thought anyway. No one fell in love that fast.

❧❦

"Come to the game today."

Megan wished she hadn't listened to Jeff's request as she sat among the players' wives. She'd managed to stall them for several months – though in truth she hadn't had a day off that coincided with a home game since she'd succumbed to Jeff and Jason's seduction. Now, everyone from the ticket-taker at the gate, to the brawny guard at the top of the seating section, to the wives seated around her, eyed her with undisguised curiosity. She tried not to squirm, but she'd never felt more like a specimen slide. At least her assigned seat was a little off to the side, rather than smack in the middle of the wives section. Nevertheless, the sidelong glances were getting to be too much. Why didn't they just ask her who she was?

"Hi," the perky blonde in the seat in front of her turned and flashed her perfect smile, perfect teeth, perfect boobs. "I'm Tiffany. I'm Chase Hamilton's girlfriend. Who are you?"

Be careful what you ask for.

"Megan Long." She tried out her relaxed, "I belong here" smile. "I'm...uhm... Jeff and Jason Holder are friends."

Heads turned. Heat bloomed on her cheeks and spread like a riot of blood-red roses over her face and neck. She wiggled her fingers at the stunned assemblage in what she hoped was a friendly, non-threatening greeting. A few returned the gesture after looking her over from head to toe, cataloguing her assets and more likely, her deficiencies to be picked apart as soon as the "club" could schedule an emergency meeting. "Nice to meet you," she said with as much hauteur as she could muster.

The stadium announcer saved them from replying by calling the fans to their feet for the National Anthem. Megan breathed a sigh of relief as her review board directed their attention to the pre-game festivities. No one said another word to her for the next six and a half innings. When they stood again for the seventh inning stretch, Megan was gone.

She didn't stop walking until she got to her car in the VIP parking lot. She cranked the engine, turned the air-conditioner to arctic blast, gripped the steering wheel to steady her trembling hands and dropped her head between them. Several minutes later, she took a deep, cleansing breath and straightened. So she wasn't part of the wives and girlfriends club. Judging from the cold reception, either Jeff and Jason lent their tickets out to a parade of women – none worthy of the other women's time, or her presence had simply stunned them into silence. Whichever it was, she wasn't going to hang around and find out.

❧

"Where did you go?" Jason asked. "I looked for you in the eighth inning and you weren't there."

"I wasn't feeling well, so I left during the seventh inning stretch," she lied.

"You didn't see my save?" Jeff sounded like a petulant little boy.

"No. Sorry."

"There'll be others." Jeff twisted the cap off the beer he'd snagged as soon as he came in and tossed the cap in the under-counter wastebasket.

"I don't know when I'll be able to go to another game," she hedged.

Two sets of blue eyes studied her.

"What's going on? Didn't you enjoy the game?" Jason asked.

"I did, but maybe I'll just watch them on TV from now on."

Jeff set his bottle on the granite counter with enough force Megan expected to see beer spewing from a certain fissure. "Tell us."

Megan cursed herself for being such a lousy actress. All the way home, she'd practiced what she would say to them so she wouldn't have to go back again and face the "club". The more she'd thought about their reaction to her presence, the more she was convinced she was the latest in a long line of women who'd occupied that particular seat, and sooner or later the quizzing would begin. She wasn't up to that. What could she say? "Oh yes, I'm sleeping with both of them. Yes, it's unorthodox, but I really do care for both men."

"Look, I'm sure the wives club was a little surprised to see someone new in your seats today, but if I go back – "

"When you go back," Jason supplied.

Megan glared at him and he pressed his lips tight and signaled for her to continue.

"*If* I go back," she said. "I'm sure they'll find their tongues, and I don't have a clue how I'd answer their questions."

"First," Jeff said, "no one besides our parents have used those tickets since we've been with the Mustangs, so any curiosity on their part was because you weren't our mother, not because of any string of women we've invited to watch us play."

"Second," Jason continued, "if you don't go back, they'll have a lot more to talk about. Rumors will fly for sure, but if you're seen in our seats enough, they'll get the idea."

"Maybe so, but they were about to pounce today. I had to get out of there before they started asking questions I didn't know how to answer."

"Like what?" Jeff asked.

"I told them we were friends, but what if they ask personal questions? What would I say?"

"Tell them the truth," Jason said. "Tell them you work at the hospital, and we come to visit the kids there. Tell them we're friends."

"I did tell them we're friends, but I could see they thought there was something more."

Jeff circled the bar and covered her shoulders with his big hands. His lips on the sensitive spot behind her ear sent a shiver of desire through her. "Tell them whatever you want, Megan. Or tell them nothing." His tongue flicked against her pulse. "We don't care what you tell them. It's up to you." His teeth grazed across the same spot, followed by another swipe of his tongue that sent liquid heat straight to her core. "You taste so damned good. Tell them to go to hell, or tell them how good it feels to have both of us inside you at the same time."

Jason's hand slipped around her waist, tugging until the barstool swung around so she faced him. Her breath caught in her lungs as he worked the buttons loose on her blouse and dragged her bra cups down to expose her breasts. "Tell them twins are twice as much fun," he said, right before he sucked her right nipple into his mouth and pinched her left one between his thumb and forefinger. Her legs fell open in primitive invitation.

Jeff's hands skimmed beneath her open collar, pushing her bra straps off her shoulders, effectively trapping her arms at her sides. Long fingers slipped beneath her breasts. He kneaded each globe as his brother continued to suck one, then the other.

Megan let her head fall back against Jeff's solid chest and forgot all about the "club". When Jeff and Jason touched her, she could hardly remember her name, much less anything as petty as a bunch of team wives with wagging tongues. Right now, the only wagging tongues she cared about were the ones driving her out of her mind with longing.

"Please," she begged.

"I love it when she begs," Jason said before he wrapped his hands around her waist and lifted her to the granite bar. Before she could protest, she was naked and lying on the cold slab with her feet draped over Jason's shoulders. The soft wool of his suit jacket slid against her legs reminding her that only she was naked. A surge of wicked playfulness pulsed through her veins. She heard the refrigerator open and close, then Jeff stood over her, shaking a can of whipped cream.

"Here," he said. "Let's decorate the pie before we eat it."

Megan arched her back off the counter as the first squiggly string of whipped cream turned her left nipple into a snow-capped mountain.

"Beautiful," Jason said. "Do the other one, then give it to me."

Jeff followed his brother's instructions, handing the can over after coating her other breast and filling her navel with the fluffy cream. She should have been embarrassed, but the look on their faces as Jason parted her folds and filled the recesses with ribbons made her desperate for what they would do to her next. Another dollop crowned her clit, then Jason put his mouth to her.

She cried out, bucking her hips to get as close to him as she could. Jeff slid his hands beneath her head. "Watch him, sweetheart. See his tongue?"

Megan groaned. When her guys wanted to play, they could be very creative. Jason's face was coated in whipped cream as he toyed with her clit and the slit below. His tongue flicked, stroked and delved inside. His broad shoulders supported her thighs, and his hands pillared her ass. He looked so damned sexy, all dressed up in his suit, with cream on his face – like a naughty boy at a party caught with cake on his face. It was enough to make a woman lose her mind, if not her heart.

"Here," Jeff clasped her hands and brought them to her breasts. "Hold these for me." He molded her palms to her breasts and pushed them together until her breasts were twin mountain peaks with snow squishing up between them and sliding down the slopes. "Fucking beautiful."

His tongue lapped the snow slowly avalanching down the outside swell of her breast. Megan arched toward him, inviting, begging for more. Every rational thought fled, replaced by need and want. As she lay there, accepting that these two could make her forget everything, she thanked the universe for putting her in their path. Thanks to one small boy who wanted an autograph, her life had changed dramatically. She no longer questioned why Jeff and Jason wanted her – they just did, and she wanted them with every fiber of her being.

She drank in Jeff's scent as he bent his head to her breast and suckled. Both men had sensitive skin so they used fragrance-free soaps that allowed their natural scent to dominate. Megan inhaled deeply, savoring the clean male smell that she'd come to associate with arousal. It was hard to be around them and not want them to touch her, to take her in any way they wanted. Together they could be very creative which always translated to great sex, and intense orgasms for her.

Jeff nuzzled, licked and sucked in orchestrated harmony with Jason's attentions, and soon she felt the familiar tension building as her body spiraled closer to the edge.

"She's close," Jason said without breaking stride. Jeff placed a palm over her stomach, pressing her back flat against the unforgiving counter. Megan tried to move her hips, but Jason's hold, and the pressure from Jeff's hand held her captive.

"Come for us, Megan," Jeff urged. His mouth closed over one aching nipple, pushing her over the edge.

The world closed in around her, and nothing existed but the ethereal plane Jeff and Jason had taken her to. Her body quaked. Her mind soared, and through it all, she felt safe and loved. The dislocation she'd felt at the stadium surrounded by the women who "belonged" didn't matter any longer, because Megan belonged here, with Jeff and Jason.

She drifted back to reality on a cloud of sated passion to find identical faces smiling down at her. She smiled back, too content to reprimand them for making her lie on the cold granite counter. What did she have to complain about anyway? They'd given to her as they so often did, seeing to her needs before their own.

"I never get tired of seeing that," Jason said as he rose to his feet.

Jeff eased her up to a sitting position and stroked her hair. "Me either. God, Megan, you are so beautiful when you come. It's like watching a miracle."

"There's nothing miraculous about it, it's all you two. You know me too well. I should be embarrassed that you can do that so easily."

"Come here," Jason lifted her off the counter. "It's our turn, don't you think?" He threaded his fingers with hers and drew her across the room. Jeff followed, coming up behind her to press his body fully against hers. His hands stroking from shoulder to elbow warmed her while the kisses he planted on her shoulder promised more.

Jason's belt jangled as he undid the buckle, then slid his trousers and boxer shorts past his hips. His erection sprang free. "Touch me," he commanded. Megan wrapped her fingers around his shaft, moving up and down in the way she knew he liked. His groan sent a surge of power through her system. They knew her body, but she knew theirs too. She had no doubt she could return the favor they'd done for her.

"Sit down, Jason. I need you."

Jason collapsed onto the nearest chair, jerking the last few buttons of his shirt open so it gaped around his stomach. Megan turned and straddled Jason's legs. He used his knees to open her, and with Jeff's guiding hands, and Jason positioning her, she slid down on Jason's cock.

"Oh, God, that feels good," she moaned as he filled her. Jason's hands cradled her hips, holding her in place. "Now you," she wiggled a finger at Jeff. He stepped closer and she worked his belt loose, followed by the button on his waistband and the zipper. "Off," she said.

She reached for his cock, but he dodged out of range. "Just a second." He returned, shaking the can of whipped cream with one hand. With the other, he urged her lips apart.

"Open up." He filled her mouth with the cool cream, then pushed his pants past his hips. His cock rose up in anticipation. "Take me in your mouth."

Megan bent and closed her mouth around the head of his cock. Whipped cream squished from the corners of her lips as he gradually pushed further in. "Ah, damn, Megan. That feels good. His fingers wiped the white foam from her mouth and spread it on his cock. "You're so damned hot, and the cream is cold. It feels fucking amazing."

She had to agree. His cock was hot, salty steel, and the cream was cold and sweet. She never would have thought the two could be so good together.

"Now," Jeff said, and Jason began to stroke in and out. Megan lost herself in the sensation of pleasuring them both at the same time.

Jeff cradled the back of her head in one hand, controlling her movements — sometimes going deep to the back of her throat, other times just giving her the head to play with. Once he pulled almost all the way out and coated his cock with whipped cream again before he drove all the way in. Megan lapped up the sweet concoction with her eager tongue, earning a growl from Jeff.

A blunt fingertip traced along her spine from her nape to her ass, raising gooseflesh in its wake. Behind her, Jason chuckled in the playful way she'd come to know. Jeff handed off the whipped cream to Jason. A moment later a cool glob coated her ass, followed by Jason's exploring thumb.

Megan moaned as Jason found the entrance he was looking for and breached it with his digit. It was too much. Between Jeff filling her mouth, and Jason filling everything else, she couldn't maintain control. Her body tensed. Jason wiggled his finger in her ass and flexed his hips, driving himself all the way to her core.

She came, contracting around the steel hard shaft inside her in rhythmic waves of ecstasy. Jason stilled as she clenched him tight. When her body relaxed its grip he flexed his hips and drove hard into her, releasing his pent-up cum with a curse.

Jeff still held her head, controlling her movements. She reached beneath her chin for his balls and tugged. He uttered a similar curse and pressed her face against his groin, erupting down her throat as he did so.

Megan smiled as Jeff released her and grabbed for the countertop to steady himself. "Damn, that was good," he said. He leaned against the counter to catch his breath. He was the sexiest man she'd ever seen in her life, standing there weak-kneed with his tie and suit coat perfectly in place, and his wool trousers around his ankles. His cock was still at half-mast, but slowly wilting.

"I don't think I can move," Jason said. He shifted and his cock slid from her. He wrapped her in his arms and pulled her naked back against his front. "As soon as I can walk, I'm going to take you to the bedroom. I want you to do that whipped cream in the mouth thing on me."

"Only if Jeff gets to switch places with you," she teased.

"Come on," Jeff reached for her hand and drew her to her feet. "Let's go. Jason can bring the whipped cream."

Megan went along, eager to have Jeff inside her again. Jason knew how to make her feel good, but what she felt when Jeff was inside her was something very different. It was as if he was made especially for her, that he completed her in some puzzling way. Sex with Jason was…just sex. But sex with Jeff was more. She liked sex with Jason, but she needed sex with Jeff. She needed to feel that connection with him, to feel him moving inside her. He touched more than her body – he touched her heart and her soul.

As he came to her in the big bed upstairs, she forgot all about the curious glances and feeling out of place. She belonged here, with Jeff. Nothing else mattered.

❧

"You know what to do?"

"For the millionth time, Jeff, yes." Megan herded him toward the garage where Jason was waiting. "If you don't hurry, Jason is going to have to drive so you won't be late." That got him moving faster. Jeff swore every time he rode with Jason that he'd never do it again.

"Okay, okay. I'm going." He turned to place a quick kiss on her lips. "I'll see you later. Thanks for doing this."

"I should be thanking you. If it weren't for you, Christopher wouldn't be alive today, much less throwing out the first pitch." She pushed him out the door before he could launch into his usual protest when she credited him with saving Christopher's life. No matter how much he denied it, it was true. After talking to Roxanne about her son's illness, Jeff had put out a call to the other players throughout the Major Leagues to help find a suitable bone marrow donor. Christopher's recovery was a direct result of Jeff's involvement.

Megan hurried up the stairs to dress. The limousine would be here soon to pick her up, then they would pick up Christopher and his parents, and arrive at the stadium in time to meet the team before the opening ceremonies. Christopher would finally be going to the game Jeff had promised him the day he first visited him in the hospital, and Megan couldn't be happier.

Not only was Jeff fulfilling a promise he'd made, but today he was announcing the new foundation he was funding that would help other kids in need of donors find a match, aptly named – The Christopher Project. That he'd taken something so close to her heart, and put his time and resources into it, made her heart glow.

Christopher was the picture of health standing on the pitching mound beside his idol. Jeff handed him the ball and stood back as Christopher hurled it toward home plate, and Jason's waiting glove. Megan fought back tears when Jason and Jeff lifted Christopher to their shoulders and slowly turned so he could wave to the cheering crowds. Now, sitting next to Christopher, she could hardly contain her joy. Christopher kept up a running commentary throughout the innings, teaching Megan all about the game he loved so much. It was a dream come true kind of day for Christopher, his parents, and her. And she had Jeff Holder to thank for it.

When Christopher and his parents waved goodbye as the limousine eased from the parking lot, Megan thought if she heard the words, "Jeff said", one more time, her head might explode. Jeff Holder had a fan for life in little Christopher, and she wouldn't change a thing.

"Ready to go?" Jeff asked.

"More than ready. It's been a long day," she replied.

"Come on then. Jason took off with Randall, so it's just you and me."

Megan rested her head on Jeff's shoulder as they walked to his car. As always, his arm around her made her feel safe, and loved. He opened the passenger door for her, then walked around to the driver's side.

"You're a good man, Jeff Holder," she said as he merged onto the freeway a few minutes later. "No wonder half the women in Texas are in love with you."

"What about you? Which half are you in?"

"Do you have to ask?"

"No, I don't think I do."

CHAPTER TEN

He sure was something to look at, especially in uniform. Megan watched from the player's family section – close enough to hear every curse and see the strain on the players' faces. She'd overcome her unease among the players' wives over the last year, adopting a don't-ask-don't-tell sort of friendship with a few. Jeff and Jason wanted her in the stands when she could be there, and they wanted her in other ways she didn't feel compelled to discuss with others. If anyone guessed how much of a friend she was to Jeff and Jason, they didn't comment. In a way, Jeff and Jason had kept their word. She wasn't exactly a secret, but sometimes she wished they didn't have to hide their relationship – especially her relationship with Jeff.

She hadn't expected it to happen, but she'd fallen in love with Jeff. Maybe she should have seen it coming from the very beginning. When they were together, alone or with Jason, she felt something more for Jeff, something that went much deeper than what she felt for Jason. She didn't have the nerve to say anything to Jeff, and if he felt the same, he wasn't saying either. Sometimes she thought Jason might suspect, but like his brother, he seemed content to keep their relationship on a friends-with-benefits status.

She'd never get tired of seeing him play. He loved the game, and his body language testified to his command of it. This was his element, and he wore the uniform with pride and confidence. The stretch knit pants coated his thighs like paint. If you were up close, you could see his powerful muscles bunch and lengthen, not to mention what you could see a little higher. He refused to wear a cup, so the fabric stretched over the real thing. On warm days like today, the short-sleeved top revealed arms toned from countless hours in the gym, and on the job. Only those with intimate knowledge knew the golden tan was almost as dark where the sun never touched his skin.

Megan held her breath as Jeff stilled, focusing everything he had on the next few seconds. It was almost over. Just a few more, and victory would be his. Jeff thrived on the adrenaline rush. He loved being the one to do the impossible. As hot-blooded as he was, when he was called upon to do what he did best, pure ice water flowed through his veins, or so it seemed to the poor souls he was sent out to dispatch. He'd been called many things, but the one he liked the most was The Terminator.

The man he faced now also had made a name for himself, and as confident as Megan was in Jeff's skills, she couldn't help but worry. Failure wasn't something Jeff dealt with well. The crowd roared, surging to their feet. Most sided with Jeff, but a few raised their voices, offering encouragement to the enemy. Megan allowed her gaze to shift to Jeff's partner in this battle. The brothers had worked as a team since their high school days when they'd discovered their unique connection afforded them an advantage over their opponents. They were the only two in their profession to remain together after so many years. It was a testament to their effectiveness, as well as their relationship. They practically read each other's minds. They shared more than their DNA, but most of the world didn't have a clue how much they actually did share. Megan knew, and held their time together close to her heart. Of all the women in the world, and they could have their choice, they'd chosen her.

Jason crouched low, his muscular torso coiled and ready to spring. Unlike Jeff, Jason wore as much protective equipment as the rules allowed. He had a healthy fear of missiles hurtling toward him at incredible speeds, not to mention the danger from their armed opposition. He didn't take chances, and for that, Megan was grateful. Jason signaled his brother. Jeff nodded, an almost imperceptible movement of his head, before he clasped his hands together, waist high.

Jeff squared his shoulders, coiled every muscle in his body, and sent the missile in his hand spinning toward his opponent. Megan refused to blink. Her eyes darted from Jeff, tried to track the missile, but failed to do so. The enemy swung out in a futile effort to fend off the attack. The missile hit Jason's specially designed mitt with a distinctive slap.

"Strike one!" the umpire called, and Megan let out the stale breath trapped in her lungs. *One pitch down. Two to go.*

∝৴৻৶

Jason adjusted his chest protector. Sweat trickled down his back and soaked his shirt where the elastic straps criss-crossed his body. His helmet hung from his right hand, his heavily padded catcher's mitt from the other. He lifted his left shoulder and wiped his forehead on his shirt. God, he hated playing in Texas in the summer. But right now, the heat wasn't his biggest worry. The man stepping into the batter's box was.

Martin McCree could be a poster child for steroid abuse. Jason hated him. Martin continued to deny his use of performance-enhancing drugs, but no one became a home run hitter with his stats overnight. Hell, few did it without steroids over an entire career. Jason hated what Martin and the few others like him did to the game. Fans couldn't trust players who worked hard and upped their game, because a few took the easy way out – choosing drugs over a healthy lifestyle and years of practice.

Jason reviewed everything he knew about the bastard's strengths and weaknesses while Martin went through his elaborate routine—scrape out a foothold for his left foot, then another one for his right; adjust his nuts, probably shrunken from the steroids; touch the necklace he wore around his unnaturally thick neck, the one he swore was the reason for his jump from the pit of Major League batting

101

averages to the pinnacle in one season; adjust his nuts again; tap the end of his bat on all five points of the plate before raising it to his shoulder.

The ump muttered low, "Strike the SOB out," as Jason donned his mask. He shared a secret smile with the ump. All Jeff had to do was get it close. If Martin didn't swing, the ump would help him out. Unethical? Probably. But he didn't give a good goddamn. Steroids were a hell of a lot further off the ethical scale than giving a pitcher a wide strike zone.

Jason didn't remember Martin fidgeting so much in previous seasons – probably another side effect of the drugs. Jason crouched, dropped his left hand between his thighs and signaled Jeff. Four fingers down for a fastball – might as well challenge Martin right off. Two fingers down for the speed – give it all you've got. Three fingers against his left thigh – throw it right down the middle of the plate. A few more bogus signs for the hell of it. Jeff nodded. *Message received.*

Jason set up, leaning to his right enough to attract Martin's attention, make him think the ball might be going outside. Martin adjusted his stance. *Idiot.* Everyone knew Jeff's go-to pitch was an inside fastball. Jason fixed his eyes on Jeff's hand, on the small orb about to be hurled right at his face, if Jeff didn't miss his spot.

A fraction of a second. That's all the time he had to see the ball, to move his gloved hand into position and intercept it before it nailed him between the eyes. Not that the hockey-style mask wouldn't do its job, but getting hit in the face hurt like hell, mask or no mask.

Jeff went into his windup. He squared his shoulders, lifted his left knee to his chest, drew his right elbow even with his shoulder – and exploded. His body fell forward, landed hard on his left foot. His right arm swung forward. Jason focused on the blur of white cowhide slashed with red as it left Jeff's fingertips. He lost it momentarily as Martin's bat cut through the air, stirring the humidity hovering like a damp cloud over home plate. Jason moved his glove, more from muscle memory than any real sense of where the ball was. His whole body jolted at the impact. His fingers squeezed reflexively around the projectile in his palm.

"Fuck." Martin spun out of the batter's box.

"Strike one!" the umpire yelled.

Jason stood, took a step forward, and threw the ball back to Jeff. He circled away from Martin to be on the safe side, locked eyes with the ump for a fleeting moment of kinsmanship before returning to his place behind the plate. *One down. Two to go.* Then they could head to the clubhouse and air conditioning. Another hour and he'd have Megan in his arms. He forced his thoughts back to the task at hand. This wasn't the time to be daydreaming. One wrong decision, one too-slow reaction could drag this game out. Get Martin out, one way or another, and then he could daydream all he wanted.

Jeff turned his back on home plate, surveying the outfield, or pretending to. It looked good for the cameras, but the truth was, he didn't see a damned thing. His eyes were open, but his vision was focused inward. In all his years as a closer for the Texas Mustangs, he'd never faced a more formidable opponent than Martin McCree. It hadn't always been that way. Last season, McCree had been an almost guaranteed out. But he'd taken the low road this season, and his stats were riding high in the saddle. Still, the man had his weaknesses, and Jason knew every one of them. Jeff had to trust his brother to call the right pitches, and he had to trust himself to throw them. That's what this little breather was really about, centering himself before he faced McCree. Three pitches, four max. The Mustangs had a one-run lead, and with two outs and no one on base, McCree was the last man Jeff had to face today, if he got it right.

McCree did his thing. Jeff waited, patient for all anyone knew. Jason set up a little off the plate. That ought to mess with McCree's mind. Only a moron would fall for that ploy.

Jeff blocked out everything else, the crowds, the noise, McCree. He read the sign, twisted the ball in his hand, found the seams he was looking for like a blind man reading Braille. He nodded to Jason, then brought his hands together waist high. Light grip on the ball, too tight and he'd lose velocity, too loose and he'd lose control. When he had it right, he focused on the image of the exact spot he wanted the pitch to go, knowing Jason's glove would be there at the exact moment the ball arrived.

Jeff squared his shoulders, filled his lungs, brought his left knee to his chest, and threw six feet and two hundred pounds of hard muscle into the pitch. His pent up breath burst from his lips as his left foot connected with the ground. Pain traveled in a lightning bolt from his foot to the top of his head, making a pit stop in the shock absorbing knee joint a fourth of the way up. Instinct told him he'd thrown the pitch as perfectly as he'd envisioned, and with a little luck from the gods, and maybe a little diamond dust, McCree would swing and miss. It would be worth the pain in his knee to see that.

A brown blur cut through his vision. Leather smacked against leather. McCree cursed. The umpire called, "Strike one!" Jeff took another deep breath and willed his body to relax.

The goddamned Texas heat had him wrapped up in a wet blanket under a heat lamp. As hot as it was for him, Jason had it worse with all that protective gear. He owed it to the team, and their fans baking in the stands to get this over with so they could all go home. Jeff resisted the urge to look into the stands. Megan was there, in the seat reserved for her. She was always there unless she had to work. He told her she didn't have to work, he and Jason would take care of her, but she'd always refused their offer, saying she loved her job too much. He understood. What she did was good, and she was good at it. But he still wished she'd make more of a commitment to their relationship. He dragged his thoughts away from Megan, and back to the game.

Two more pitches and they could all find some air conditioning. Another hour, two if he got stuck doing post game interviews, and Megan would be in his arms. Being hot and sweaty had its place – the bedroom. He took his cap off and wiped his face on his shirtsleeve. Jason waited until Jeff replaced his hat before making eye contact. Beneath the mask, Jeff saw the gleam of excitement in Jason's eyes. Martin could be damned predictable, his greatest weakness, and Jason could read him better than a fortuneteller. Martin was going down.

❧❧

Jason crouched behind the plate. This time his fingers flashed a different code. Only he and Jeff knew it was mostly nonsense. Only the first one meant anything – do it again. Jeff nodded, took a second to focus, and went into his windup. The pitch left his hand like a bullet shot out of a long-barrel gun – straight and true. Martin McCree tensed, swung his artificial muscle and kiln-dried lumber in another futile attempt to connect. The ball slammed into Jason's glove with the impact of a car into a brick wall.

"Fuck," Martin hissed.

"Strike two!" The umpire called.

Jason stood, shook his gloved hand to get the blood flowing to his stinging palm. A glance at the centerfield scoreboard confirmed his suspicion. Ninety-nine miles per hour. Martin didn't have a chance. Jason slid his mitt and mask off, and headed to the pitching mound. His hand could use a short break, and it would do McCree good to think he needed to consult with Jeff about the next pitch.

The umpire called time as Jason approached the mound. He handed the ball to Jeff and ducked his head so the cameras couldn't read his lips. "Shit. You almost broke my fucking hand."

Jeff held his glove up, blocking his lips from the prying eyes. "Works for me. You spend some time in the hospital, and I get Megan all to myself for a while."

"Dream on, brother. One more and we're done. Don't fuck it up. It's too hot to stay out here a minute longer than we have to." He turned and walked away before Jeff could respond.

Jason adjusted his chest protector. "Guess we better not try that again," he said to himself, loud enough Martin couldn't help but hear, then he pulled his mask on, crouched low. "Let's see…something different this time…" He flashed Jeff the pitch call, pausing after the last set of signs long enough that surely, the live broadcast had moved on, then he flashed one more sign. His middle finger descended in an age-old sign that had nothing to do with baseball, and everything to do with relaxing his brother.

Jeff's lips curved up in a knowing smile. Jason noted the quick tension in Martin's thighs. Let the bastard wonder what was up with

Jeff's smile. Jason raised his glove, shifted a little to the left, exaggerating his movements a little so Martin couldn't miss it. Jeff paused, hands together at his waist. Jason relaxed and focused on Jeff's right hand and the speck of white he could see between his fingers. The ball spun through the thick air like a comet through the night sky. McCree swung even as he danced back from the plate. Jason closed his fingers, trapping the ball in his mitt.

"Steeeeriiiiiiikkkkke three!" the umpire shouted with more enthusiasm than was probably warranted for the occasion, but Jason couldn't argue with him. McCree, however, had no qualms about doing so. The man went into a rage—something else to attribute to the drugs – and cracked the bat against the plate. Jason knew some colorful language, had used some on occasion himself, but the string of invectives that followed Jeff and him off the field was enough to make a sailor blush.

He met Jeff halfway to the dugout and slung an arm around his shoulder. "The moron would still be at bat if he hadn't swung." He chuckled. "That was some inside heat, bro. You damned near took his kneecaps off."

"I wouldn't mind putting him on the bench for a few games, or the rest of the season."

"Well, you almost did. Better luck next time." He gave Jeff's shoulder a squeeze. "See you at home. Don't take too long." Jason ducked his head to avoid eye contact with the horde of reporters storming the field, and his brother. Jeff was good at the press thing. Let him answer their inane questions. Megan was a quick shower, and a short drive away.

✑✐

Megan hung her car keys on the key rack inside the kitchen door. She needed a shower and a drink. She grabbed a soda from the fridge, swept her limp ponytail to one side, and pressed the can to the back of her neck. One foot hooked the bottom of the door and swung it shut while she tugged the freezer door open with her free hand. Frigid air met heated skin from her toes to her hairline. She closed her eyes and silently thanked whoever invented the side-by-side refrigerator/freezer. She savored the cold for a minute, then headed for the pool to complete her cool-down.

The front door opening and closing echoed through the cavernous house, followed by heavy footsteps across the hardwood floors, punctuated by short silent pauses, much like missed heartbeats. That would be Jason coming home. The man couldn't sneak in if he had to. Megan paddled her floating lounge chair to the middle of the indoor pool so she could see him coming. As many times as Jason had done this, it was still something she didn't want to miss.

He walked through the open French doors, into the glass-enclosed pool area. Megan eyed him appreciatively as he crossed the rough flagstones to the flat rock that doubled as a diving board. He was a magnificent specimen, she'd give him that, but he had the manners of a caveman. "You know you're going to pick those up, don't you? I'm not your maid."

He raked his longish hair back with one hand and bounced on his tiptoes, making all sorts of things bounce too. The man had as much modesty as he had manners – absolutely none. "I know. I promise to pick the clothes up, but first I need to cool off. It was hotter than hell out there today." He executed a perfect dive and stroked underwater until he surfaced next to Megan's wildly rocking chair. "You're too pretty to be the maid."

Megan put her hand on his head, shoved him under the water, and held him there until he came up sputtering.

Jason clung to the side of her chair while he kicked them both to the shallow end. He sat on the built-in bench, his arms stretched along the pool edge. "I keep my clothes on in front of company. It's not like *you* haven't seen it before. He manipulated her chair with his toes, pushing it away, then reeling it back in so the cool water rippled over her submerged midsection.

"We were talking about your slovenly ways. You're only a slob because it annoys Jeff."

He flashed an unrepentant grin. "Picked up on that, did 'ya?" His grin faded. "Why don't you get off your throne and make me forget I have a brother."

His voice had gone from light and teasing, to dark and hungry in the space of a heartbeat. Megan let her gaze slide from his full lips to the scar on his otherwise smooth chest, then lower. He'd been flaccid when he dove in the water, but that wasn't the case now. A wave of heat washed over her and set her skin on fire. It never occurred to her to say no, she never had before. Jason hooked one foot on the edge of her chair and Megan tumbled out at his feet.

"Come here." He wiggled a finger in invitation. His dark blonde hair was plastered to his head like a sleek helmet, leaving the sharp lines of his face unobscured. She recognized the determined set of his jaw, and the sparkle of lust in his eyes. It had been like this from the very first when she'd met the twins. Even a nun wouldn't be immune to a look like that, but as arousing as it was, it was nothing compared to the way she felt when Jeff looked at her. That didn't mean she wasn't going to take what was being offered. A round of sex with Jason would be fun, and it was always satisfying.

Megan moved closer in the hip deep water until her legs straddled Jason's. "Whoa." His hand spanned her stomach as he stopped her progress. "You're wearing too many clothes."

She stood mute as Jason loosened the ties at her hips and tossed her bikini bottom over his shoulder. It landed with a slap on the flagstone deck. His hands framed her hips as his eyes surveyed her exposed flesh, lingering on her neatly trimmed mound. After all this time, he still looked at her as if he'd just unwrapped a work of art. His thumbs swept across her skin in a sensual arc, fanning the flames of her desire into a full-blown conflagration. With every callused sweep, her knees weakened until she had to lean into him for support. Jason took her weight easily, guiding her down to his lap.

Her hands drifted to his shoulders, and she dug her fingers into the hard muscles there. There wasn't an ounce of extra fat on his or Jeff's body. At twenty-eight, they had the kind of physiques you saw in fitness magazines, the kind that made women drool. Megan wasn't immune to their sexual appeal, or to the men they were inside, especially Jeff.

She couldn't say when it had started, this growing need for something permanent, for a family, but every day it grew stronger. She wanted kids, and she wanted them with Jeff.

Jason's hand slid from her hip, over her ribcage and to her nape. Gentle pressure brought her face down to his, while his other hand worked the fastening at the back of her bikini top. His lips commanded, and Megan responded, opening for his tongue to explore. He tasted like the peppermint gum he chewed while at bat, and it drove her nuts. It always had. Her top slipped away, landing on the flagstones next to her bottoms. Warm water lapped at the undersides of her breasts, a gentle, teasing caress. Her nipples hardened in the moist air, begging for Jason's touch.

His hands dove underwater, found her ribcage, and slowly worked their way to her front. He lifted her breasts in his callused palms and squeezed. Megan's heart thudded against her ribs. She dared to glance between them to see his hands molding, squeezing, manipulating. Her pale breasts were generous, but not overly large. But in Jason's huge hands they looked small, even when he plumped them together. Her nipples had darkened, hardened into aching pebbles under his gaze. If he didn't touch them soon she thought she might scream.

"Beautiful," he breathed against one aching nub. "You are so fucking beautiful."

Jason never failed to make her feel cherished. He meant the compliments, every one of them, but in her heart she knew it was only his appreciation for a woman's body – nothing more.

Jason lowered his head, drew one throbbing nub into his mouth, and Megan forgot that it was just sex. A stab of pure lust shot from her nipple to her womb, and drove every rational thought from her brain.

His hands explored at will, while his mouth moved from one breast to the other, tasting, taking, teasing, until Megan ground against him in frustration. Her pussy clenched with each pull on her nipple. Her core turned to liquid. Jason might not be able to give her his heart, but he could give her this. His rock hard cock pressed against her stomach, a testimony to his need. Megan wanted nothing more than to assuage that need, and sate hers at the same time, but what he was doing to her breasts felt too good to stop. She speared her fingers through his wet locks, and held him to her like a drowning victim clinging to a life preserver.

"I love your tits." Ahh, and she loved it when he loved them too.

Her head fell back. Her long hair fanned across the water. A primal moan worked its way from her chest to her throat and echoed off the glass walls surrounding the pool. She was close to begging when his hands left her breasts to cradle her hips once again.

"Yes," she sighed. Every cell in her body was tight with need. "I need you."

Jason guided his cock to her entrance and pressed her down. She wanted to sink fast, take him all at once, but he wouldn't allow it. He eased her down, one delicious stretching, filling inch at a time, until her inner thighs rested on his. Hot steel impaled her.

"Oh God!" Her body adjusted quickly to the invasion. Megan dropped her forehead to Jason's and closed her eyes. He held her still for a moment, and when she relaxed in his arms, he flexed his hips and worked himself impossibly deeper inside her.

"Ahh, baby. You feel so damned good." His voice was hoarse with desire. Megan wiggled as best she could without shredding her knees on the concrete bench. Jason's hands tightened on her hips, holding her still. "Don't, baby. Let me do all the work."

CHAPTER ELEVEN

"Like hell you will."

Megan fought her way up from the sensual haze that engulfed her. Her breath quickened and her insides turned to liquid heat. Jeff.

"I see you started without me." The voice was near identical to Jason's, but there was something about the way he delivered his words that sent her libido into overdrive. Everything that came out of his mouth sounded like a sensual caress, a forbidden touch. Sex. Hot, steamy, fuck me now, sex, and ...love.

Fabric slid against fabric. The rasp of a zipper seemed muted by the thick, moist air. She didn't have to turn around to know that in a minute, Jeff would have his clothes neatly folded and placed well out of the way of splashing water.

"You're late," Jason replied. "Maybe she doesn't want you."

The splash from Jeff's sleek dive barely registered on the surface, but below, a tidal wave washed between her body and Jason's. Jeff surfaced behind her. His breath fanned along her spine as he placed hot kisses from the water line to her nape. Then he was there, his heat pressing against her back. His erection nudged her lower back, sending a shaft of longing through her. Megan shuddered with desire as Jeff's hands rested on her shoulders and, aided by the slickness of the water, slid along her arms to her wrists.

Long, competent fingers shackled the delicate bones there. She loosened her hold on his brother and let Jeff pull her hands up, placing her palms on top of her head, bringing her breasts above the water line. His hands stroked back the way they'd come, past her shoulders, along her back and then around to cup her breasts. He massaged gently at first, then he found her nipples. He pinched the sensitive nubs between his thumb and forefinger, tugging and applying pressure until she cried out. A lightning bolt shot from her nipples straight to her pussy making her clench hard around Jason's cock.

"Ah, Christ, Megan!" Jason cursed through gritted teeth. "Not yet, baby. It feels too good."

"Finish him, sweetheart," Jeff crooned, his lips moving over the shell of her ear as he continued to torment her breasts. "Get him off, and then it'll be just you and me. I'll make you feel good, I promise."

"Shut up, Jeff." Jason had regained some control over his body. "I found her first."

"Maybe, but she wants me, don't you, sugar?"

Jeff's erection pressed against her lower back, his chest against her shoulders. Sandwiched between matching bookends, it was nearly impossible to think, much less speak. Megan moved her lips, tested the motions necessary to form the words before she attempted to speak.

"Both," she mumbled. "I want…"

"Yeah, I want too," Jeff said. He tucked her hands over her breasts and pressed them hard against her chest. "Hold these for me," he commanded.

Megan did as she was told, though she found it difficult to keep up the pressure, no matter how wonderful it felt. Jeff leaned to one side, snagged a foam float, and pulled it to the edge of the pool. A few more tugs and the doublewide float was centered behind Jason's head.

Jeff's hands cupped her ass from below. "Lift her up, Jase."

Water sluiced down their bodies as the two men lifted her from the pool. When they were finished relocating, Megan was still impaled by Jason's cock, but now he sat on the foam mat with his legs dangling in the water. Jeff's hand on her shoulder pushed her forward. She followed Jason down, her pussy stretching to take him at the new angle. His hands soothed down her back as she wiggled to find a comfortable position.

"Don't move." Jeff bounded out of the pool, crossed to a table nearby for a tube of lubricant they kept there. A ripple of desire worked its way through her body as Jeff's intent registered. They usually took turns, but the times when they did take her simultaneously, it was an incredible experience. Behind her, Jeff snapped the lid shut on the tube, and weakness took hold of her body.

She sank, boneless against Jason's powerful torso, drawing what strength she could from him, as her body seemed incapable of functioning on its own. She turned her face into his neck, and his arms came around to cradle her shoulders and her head, stroking, comforting, assuring. "It's okay, baby. Just relax. Let us love you." His words rumbled through his chest, then whispered against the top of her head. Her shoulders slumped and her fisted hands uncurled. "That's it. You know it's going to feel good."

Her body relaxed, but her mind was another thing. Jeff parted her ass, slicked lube everywhere, on her, in her, over her ass cheeks. Her brain conjured things she could only imagine. His fingers circling. Swiping. Plunging. The look on Jeff's face, as he prepared her for his entry. Somehow, she knew he would have the same focused concentration he had when he threw a pitch, and her pelvic muscles clenched at the thought. God, he was sexy when he had that look on his face. Single minded focus. Determination. Dominance.

"Good, Christ." The curse came from behind her. "God, Megan! When you squeeze my fingers like that, all I can think about is how it's going to feel when you come, and I'm inside you."

"I...I'm sorry," she whimpered.

Jason smoothed a hand over her wet hair. "Don't be. Shhh. You want this, don't you?"

If she wanted it any more, she'd die. "Yes," she whispered.

Christ, she sounded like a kitten, mewling for milk. Her apology and that one word confirmation had Jeff so hard he could drive nails with his cock. He needed to calm down, focus on taking her slow so he wouldn't hurt her. He couldn't take his eyes off her pussy lips, stretched thin by Jason's cock. He could see his brother's ragged heartbeat in the thick vein along the underside of his shaft. If he waited any longer to join Jason inside her, he'd blow like a volcano. Hell, there was no guarantee he would last more than a second inside her tight little ass, either.

She had an ass any man would want to fuck. Sweet, round, soft. Every time he saw it, he wanted it, wanted her. He was too big to do it often, especially in tandem with Jason, but they'd done it enough he knew she could take it. Thank God she'd said yes, because once he'd put his fingers in her tight hole, he'd committed himself to fucking something. Her kitten soft voice made his balls draw up tight and his cock throb. She was his, and he was going to have her. Now.

He parted her with both hands, kneaded the soft globes as he flexed his knees and brought the head of his cock to the sweet rosebud. His cock had enough lube on it to slide through a garden hose, but he'd be careful with her. He'd take his time, ease into her, even if it killed him.

Jason crooned nonsense as he stroked Megan's head from temple to crown. Her back rose and fell with each slow breath. Jeff timed his entry, watching until she'd filled her lungs. Then as the breath passed her lips, he pushed hard, breaching the tight ring of muscles. She gave a startled cry and tensed. Jeff ground his teeth as her body closed around his shaft. He would not go off, not until he took her completely.

He waited until Jason's ministrations calmed her once again, then he pressed in another inch. Now that he was inside, he let her ass cheeks close around his shaft. She felt like heaven – tight and hot where she held him inside her – soft and warm where she cradled the rest of his shaft. "God, Megan...You're so fucking tight."

He stroked her soft globes, ran his hands in hard circles, then swept up and across the small of her back. Eventually, he wrapped his hands around her hipbones and held her steady.

"Can you take all of me?" he asked.

She nodded her head against Jason's shoulder. No one had ever trusted him the way Megan did. A now familiar warmth spread through his body as his love for her enveloped his heart and squeezed almost as tight as her ass was around his cock. She looked so damned vulnerable lying there draped over Jason. He'd have her again, like this, when they were all alone and he didn't have to share her with his brother. His cock grew harder at the mental image of Megan beneath him, offering her ass, giving him everything.

"Tell me if it hurts. I'll stop." He pressed again, this time inching in with one long, slow thrust that had sweat beading on his forehead and his balls burning with need. It was torture. It was heaven. Every inch stole a little bit more of his sanity. God, she was beautiful in her submission. His heart lurched at the amount of trust she gave to them.

It was all he could do to hold still once his pelvis pressed up against her pillow soft ass. He clenched his jaw tight, stroked his hands over her back and along her spine and down her legs. Once, she wiggled her ass, and he clenched her hips to hold her still.

"Don't do that," he admonished. "Let us do all the work. I'm going to pull out a little, then push back in. Real slow." He caught his brother's eye over Megan's head. "You know what to do."

Megan dug her fingers into Jason's shoulders as both men set up a torturously slow rhythm. When one slid out, the other slid in, like pistons in a two-stroke engine. They filled her body, her mind, her heart. She felt weak. She felt powerful. Love and need and hunger ravaged her body. She'd never felt more loved, more cherished. Their hands stroked every inch of her skin, in a sensuous massage that both relaxed and aroused. Love infused every tender touch and warmed her from the inside out.

Her body adjusted to the fullness, but she needed more. She braced herself upward, changing the angle so her clit rubbed against

Jason's pelvic bone. The angle allowed Jeff to go even deeper, and faster. Megan groaned as the new sensations pushed her closer to the edge.

Her hair hung over one shoulder, leaving crystal drops of water on Jason's chest and shoulders. When it swung over and splattered his face, he lifted it so it hung down her back like a curtain of black velvet. Rivulets of water collected and ran along her spine. She heard Jeff's hiss as the cold water made it to his cock.

"Son of a bitch," he snarled. "That's fucking cold!" Megan smiled down at Jason who smiled back at her.

Both men took advantage of the new position, cupping and fondling her breasts. Jeff's fingers ran through the cold river running along her spine, then transferred the damp chill to her burning nipples, making them tighten into hard aching buttons. Megan arched away from Jeff's cold fingers, then just as quickly thrust her chest forward, begging for more. Jeff obliged, wetting his palm and capturing her breast in a firm caress.

Megan writhed between them. Where Jeff tormented, Jason soothed, chafing her tender skin with his callused palms, replacing cold with burning heat. She was trapped between heaven and hell, needing the release held just out of her grasp.

Jeff changed the tempo. Jason closed his eyes and clenched his jaw. It was awkward for the span of two strokes, until Jason adjusted to the new rhythm. Megan moved her hands to Jason's biceps. He slid his hands up to support her arms as both men thrust into her hard, at the same time.

Jeff's hips ground her clit against his brother's pelvis. What had been a slow climb to the top became a desperate scramble to the peak. Her breasts bounced with each powerful thrust. Her pussy ached, her ass burned. Deep in her gut, her orgasm coiled tight. Blood roared past her ears, muting the voices urging her on. Jeff flicked a finger over her clit.

She went over the edge. Jason clamped his teeth hard over one nipple. She screamed. Pain and pleasure melded into one as she escaped earth's bonds. Nothing could ever feel that dangerous, or that good, again. Simultaneous curses from Jason and Jeff told her they had found the same unearthly plane. They shoved into her as their cocks pulsed, flooding her with their heat. She took it all, savoring this part of them that they gave to her, and her alone.

She collapsed against Jason's laboring chest. Jeff stroked her back for several minutes, then as he grew soft, he slipped from her. He pressed his lips to her sore ass. His breath fanned against her tender skin until gooseflesh covered her body. He laughed and did it again. She reached out in a weak attempt to swat at him.

Jason shifted his hips, slipping from her. Jeff stood over them. "Let's get cleaned up, then I need food."

Megan rolled off Jason. He got to his feet and both men offered a hand to help her up. Her knees refused to hold her. She fell into Jeff, and he caught her to his side and helped her to the open shower in the corner. Designed for one person to rinse off, the three of them pressed close, skin-to-skin under the spray. Megan felt like a ragdoll, supported by one, then the other, as they bathed her body, taking extra care with the tender flesh between her legs.

Jeff dried her while Jason supported her. When they were all dry, Jason carried her to her bedroom. Megan closed her eyes as Jason deposited her on the bed and pulled the duvet over her. "Rest. We'll order in tonight," he said. He placed a kiss on her forehead, then walked to the door where Jeff stood, watching. "She's exhausted."

"We should have been easier on her," Jeff said in a voice just above a whisper. Their concern was touching, but unnecessary. Megan hadn't felt this good in a long time. She'd been thoroughly loved by the two most incredible men in the whole world, and now, they were taking care of her as if she were spun glass. What more could a woman want? She loved them both in her own way. They were so much a part of her now she couldn't imagine her life without them.

"We were doing fine until you came home and stuck your dick in where it wasn't needed," Jason said.

"*I* needed her."

"And that's supposed to make it okay? Christ, Jeff."

"You know I can hear you, don't you?" She couldn't let them argue over something she'd enjoyed so much.

A chorus of apologies sounded from the doorway. Megan rose up on one elbow. With towels wrapped around their waists, they looked like they'd been caught playing pranks in the locker room, and it was all she could do to keep a straight face. "I appreciate your concern, but I'm fine. More than fine, actually. I loved it. I'd invite you both to come snuggle with me, but I'm starving, and if I invited you to bed, I'd never get anything to eat. So scram, both of you, and let me know when there's food downstairs."

Megan waited until she heard their doors open and shut before she curled on her side and closed her eyes. Her pussy and ass still throbbed from their penetration, but it wasn't the least bit uncomfortable. She squeezed her thighs together, savoring the pressure on sensitive skin. Jason was right, she was exhausted.

She placed her palm over her stomach, reliving in her mind the feel of them emptying into her. How could a man possibly understand how that felt, or how much she loved knowing she held a part of them inside her still? Maybe one day she'd have an even bigger part, a baby. Jeff's baby.

∽∾

Jeff paid the delivery boy and carried the food to the big granite island in the kitchen. He'd taken the lids off the foil containers and set out plates and silverware when Jason and Megan came into the room. Megan placed one hand on his stomach, just above the waistband of his jeans and slid it in a provocative caress around to his side. She rose on tiptoe and kissed him on the cheek.

"Uhm. You smell good, and so does this." She indicated the Mexican food spread out on the island.

Jeff smiled and watched her sidle around the corner and take the middle of the three seats on the other side. Jason followed, taking his place beside Megan. Jeff crossed to the Subzero refrigerator, took three beers out and slid them across the smooth counter. "You smell pretty good yourself. Did you get enough rest?"

Before she could answer, Jason pointed a remote at the under-counter television, and the unit blared to life. He flicked through channels and Megan raised her voice to talk over the noise. "I did, thanks. And thanks for getting dinner."

"It's the least we could do," Jeff answered as he joined her and Jason at the island. "I should have left when I saw you with Jason, or just watched. What can I say? You make me crazy."

"Hey! Look who's on TV." Jason pointed at the small television.

Jeff groaned. "What the hell is..."

"Shhh!" Jason increased the volume. "I want to hear this."

Megan laid her hand on Jeff's arm. He turned his head and the understanding in her eyes was cold water on his anger. How did she do that? Diffuse his anger with a look or a touch? Calmer, he turned back to the press conference, and the one player he had zero respect for. Martin McCree.

It was enough to ruin your appetite, the way he stood there denying his steroid use. Anyone who believed what McCree spouted should also be interested in prime real estate in South Florida. Both were bogs, that once you sunk your feet into, you'd never be free of.

"Turn it off," Jeff barked. "It's ruining my appetite."

"But..."

"Turn. It. Off."

Jason lifted the remote and a game show filled the screen. "There. What's with you anyway?" he complained.

"I can't stand that guy. I have to see his face on the field, but nothing says I have to invite him into my home."

"I can't stand him either, but it's kind of funny, watching him dig his own grave. You know, sooner or later, he's going to test positive. No way did he get all that muscle on his own."

"Well, up until then, I have to pitch to the bastard and hope he doesn't hit one right back at my head."

Jason helped himself to another taco. "Just keep throwing him what I tell you, and he won't hit it. He might have more muscle now, but he's still dumber than a bag of peanuts."

"Is he a problem?" Megan asked.

"He's the biggest problem in baseball right now. So far, I've been able to hold him off, but as the season goes on…"

"As the season goes on, he'll be out on his ass for fifty games."

"Not unless he takes a drug test. So far, he hasn't come up in the random selection, and it doesn't appear anyone on the Health Policy Advisory Committee is going to call for one."

"Why not? If it's clear he's cheating, why doesn't someone do something?"

Jeff shook his head. Megan was as honest as the day was long, and thought everyone else should be too. "It's not that easy, sugar. Even though everyone in the league is sure McCree is, or was, using steroids, no one wants to be the one pointing a finger. Maybe he did build all that muscle over the winter. Theoretically, it's possible. Don't worry. His name will come up in the random drug test selection soon enough, and then we'll see."

"So, you and all the other pitchers are supposed to let him keep this up?"

"For now, that's all we can do."

"It doesn't seem fair to me. That's all I'm saying."

Jason slid his empty plate a few inches and rested his forearms on the countertop. "I say we forget all about illegal steroids and put in a movie or something. Tomorrow's game is late, so we can sleep in tomorrow."

"Sounds good to me," Jeff said. He stood, gathered the empty food containers, and dumped them in the trash basket under the sink. "What about you?" he asked Megan.

"I'm in, as long as I get to choose the movie."

Jeff braced both hands on the counter and dropped his head between his shoulders. Megan always chose a lame-ass romantic comedy, or worse, something where everyone wore too many clothes and spoke with accents he couldn't understand. But, then again, maybe she did deserve to choose after the way they'd taken her earlier.

"Okay with me," Jason said in uncharacteristic agreement. Jeff shot him a look. Jason raised his hands in mock surrender. "Hey! What did I do?"

"You just condemned us to an evening of chick flicks, you idiot."

Megan's laughter had both men frowning. "What's so funny?" Jeff asked.

"Nothing," she replied. "What if I promise no chick flicks?"

Jeff was instantly suspicious, but he had no reason to suspect Megan had any other motive. The truth was, he didn't care if she put in a chick flick or not, as long as he got to hold her for a while. He could amuse himself in other ways while she watched the movie.

"Deal," he said. "We'll clean up in here. You go on and get the movie started. We'll be there in a few."

Jason grumbled something beneath his breath, but he kissed Megan on the cheek and sent her into the den. "Sorry. I thought we should humor her tonight. You know, after what we did earlier."

"I agree. We were pretty hard on her, but Christ, I couldn't wait to be inside her. When I came in and saw you with her, I had to have her too." Jeff ran a hand through his hair and stared blankly at the door Megan had disappeared through.

"Don't worry. She looks fine. She sounds fine. And it isn't like we haven't done it before."

"I know. We usually work our way up to it, you know? Today, I just did it."

Jason picked up a dirty plate and rinsed it in the sink, then opened the dishwasher and placed it in the bottom rack. Jeff leaned his hips against the island and watched. "You know how to load the dishwasher?" he asked with mock amazement. "I didn't think you even knew where it was."

"Shut the fuck up, asshole. Just because I don't dust every piece of furniture I walk by, doesn't mean I don't know how." He glared at his brother. "Hand me another fucking plate, or you can do this all by yourself."

CHAPTER TWELVE

Jason propped his feet on the coffee table, more to annoy Jeff than anything else. Old habits were hard to break. Ever since they were kids, he knew how to push his brother's buttons, and he did it often. If Jeff ever bothered to look, he'd find Jason's bedroom every bit as neat as his, maybe neater, but that was Jason's little secret. A guy had to have something that was his own.

A plate in the sink didn't bother Jason, but it made Jeff crazy. How was a brother supposed to ignore opportunities like that? Jason couldn't, anymore than he could stop breathing.

It didn't help that every day he felt Megan slipping away from him a little more. Or maybe he was slipping away from her; he couldn't tell. All he knew was his alone time with her had dwindled to almost nonexistent in the last few months.

This afternoon, he seized the opportunity to have Megan all to himself for a while, and she hadn't exactly pushed him away. When Jeff walked in though, he really hoped Megan would say she wanted to be alone with him. Instead, she allowed Jeff to join them. He did a good job of hiding his feelings, or at least, he thought he did.

Megan had been curled up on the sofa under a throw when he and Jeff came in. She looked so soft and warm, he wanted to take her in his arms and hold her, but the minute Jeff sat on her other side, she practically crawled into his lap. That's where she was now, still looking like a kitten cuddled up next to the stove. They looked so damned cozy. Jason swallowed hard, and tried to concentrate on the movie. It was an old one, but a favorite which they'd watched many times. Only tonight, he stared at the screen with sightless eyes.

What the hell was happening? He'd never felt so much on the outside, so alone. Things were changing. He'd known it for some time, but it had never hit him with such force before. Megan shifted in Jeff's embrace. Jason knew without looking that they were getting more intimate. She parted her legs and squirmed her delectable bottom around to allow Jeff better access. Jason could smell her unique scent, stirred by their slight movements. Even after their earlier encounter, he should be hard as a post watching them get it on, but he remained flaccid. If he turned to them, he'd be invited to play too, but he couldn't bring himself to do it.

A hole opened in his chest. He'd never turned down an invitation to touch her, and she'd never turned him away. Yet, somehow, tonight, he felt like he was on the outside, looking in, and even being on the periphery felt wrong. Hell, he felt like a Peeping Tom.

Shit. He'd watched Megan and Jeff together plenty of times and never felt like a pervert before. So why now? What the hell was wrong with him?

"Jase," Megan ran her dainty foot over his bare forearm. His skin tingled at the invitation. But where there should have been a reaction – nothing. Abso-freaking-nothing. His gut churned and the gaping hole in his chest threatened to swallow him whole. He tried to focus on the television, realizing his vision problem was caused by excess moisture. Christ. He had to get out of there before he did something really stupid.

"Thanks, but you two have a good time. It's been a long day." Did he sound normal? He couldn't tell for the blood rushing past his ears as he stood. "I'm going to bed."

Megan's concerned voice followed him out of the room, wishing him a good night. He shouted his response over his shoulder. Looking at them was out of the question. Just being in the same house tonight felt like a challenge, one he wasn't sure he was up to.

Up to. That was hilarious. He knew his inability wasn't physical. It was all in his fucked up head tonight. He closed the door behind him and pulled his T-shirt over his head as he crossed the room to the walk-in closet. Everything was in its place. Shoes on their custom built racks, ties hung from their miniature hangers. Rows of color-coordinated shirts, slacks and suits. His life outside this house was every bit as orderly. Maybe he needed to shake things up. Maybe he needed his own woman. One he didn't have to share. It had been a long time since he'd thought about going solo. Where the hell was he supposed to find a woman? It wasn't like he could go out to a club and pick one up. The tabloids would have a field day with that. Just ask A-Rod.

He held the T-shirt over the hamper, staring at the mound of clothes in the bottom, then swung his hand away. The shirt fell in a crumpled heap on the floor. His jeans joined the shirt. He lied to Jeff and Megan. He wasn't in the least bit tired, but he couldn't go back in there. They had another game tomorrow against the Miners, and that meant facing McCree again. Today's stats and analysis would be up by now, so he grabbed his laptop and settled against the headboard to do a little studying.

He didn't really need another woman. He had Megan, if he wanted her. But…did he want her if he couldn't have all of her?

Memorizing stats wasn't what Jason had envisioned for the evening, but it was a hell of a lot better than his only other choice. Besides, Jeff couldn't throw the same pitch sequences tomorrow that he had today, especially not to McCree. His brother relied on him to know the batters, to ferret out their weaknesses and to call the best pitch sequence possible. He powered up the computer and entered the password for the Mustangs' database. A complex grid filled the screen.

"What's wrong with him?" Megan asked.

Jeff stroked his long fingers through her slick folds. His lips tugged at her earlobe. "Who?"

"Jase." Megan tilted her head to one side to allow Jeff better access. Her knees slid further apart.

"Who cares?" He dipped one finger inside her and unerringly found the spot guaranteed to turn her into a puddle of goo. Tonight was no different. She lifted her hips to meet him.

"About?" She'd lost track of the conversation. It was something important, or at least it seemed important at the time. Jeff stroked her tender folds. Her insides heated, throbbed for his touch, for the blissful release that hovered tantalizingly close.

"I don't want to hurt you." Jeff's voice was a soft whisper against her temple.

"You won't," she assured. "It feels so good…" Whatever they'd been talking about no longer mattered as she gave herself over to the sensations. So good. Jeff had always known how to touch her, how to make her lose herself. His heat enveloped her, wrapping her in bone melting sunshine. Being in his arms was better than soaking in a hot tub. He had the ability to heat her to the core.

"You're so perfect." Jeff's free hand covered her breast and squeezed. Electricity shot through her as if he'd closed an unseen circuit. She squirmed as her whole body jolted then clenched tight. "So responsive, so sweet…," his lips switched from words to actions.

It was late when she curled up beside Jeff in his bed and drifted off to sleep. She wanted to say goodnight to Jason, but the band beneath his door was dark. Whatever had been bothering him, and something sure as heck was, it would have to wait.

❧

Jason cursed under his breath as he made his way to the clubhouse, practically daring anyone to get in his way. Christ, he needed to get a grip. Jeff had been right about McCree weeks ago. He should have listened, but he'd been too focused on his relationship, or lack thereof with Megan to hear what his brother was saying. This was the second series they'd faced the Miners, and McCree was still playing, and still a threat that couldn't be ignored. The scoreboard testified to that fact. He'd called a sequence of pitches that should have gotten the bastard out, but as the season wore on, McCree was learning to read the pitchers better.

Jeff was going to be pissed. Not only had Jason called the pitch that cost the Mustangs the game, but he'd left his brother out there on the field to face the press after the blown save. Reporters were your best friend if you were winning, but let the best closer in baseball blow a save, and they would descend like a flock of vultures. He should have stayed by Jeff's side. The loss was more his fault than Jeff's. Hell, he'd called pitches the entire game, and every fucking time McCree came up to bat he'd had a hit.

He kept his head down, his eyes diverted, and a scowl on his face. The last thing he needed was well meaning teammates offering up platitudes. He'd had enough of that in the dugout during the game. "Don't worry, we'll get him next time," was the favorite, and probably the least welcome one. *Don't worry.* Jason worried day and night about facing McCree. After all, it wasn't only his career in the spotlight. It was Jeff's too. More Jeff's than his own. Most people placed all the blame on the pitcher, but if the pitcher threw what his catcher called, then it was the catcher's fault, plain and simple.

By the time Jason was dressed and heading home, he still hadn't seen Jeff. That couldn't be good. Guilt clung to him like a pair of sweat-soaked socks, and stunk just as bad. The stink followed him all the way home, and to the pool where he knew he'd find Megan. Not that he was going to do anything with her. It had been weeks since he'd so much as kissed her, but he needed a few minutes to get his head on straight.

Her eyes held no pity, no censure, even though he knew he deserved at least the latter.

"I won't say it. You're always harder on yourself than anyone else could be."

"You know as well as I do, it's my fault." Jason stopped with his toes at the edge of the pool. He'd been on the edge of the unknown for a while now. He wished to hell, he knew what was going to happen when he took the next step. He hoped to hell, he had the courage to take it before someone or something pushed him. It wasn't the stepping that had him running scared. It was not knowing what was beyond the edge.

"Baseball is a team sport. You aren't responsible for the missed plays, the poorly thrown pitches, or the missed opportunities at the plate."

"I know all that, but…"

"No buts. You aren't the only player on the Mustangs, any more than Martin McCree is the only player on the Miners. Any number of plays could have changed the outcome of the game, and you know it. Don't take it all on yourself."

She looked like an angel floating on the water in her favorite lounge chair, paddling around with her hands and feet. She'd learned a lot about baseball over the last year or so, and everything she was saying was true. Inning ending strikeouts with runners on base, the walked batter in the fifth who ended up scoring, were a few of the things she was talking about. "You're right. I know it, but I can't blame my own failures on other people's mistakes. Maybe I'm not entirely to blame, but I let myself down. Hell, I let Jeff down."

"Why don't you come for a swim? Cool off a little, then when Jeff gets home, we'll have dinner."

"No. I'm going to go out for a while. You and Jeff can have the house to yourself tonight. We're off tomorrow, then on the road for nine games. I'll be okay."

"You're going out? Again? What's going on, Jason? You know we miss you. You haven't been with us in ages."

Jason's smile faded, and he focused on something across the pool. "I know. It's not you, Megan. You know how I feel about you, but I think it's time for me to move on, find my own woman. You don't need me, and I'm…well, I feel like I'm in the way here. I'm coming between you and Jeff."

Megan stopped paddling. "Is there someone else?"

What if there were? Would it make a difference? "Maybe." It was a lie, but Megan didn't have any way of knowing that. Jason stared off into space until Megan's direct gaze made him uncomfortable, a tactic that worked on him every time. He squirmed on the inside, determined not to let her see how close he was to the edge. "We have something good here – "

"Don't you mean had? Jason, you haven't been with us in weeks. You haven't been with me in weeks. Jeff's been so preoccupied with the season I don't think he's even noticed, but I have."

"I'm sorry. Really. But this has been coming for a long time. Don't tell me you didn't think so too. You're awesome, Megan. We're lucky bastards to have found you, but you're in love with Jeff. I know you want a family, and as long as I'm around, you'll never have that. I love you, but not the way Jeff does."

"I'm sorry, Jason."

"Don't be. I just want you to be happy."

"I know. I want that for you too. Loving Jeff doesn't mean I haven't enjoyed our time together. You're right though. I do want a family, and I think Jeff may be ready for that too."

"But big brother is hanging around."

"You know he doesn't think of you that way. You're only five minutes older than him."

"Maybe it's not like that, but in this case, three's a crowd. I need to move on, let the two of you have the life you want, and deserve."

"Jason, please. Don't go out tonight. Stay home, with us. Now is not the time to be talking about making changes. All of this can wait until the season is over."

"No, it can't." Suddenly, he could see what was over the edge. It was a blank page. A lonely, singular existence. He and Jeff had always been a team, then Megan had joined them, and he thought they'd completed their team. They worked well together, but this wasn't a game he could win. Just like on the field, he'd done his part. It wouldn't do any good to second-guess the plays. It was time to take responsibility. Time to make a trade. "I'll see you in the morning."

He stopped at the French doors separating the pool enclosure from the family room and turned. "Don't mention this to Jeff, okay? He has enough on his mind without worrying about me."

It wasn't the first save he'd blown, and it wouldn't be his last. Jeff's patience wore thin as he fielded one stupid question after another. He needed to catch up to Jason. The look on his brother's face when McCree sent that pitch into orbit had said it all. Jason blamed himself for the blown save. The media didn't see it that way. As far as they were concerned, it was one hundred percent Jeff's fault. Maybe it was. The game evolved on a daily basis. If you didn't stay on your game, you'd become a has-been before they put your name on a locker. Before he had to face McCree again, he had to come up with something the asshole hadn't seen. Maybe not a new pitch, but a new sequence or maybe adjust the speed on his breaking ball – something. Inside heat wasn't enough anymore, not if he was going to keep McCree from sending his pitches into orbit. Even if the league came to their senses and benched McCree, there would always be another one, another player willing to risk their health and career for the chance at the record book. Hell, he wanted his name next to a Major League record too. And the only way he was going to get it was to keep working on his pitches.

He was still mulling over the possibilities when he pulled his car into garage. Megan handed him a cold beer as he entered the kitchen through the connecting hallway, then she went back to tossing a salad. Watching her do these little domestic things in his kitchen – no, their kitchen – put things in perspective. Maybe his job wasn't the nine to five variety, but there was no reason he had to bring his work home with him. He'd rather spend time with Megan and Jason, than think about McCree. Besides, they'd be on the road for over a week, and there would be plenty of time to work on a solution to that problem. Tonight, he wanted to be with Megan, to hold her in his arms, to make love to her and forget baseball.

It wasn't until Megan carried the salad to the table, that Jeff noticed there were only two place settings. "Where's Jase?"

"He went out."

Jeff helped move the rest of the serving dishes to the table, then they took their seats next to each other. "He does that a lot these days," he said.

"I didn't think you noticed."

He helped himself to salad and took a large helping of casserole. "I noticed. Do you know what's up?"

"You should ask him. I think I know, but please, will you talk to him?"

"Maybe. Maybe not. Jase has always kept things to himself, even when we were kids. Of course, I could beat it out of him then."

"I don't think that's a good solution now. Why don't you just ask him? For me?"

Whatever was bothering Jase, he'd eventually get around to talking about, but Megan's concern made him wonder if she knew something he didn't. Jason was a big boy; he certainly didn't need Jeff to sort out his life for him. "We aren't kids anymore. He's a grown man, he can work it out on his own."

"Please?" she wheedled. "I'm worried about him."

The quiet way she said those last words made him take notice. He knew she loved Jase. How could she not and do the things they did together? It wasn't like her to share herself with someone she didn't love, but how deep did her feelings go for his brother? He dropped his fork and stared at his plate. Had they had a fight he didn't know about? Is that why Jason had been scarce the last few months? Something foul churned in his stomach. Jealousy? No. Megan loved him, and he'd always known she loved Jason too, so it couldn't be jealousy. That didn't make sense, but something had soured in his stomach when she admitted she was worried about his brother. Christ, what was wrong with him?

"He'll be fine. I've got to pack. We're leaving early tomorrow because of the two-hour time change." Jeff shoved back from the table, unable to look at Megan. He couldn't bear to see the hurt he'd put there on top of her worry for Jason. Everything she felt showed on her face, it always had. So, how had he missed how she felt about Jase?

"Jeff, wait!"

He concentrated on putting one foot in front of the other until he was far enough away from the kitchen he couldn't feel her confusion or her concern any longer. Shit. This was the last thing he needed – his personal life falling apart when he needed to be concentrating on pitching. More specifically, on how to shut down Martin McCree. When you only threw a few pitches, and only in games when your team was ahead by a small margin, every outing had the potential to be a career maker, or breaker, depending on the outcome. A good inning was nine pitches or less, and unlike a starting pitcher, he was expected to have a zero earned run average. Anything less meant he wasn't doing his job.

He pulled a suitcase off the closet shelf and flipped it open on the bed. Ten days in hotels, eating in restaurants, and sleeping alone. He crossed to the dresser, yanked open a drawer and without bothering to count, tossed a handful of boxer briefs into the open suitcase. A couple of handfuls of socks followed. He frowned as half of them bounced and scattered across the bed. Well, hell. He picked up the stray socks and neatly tucked them into the suitcase, counted his boxers and added a few more in precise stacks. Slovenly living wouldn't make his situation any better. By the time he finished packing, he'd almost convinced himself the time on the road would be a good thing. With nothing else to do, he could concentrate on finding Martin McCree's weakness. Then, the next time he had to face the bastard, he'd be ready.

Maybe it wasn't rational, but Jeff couldn't help thinking McCree could be the single biggest challenge of his career, now, and in the future. If he could find a way to win the battle with the steroid-pumped hitting monster, he'd carve a place for himself in the record books. Jeff closed his suitcase and set it beside the door. He undressed and stretched out on the bed, thinking about what he wanted to accomplish in his career. He might never be the caliber of closer Mariano Rivera or Trevor Hoffman, but if he played it right, he could be a name people remembered. But first, he had to get the better of Martin McCree.

He heard Megan's footsteps sometime later. She paused outside his door, and he felt a pang of guilt at the way he'd left her sitting at the table. He should call to her, ask her to come in so he could apologize, maybe lift the covers and invite her to join him. That's what she would expect the night before a long road trip. She would come to him, he knew she would, but he couldn't shake the feeling that she might give herself to him, but all the time, she'd be wishing she were with Jason.

Damn. He flashed back to that time he'd found them in the pool together. How long ago was that? A month? Two? He couldn't remember, but that was the last time they'd been together as a threesome. He'd walked in, practically demanding to join them. Had he invited himself into something where he wasn't wanted? A cold chill shivered down his spine and shriveled his scrotum as that thought settled in his brain.

Was that why Jase had been so distant? Had the relationship between Megan and his brother developed into something more when he hadn't been looking? That would account for Jason's aloofness for the last few weeks, and Megan's concerns.

Jeff tossed the covers aside and turned on the lamp next to the bed. Naked, he paced the length of the room and back again. The same nauseating feeling he had during dinner gripped his gut. Jealousy. Doubt. Disgust.

He'd made love to Megan several times since that evening in the pool. The thought that he'd been making time with his brother's woman turned his bowels to water. Surely, if she loved Jason that way, she wouldn't have welcomed him to her bed. Would she?

Christ. When had he begun to think of Megan as his? He hadn't really had any qualms about sharing her with Jason because he always thought there was nothing more than sex between Jason and Megan. Blind. He was fucking blind. How could he not have seen it? He'd come to think of Jason as the extra, the one they brought into the relationship for fun. Jeff stopped pacing and stared at his reflection in the darkened mirror. Dear God. It was him. He was the extra.

And he was in love with Megan.

His knees gave out, and he felt behind him for the edge of the bed. He stumbled back and sat, propping his pounding head up with his hands. His elbows dug into his thighs, but that was nothing compared to the churning in his gut.

Now he admitted to himself just how far gone he was. He'd actually been thinking of a future – with Megan. Kids. A family. Marrying her. Christ. When had that happened? And how blind could he be? Sure, she wanted those things, she'd said so often enough. But now he knew when she talked about those things, he'd seen himself as the father.

And she'd been seeing Jason. Well, shit. How freakin' fucked up was that?

CHAPTER THIRTEEN

Megan stared at Jeff's retreating back. To be such simple creatures, men could be totally incomprehensible at times. First Jason, now Jeff. She felt like the ballerina in the jewelry box she had when she was a kid, wound up, and dancing in circles until she was dizzy and confused. And, like that tiny ballerina, once they slammed the lid down, completely in the dark.

She cleared the table with more than a grumble at being left to do the kitchen clean-up by herself. It would serve them both right to wake up to a dirty kitchen. Megan flicked off the light and headed upstairs to her room. A strip of light spilling across the carpet told her Jeff was still awake. She paused outside his door, her emotions warring inside. It was tempting to tell him what she thought of his behavior, but another part understood the stress he was under. Stats were everything in baseball. A player's value and popularity was only as good as their last game. Still, that didn't excuse his behavior. She hadn't done anything wrong.

All she'd done was voice her concerns about his brother, something she thought she had every right to do. She'd promised Jason she wouldn't tell Jeff, but she didn't promise she wouldn't get Jeff to talk to him.

Jeff's reaction didn't make any sense. Jason and Jeff were close, so close it was surprising that Jeff didn't know what was going on all ready. Maybe he did, and he didn't want to talk about it with her. She swallowed that thought like a hot lead ball. They were pushing her away – both of them.

She made it to her room across the hall, barely. She sat on the end of the bed and stared across the darkened room at the closed door. Her heart continued to pump, oblivious to the grievous wound inflicted on it moments ago. Tears formed and she swiped them away with trembling fingertips. How had her world shifted so completely without her knowing?

Jeff and Jason didn't want her anymore. Pain knifed through her, doubling her over. She loved them, and they loved her. How could things have changed so much, so quickly, without her knowing? Because she was a blind fool, that's why. She'd wanted it so much, she let her guard down, and Jason had moved on, and now Jeff.

It had been so easy to let her dreams blossom into a full-blown fantasy – one that included children and a lifetime with the man she loved. Jason had seen it. Hadn't he admitted as much earlier today? So what had happened with Jeff? Why was he pushing her away? Even Jason said Jeff loved her.

She saw it now – crystal clear. Jeff loved her, but he wasn't *in love* with her.

Megan crawled onto the bed and curled into a tight ball on top of the covers. Tears flowed like blood from an open wound. She felt as brittle as glass. She clutched her midsection in tightly wrapped arms, as if doing so would keep her insides from shattering. Vignettes of time spent with Jeff tormented her with all the reasons she believed he loved her. Memories of his touch, his smile, his words were etched on her glass heart. No matter how many times she revisited those moments, she couldn't reconcile the man she loved, and who she was certain loved her, with the man across the hall.

Footsteps woke her. She lay still; listening as Jason moved past her door then opened and closed his own. She could go to him, talk

135

to him about Jeff. No sooner had the idea formed than she dismissed it. Jason didn't need her dragging her personal drama to his door, not in the middle of the season. He had his own set of worries. The media might not focus on him, but team management did. Calling pitches was his job, and getting McCree out was as much his responsibility as it was the pitchers'. No, she couldn't dump her insecurities on Jason's shoulders.

Daylight glimmered on the horizon when she dressed and made her way downstairs. She was working the late shift today, so the morning was hers. She made a point of attending the home games as often as her schedule permitted, but traveling with the team was out of the question, so they'd made a tradition of sharing breakfast on travel days.

Coffee was first on the agenda, then breakfast. Lying awake most of the night, she'd come to a conclusion. She'd keep her insecurities to herself. That meant acting as if nothing had happened. And in truth, nothing had. She'd played the evening over and over again in her mind, and though she'd been hurt by Jeff's behavior, she wasn't sure he was even aware of what he'd done. That didn't make it hurt any less. If anything, it made it worse. If Jeff didn't know he'd hurt her, then that in itself told a story. Her feelings were one-sided. It was a bitter pill to swallow, but really, it was her own fault. She'd come into this relationship with nothing more than the promise of great sex, and they'd delivered on that time and again. It was her own stupid fault for falling in love with one of them.

"Are you okay?" Jason asked.

Megan added a couple toast slices to a plate and handed it across the table to him. "Fine. Jelly?" She held up the jar of grape jelly.

He shook his head. "No thanks." The jelly jar hit the table with enough force to rattle the silverware. If he weren't in such a hurry, he'd have pressed her for details, because she most certainly wasn't fine. Judging by her red-rimmed eyes and puffy face, she'd been crying. Jason racked his brain for anything he might have done to make her cry and couldn't come up with anything. She seemed fine when he left. Concerned for him maybe, but not on the verge of tears. That left Jeff. He wondered what his brother had done or said, but it was going to have to wait. The limo they'd hired to take them to the airport would be there in a few minutes. Not enough time to dissect, then fix the problem, and sew everything back up neatly.

Jeff came into the kitchen as the limo driver honked his horn. He leaned over Megan's shoulder, grabbed a slice of toast from her plate and landed a perfunctory kiss on the top of her head. "Gotta go. Thanks for breakfast." Jason watched his brother's retreating back. Something was definitely up between Jeff and Megan. The protective shell Megan pulled around her when Jeff walked in would make an armadillo jealous. Jason thanked Megan for breakfast and stooped to kiss her full on the lips before he left. It wasn't much of a kiss, he didn't feel he had the right to anything more, but she softened under his touch. Yet, there wasn't a spark of interest. He might as well have kissed his sister.

"See ya when we get back. We'll call."

Jeff had already loaded his luggage and slid into the backseat by the time Jason came out. He stowed his own suitcase, then pulled the door shut behind him and settled into the seat across from Jeff. His brother looked like shit. He was impeccably groomed, as usual, but his eyes looked like cheap animation for a Visine commercial. Jason had seen vampires with more color.

"Want to talk about it?" Jason asked.

Jeff glanced at him, then turned his attention to the landscape. "No. There's nothing to talk about."

"Uh huh." Jason recognized the tone and the body language. Jeff wasn't going to talk. That didn't mean he couldn't have his say. "Look, asshole. I don't know what you did to Megan, but you'd better find a way to make it right. Send her some flowers or something. Better yet, call her. Ten days is a long time to let something simmer."

"Shut the fuck up! You don't know what you are talking about. If you think Megan has a problem, you call her. She'd rather talk to you anyway."

"What the hell? I don't know what happened last night, but Megan was fine when I left the house, so that means you did something to her. Did you see her eyes? No, of course you didn't. You didn't take the time to look at her, did you? Whatever you did, it made her cry. All night long, from the looks of it."

"I didn't do anything."

"Then maybe that's what's wrong. She wanted something and you didn't give it to her."

Jeff continued to stare out the side window at the passing cars and billboards. Jason waited. Sometimes he knew what his brother was thinking, as if they shared the same internal circuit boards. But other times, like now, he didn't have a clue what was going on inside that head that looked so much like his own. So he waited. When Jeff finally spoke, the defeat in his voice shocked Jason.

"I can't give her what she wants." The words sounded like they'd been wrenched from him with a rusty crowbar. Jason stared at the man across from him. This wasn't the confident, over-achiever brother he knew.

"What, exactly, does she want?"

"I don't know, exactly. All I know is – it's not something I can give her."

The finality in Jeff's statement stopped Jason cold. He'd felt like a third wheel for so long, it hadn't occurred to him that maybe things weren't so great between Jeff and Megan either. He'd been certain Megan loved his brother, and wanted to make a life with him. Maybe that was it. Maybe she'd asked for more and Jeff had said no. It would be just like his brother to do something stupid like throw away the best thing that ever happened to him. What he couldn't figure out was why.

It didn't make any sense. Jeff had to know how Megan felt about him. Hell, if Jason could figure it out, then anyone could, even

Jeff. That only meant Jeff didn't return her feelings, but if that was true, then why was Jeff so down?

The limo weaved through the early morning traffic and deposited them on the sidewalk in front of the terminal. Worries about Jeff and Megan took a backseat to getting through security and the inevitable autograph-signing as they were recognized by fans. He usually didn't mind interacting with the fans, but today, when things weighed so heavily on his mind, it was more difficult to put on a smile and say the right things. All he wanted to do was get to the VIP lounge and find a quiet place to think.

❧ ❧

Jason climbed out of the cab and tossed the driver a twenty. He joined his brother at the stadium gate where Jeff was talking to the guard on duty.

"Yeah, we're early," Jeff said. "I need a little extra time to get loose."

"Sure thing, Mr. Holder You being loose probably isn't a good thing for the home team, but hey! I've always been a Mustangs fan, so you go on in and make yourself at home." His gaze shifted to Jason. "You too, Mr. Holder."

Jason shifted his duffel bag to his left hand and extended his right to the guard. "Thanks…"

"George. You can call me George."

"I'm Jason, and this is Jeff. No need to be formal." George's smile could light up the ballpark if the power went out. "We appreciate you letting us in, George."

"No problem. Hey, since you're here, and all…could I get your autographs?"

"Sure," Jeff said. "Do you have a piece of paper or something?"

George flipped a page over on his clipboard and handed it to Jeff who signed and passed it to Jason. He signed his name and handed it back. They shook hands all around before Jeff and Jason headed into the tunnel leading to the clubhouse. They changed into practice gear in the visiting team's locker room and headed out to the bullpen.

"I want to go on record as opposing this."

"Just shut up and catch, will you? I'll work this out on my own."

Jason caught the warm-up throw and returned it with more force than was strictly necessary. "I'll shut up when you start acting sensible. You can't keep throwing this much every day. It's not good for your arm."

"It's not your career on the line, Asshole. McCree is hitting everything thrown at him these days. I can't keep throwing him inside heat. I've got to find a way to get McCree out, and working a curve ball into my portfolio might do the trick."

"I doubt it. Your curve ball sucks, bro." They were halfway through their road trip, and Jeff had dragged Jason to the field every day for a few extra hours of pitching practice. His curve ball had started off bad in high school, and from what Jason could see, it hadn't improved one bit.

"I haven't heard you come up with a better idea."

"That's because I don't have one. McCree is a stupid shit. He's digging his own grave, one steroid shot at a time. Eventually, that's going to catch up to him and he'll be out for a lot more than one at bat."

"Until that happens, and I have little faith that it will, he's still a problem. I can break records, but the one I'd like most to break is McCree's homerun record."

Jason slid his mask into place and crouched low. They'd had this same conversation at least a million times over the last few days. Jeff wasn't going to budge. Jason could refuse to help, but knowing Jeff, he'd ask one of the other team members to catch for him. In the meantime, he'd continue trying to talk some sense into his hardheaded brother. Besides, they were on the road, what else did they have to do?

"You should be working with Nate. He's the pitching coach. It's his job to figure what pitches you should be throwing."

"Yeah? How's that working out for Andy, or Jose, or any of the others? They've been listening to Nate and their ERA's look more like shoe sizes."

"Maybe so, but throwing the same bad pitch over and over isn't going to help any. If you're determined to throw a curve, you need someone who can help you fix whatever's wrong with it. I'm not that guy."

He caught another lousy pitch and stood to throw the ball back. "Have you talked to Megan?"

"No."

Another curve ball — worse than the previous one. "Why the hell not?"

"Why don't you mind your own fucking business?"

Jason cursed as the next pitch went so far outside it was a wonder it stayed in the ballpark. It hit the back wall behind him and spun in the dirt until he ambled over and picked it up. He turned it over and over in his hand looking for damage before he threw it back again. "That one will get McCree out. Can you do that again? I think that's the one."

"Shut the fuck up and catch or I'll shut you up myself."

Jason slid his mask to the top of his head and faced his brother. "What the hell is wrong with you? You can't even take a joke anymore."

"My career is no joke." Jason watched his mirror image go into a rage, totally at a loss as to what was going on inside Jeff's head. "If you aren't going to help me, then get the fuck out of here. I'll find someone else."

"Look, Jeff, you don't need to do this."

"Like hell I don't."

"You don't." Jason scanned the empty stadium. At least there wasn't anyone else around to witness his brother's meltdown. "Come on. Let's go get some water bottles and cool off." He headed toward the clubhouse, hoping Jeff would follow. Absolutely nothing good could come from Jeff's obsession, and that's what it was, an obsession with striking out Martin McCree. But as focused as Jeff was on that one goal, Jason had the feeling there was something else going on that Jeff wasn't talking about. He was using the McCree situation as an excuse to ignore whatever else he had going on inside his screwed up head.

"I don't want water. I need to pitch."

"You're right about one thing. What you want and what you need are two different things. You've just got them backasswards." Jeff followed him. Jason tossed his glove and helmet on a nearby table and wiped his sweaty face on his shirtsleeve before he pulled two cold water bottles from the refrigerator and handed one to Jeff. "Look, Jeff. At the risk of inflating your already enormous ego, you're one of the best relief pitchers ever to play the game. Giving up a few homers to McCree isn't going to change that."

"That's what you think. The press is eating this up. Did you see the Sports Center report the other day? Hell, they ripped me to shreds over one homer. Don't they have a clue what's going on? It's like going up against Godzilla with a fucking spit wad."

Jason smiled at the apt description. Everything Jeff said was true, but it still didn't account for his brother's attitude. This sour, obsessed man wasn't Jeff Holder. "You've had your share of success against Godzilla. You struck him out twice in the first series this year. You'll do it again."

"When? We only face them one more time in regular season, and if the team doesn't start playing better, there won't be a playoff for us."

"All I'm saying is you're letting this get to you. This obsession is affecting your pitching, Jeff. You blew a save the other day because you missed your spot. That was supposed to be inside and you threw it right over the plate. Served Hanson a freakin' meatball. The only thing you could have done to make it better for him was to put red sauce on it."

"You think you could do better? Huh? Why don't you go stand on the mound and show me how easy it is." Jeff's face had gone purple and he'd closed the distance between them until Jason had to take a step back or breathe the same air as his brother.

"Whoa! I never said it was easy. All I'm saying is — you used to think pitching was fun. It was a challenge, but it wasn't the end of the world — "

"If I lost my edge? Is that what you were going to say?"

"No —"

"I haven't lost my edge!" Jeff raked his hands through his hair and paced away. Jason sucked in a clean breath as Jeff left his space. "I haven't." Jeff dropped into one of the club chairs lining the walls. His shoulders sagged and he folded in on himself like a deflating balloon. "I haven't."

Shit. Jason didn't have a clue what to do. He'd never seen Jeff like this, didn't want to see it now. For a guy with an ego roughly the size of Texas and Alaska combined, Jeff didn't implode — ever. The pathetic mutterings that followed his first outburst shook Jason as nothing else could. He'd seen other ball players lose confidence in their abilities, but never Jeff. From the first moment he'd put on a glove when they were all of eight years old, Jeff had known his value as a pitcher. It had taken Jason longer, years longer, to develop into a decent catcher and win a place in the batting order, but Jeff had always had enormous talent, and confidence to match it. Watching him now sent a chill down Jason's spine. What the fuck was wrong with his brother?

"What the fuck is wrong with you?" He wasn't a shrink. So sue him.

"I don't fucking know!" Jeff looked at him, and the blast of uncharacteristic uncertainty in his eyes hit Jason like a wild pitch to the side of the head.

"Then you damn well better figure it out." He glared at his brother. If looks could kill, he'd be bloody on the floor by now. "Get yourself someone else to help you fuck up your arm. I quit." Jason picked up his helmet and glove and headed toward the hallway leading to the locker room. His brother's voice stopped him.

"I don't need you."

Freakin' pathetic. "Look, Jeff. I don't know what's going on in your head right now, but I can tell you this. If your career goes down the tubes, it won't be McCree's fault. You'll be the only one to blame."

CHAPTER FOURTEEN

Jeff stewed in the bullpen. He'd been sitting on his ass for the better part of two weeks, watching his team lose game after game. The season had gone from bad to worse. They still had to face the Miners one more time, and Megan was in love with his brother. From his perspective, things couldn't get much worse. Of the three worries on his mind, the only one he had any control over was the Miners, and only if the rest of the team could score enough runs to give him a chance at a save.

How the hell was he supposed to stay in form if his ass never left the bench? The team was doing their best, but lately that hadn't been good enough. At this rate, they weren't even going to make the playoffs. The best they could hope for was a wild-card spot, and that was looking less likely every day. He tried to keep his frustration to himself. Venting in front of the team wouldn't help, wouldn't change a thing. It would only make him look like an ass, looking out for his own interests. He had goals like every other player in the major leagues, but when you only played an inning or two, and only if the team was ahead by a few runs, then the window of opportunity to reach those goals was mighty slim.

Jeff glanced at the scoreboard and winced. He wouldn't be warming up for this game – not unless a miracle happened. He wouldn't be setting any records this season, but the one thing he could do was get the best of Martin McCree. The press would be all over that, and at least he'd salvage something from this season. Maybe Megan would take notice. It hadn't escaped him that Jason was having a fantastic season. His stats were as good as any in the league. As a catcher, he was one of the best in the game, and his batting average was close to tying the team record. He'd never thought that sort of thing mattered to Megan, but he couldn't dismiss the coincidence. His own star was, at the very least, stuck in limbo, while Jason's was rising, approaching the stratosphere. He couldn't really blame her for falling for Jason, but it still hurt like hell.

He blew two more saves before the road trip ended. His curve ball was every bit as bad as Jason said it was, and his attitude had the entire team walking out of their way to avoid him. It wasn't any secret the manager was pushing the starting pitchers and middle relievers to go more innings, hoping he wouldn't have to call Jeff to the mound. Management had lost confidence in his ability. In a few short weeks, he'd gone from a sure thing to a long shot.

The press was all over the story like maggots feeding on rotting flesh. They used words like *slump*, and said he'd lost it. They never bothered to define what 'it' was, but Jeff knew what it was. 'It' was everything. He'd lost his confidence, his talent, and, he'd lost Megan. Without those three things, he was nothing. Hell, maybe the first two were what had driven Megan into Jason's arms in the first place; or maybe that's all he was to her to begin with. She hadn't been that close to Jason before this McCree thing.

He thought Megan was different. He thought she'd been with him because of who he was, not because he could throw a baseball. All through high school, girls had been easy conquests – mainly because of his achievements on the ball field. He was a big man on campus, and on the field. He won every award there was to win, and his photo had been in the local papers every week during the season, and he'd even made the state-wide paper a few times. College scouts, as well as major league scouts had watched Jason and him play. At the end of their junior year, they signed with the University of Texas.

Nothing changed for him at UT other than he didn't have to sneak around anymore. He shared a dorm room, and later an apartment with Jason, and they both brought women home on a regular basis – and shared those women, more often than not. He never thought much about their sharing. He and Jason practically shared one brain sometimes, and the women didn't seem to care which one they were with. Quite a few subscribed to the "two is better than one" theory of sexual fulfillment, which hadn't bothered him or Jason at all. They managed to keep their sexual escapades from becoming common knowledge, and then they were drafted by the Mustangs. For years, they'd been too busy building their careers to notice the women throwing themselves at them, but in the back of their minds, they'd been looking for someone. Someone like Megan.

Jeff tried to concentrate on the novel he picked up in the airport, but all he could think about was how quickly his life had gone down the crapper. He had the whole row, and then some, to himself on the team's charter flight. He knew the drill. Most of the team was pissed off at him for various reasons, and the ones that weren't were afraid his slump might be contagious. He couldn't blame them. Lately, he didn't even like himself.

"Mind if I join you?" Jeff looked up from his book when Andy, the team's assistant manager joined him. He closed the book and tucked it into the seat pocket as he told himself to relax.

Hell, yes! "No." If he needed confirmation he had loser's plague, this was it. "Be my guest."

He had to hand it to Andy. He was professional in the way he delivered his news, looking straight ahead as if they were talking about the weather, or the movie playing on the seat back screens. "Doyle wants to see you in his office when we get back."

"Trading me already?" Fear gripped his stomach and twisted it into a knot.

"Just be there. He wants to have this talk before you go home today." Andy unfolded from the cramped seat and returned to his seat in the first class section with the management team.

Jeff slid the book out of the seat pocket and flipped it open to a random page. He tried to focus on the words, but his mind was already in Doyle Walker's office. Shit. Could they trade him? Would anyone want him if they tried? He wondered if it were possible to keep this meeting quiet, all the while knowing it couldn't be done. Everyone on the plane knew he'd been summoned, and there'd already be as many guesses as to what would be said as there were players on the team.

Jason took the seat vacated by Andy. "Got called to the principal's office?"

"Yeah."

"What did Andy say?"

"Nothing. There's a meeting this afternoon."

"Trade?"

"How the hell would I know? I don't think they can trade me, at least not without my permission."

"You gonna give 'em permission?"

God, he needed to move around, but he didn't dare let his head drop back against the headrest. Even that small gesture would telegraph defeat to everyone looking at him, and they were all looking. He could feel their eyes on him, watching his body language. They'd form their opinions based on how he reacted in the next few minutes, hours, days. Any weakness on his part would only fuel the speculation. "No."

"Good." One word from his brother and an invisible weight lifted off his shoulders. He almost smiled at the relief. At least someone wanted him to stay. "Because I'd have to ask to be traded too, and I don't want to go anywhere else."

"No worries. Doyle probably just wants to chew my ass for a while. I can take it."

"I'm sure you can, bro."

Silence stretched between them. Jeff thumbed the pages of the book to keep his hands busy.

"Are we alright now?" Jason asked.

Damned if he knew, but he couldn't say that, not when Jason was making an effort. "Yeah."

"Good." Jason shifted in his seat. "That's good."

"I've got to do this…thing when we get back…" Hell, he couldn't even say it. He didn't want to think about what he faced. Trade. They wouldn't send him down to the Minor League. That would be a death knell to his career for sure, but they would trade him.

"I'll let Megan know you'll be a little late."

Jeff nodded. For once, he was glad there wasn't another soul in hearing distance. He didn't want to talk about Megan at all, but stopping to call her was out of the question. "Thanks. As long as you're there, she won't miss me."

Jason ducked his head and spoke low so Jeff had to lean in to hear him over the drone of the engines. "Is that what you think? If it is, your head is further up your ass than I thought it was."

Jason was several rows away before Jeff composed himself enough to consider answering his brother. He thought about following Jason up the aisle and beating the shit out of him, but he was in enough trouble already. Adding a fistfight on top of everything else wouldn't help. Besides, what was between Jason and him was family business, personal. It had nothing to do with the team, and right now, he needed to focus on his job. If he could get that right, maybe everything else would fall into place.

❧

After a week and a half, Jason didn't have any more of a clue what was going on in his brother's head than he did when they'd left on the extended road trip. Phone calls to Megan told him she didn't know anymore than he did, and her reluctance to talk about it sent his suspicions into overdrive. To make matters worse, Jeff was obsessed with Martin McCree. The Miners would be back in Dallas for the last regular season series, and Jeff was determined to get the man out.

Jeff had only been called on to close three of the eight road games, leaving him plenty of time to obsess, and to work on his pitches. Like most pitchers, Jeff had an ego only eclipsed by a full harvest moon. If McCree won the last battle, Jason couldn't imagine how that would affect Jeff's confidence. It had already taken a hit, and now it looked like the team management had noticed too. If they talked about a trade, Jeff would go ballistic. Then there was Jeff's relationship with Megan. If that went any further south, heaven help them all.

❧↩❧

Jeff left his duffel and suitcase in his locker and headed to Doyle's office. He'd taken his time, waiting until the other players left before he made the walk every player hated. He'd never had reason to hate it before today. Doyle had brought him up from the Minor League after just a few months and put him in the bullpen as a middle reliever. He'd taken a chance on Jeff, and Jason too, and for that Jeff would always be grateful. Over the years, the three of them had become friends, but this was business, and Doyle was in the business of winning.

Jeff knocked on the open office door and Doyle waved him in from behind his cluttered desk. As usual, everything else in the office was organized and proclaimed the winning heritage of the franchise. Photos of Doyle with every celebrity and dignitary imaginable lined the walls alongside plaques and trophies declaring one winning season after another. The only thing missing was a World Series trophy, and there wasn't a person associated with the team who didn't want one of those more than they wanted their next breath. Doyle would give his right arm, and divorce his wife, if that would get him one.

"Close the door, Jeff." Three words that more than anything else signaled this was serious business. Jeff closed the door and leaned against it, eyeing his friend across the expanse of hardwood floor and the custom-made Mustangs rug that took up most of the floor space between the door and the desk. Hell, he couldn't even say he'd been called on the carpet.

"You wanted to see me?"

"Yeah. Come on in. You can relax, I'm not trading you." The knot in his stomach unwound a little at the news, and he pushed away from the door. Doyle walked around his desk. "Let's sit over here." Jeff followed him to the casual grouping of sofas and chairs on the other side of the room, declining his offer of something to drink. Some of the tension in his shoulders eased. Doyle never did his dirty work without a massive chunk of carved wood between him and his victim. Maybe this wouldn't be so bad after all.

"What's this about?" he asked as he sank into a plush armchair and crossed one ankle over his knee. Doyle folded his lanky frame onto the opposite sofa and propped his heels on the coffee table.

"I'm worried about you. What's going on, Jeff?"

"Nothing is going on."

"Don't lie to me. I'm not asking as your manager, I'm asking as your friend. We've known each other for a long time, Jeff. Every player is entitled to a slump now and then, but this isn't like you. Talk to me."

Jeff revised his previous thought. This was that bad. Worse. He might be able to lie to the press, but Doyle wasn't going to settle for his usual B.S. He never had. Jeff didn't know what to say, hell, he didn't understand it himself so how was he going to explain it to someone else? Instead of talking, he studied the shoe dangling over his knee. Maybe he could get Megan to find him a new pair of dress shoes. Then he remembered Megan wasn't his anymore and he frowned at the thought. It didn't matter. She never would have gotten the shoes for him anyway. She could be accommodating, but she drew the line at being a doormat.

Patience wasn't one of Doyle's virtues. "God damn it! Tell me what the hell is going on inside that head of yours or so help me, Holder I'll trade your sorry ass faster than you can say bite me!"

Everything that he'd lost, and stood to lose, churned in his gut and control slipped from his grasp. "You want to know what's going on? I'll tell you what's going on!" Unable to sit still any longer, he jerked to his feet and took long, angry strides across the room and back again. He faced Doyle with his feet braced shoulder-width apart and his hands fisted on his hips. "My life is hell. McCree is making a laughing stock of everyone in the league. My brother is f..." He couldn't say it, couldn't do that to Megan. "Jason is...Megan..." Shit. "I'm in love with Megan, and she's in love with Jason."

As soon as the words were out of his mouth, he wished he could take them back. He thought this was what a spent condom must feel like, limp, used-up and unwanted. Deflated, he sank back into the chair he'd vacated earlier. His head felt like a lead weight dragging his shoulders down. His elbows dug into his thighs as he sat hunched over, staring at his shoes. Christ, he was falling apart.

"Forget about McCree for the moment," Doyle said in his calm manager voice. "Let's talk about Megan. She's the woman who's been living with you and Jason for the last year or so?"

His head shot up and his gaze locked on Doyle. "How do you know about Megan?"

"Do you think there isn't anything I don't know about your life? I know you both sleep with her, and I know you do a damned good job of keeping your private lives private."

"Obviously, we don't do a good enough job. How did you find out?"

Doyle shrugged. "I'm an observer. It's what I do. I watch my players on the field and off. Neither one of you date. You never bring a woman to any of the team functions, and the only person who ever uses your player tickets is a woman named Megan. She's at most home games, but she always comes alone."

"That doesn't mean we're both sleeping with the woman."

"No, it doesn't, but she picked you both up once after a road trip. She was late, and everyone else was gone. Do you remember?"

"Yeah, I remember." They'd come home from one of the longest and most successful road trips ever. Twelve days, and twelve wins. They'd set a team record with that string of wins. Jason had added a couple of homeruns to his stats, and Jeff had six more saves. Megan had missed them, and she was more than ready to celebrate their homecoming. As a matter of fact, the celebration began on the way home. She'd driven, telling them in excruciating detail exactly what she was going to do to them, and what she wanted them to do to her when they got home. They'd done it all, and then some.

"I'd gone to my office to get something I needed for the game the next day, and when I came out...Let's just say her greeting was enthusiastic – for both of you. I knew then."

"That was what, a year ago?"

"Something like that. So, what's changed? If she's been with you and Jason this long, why have her feelings changed? I don't get it."

"Neither do I, and I don't want to talk about it. It's none of your business."

"If it's fucking with your head, and your game, then it's my business."

Jeff sighed and flopped back in the chair. His arms hung like limp noodles over the chair's wide arms. Doyle was right about one thing. The whole situation was fucking with his head, but it still wasn't any of the older man's business. He couldn't very well tell him that, even as a friend. Doyle had all the power in their relationship, especially when Jeff wasn't holding up his end of the business arrangement. He'd been hired to win games, and in the last few weeks, he hadn't delivered. He had to get his head on straight, or Doyle would hand it to him on a platter, right next to his trade papers.

"I can't think about that now. I've got bigger worries."

"McCree?"

"Yeah. The press is feeding on his run at the homerun record. The son-of-a-bitch is making a mockery of the game, and there isn't a fucking thing I can do about it."

"How's the curve ball coming?" Jeff raised his head from the back of the chair.

"Is there anything you don't know?"

"I don't know if you jack off right-handed or left, but I'd guess right."

"Shit."

"Forget about McCree. Sooner or later he'll get caught, and his record won't mean shit. We need to win games. That means beating the entire team, not just one player. We only have to face the Miners one more time in regular season. We'll deal with McCree, even if we have to walk him every time he comes to the plate."

"I can't forget about him. This is a war I'm determined to win."

"With that lousy curve ball? I don't think so. Forget McCree. I'm telling you to let it go, Jeff. This is one season, and in the grand scheme of things, it doesn't mean shit. You'd do better to concentrate on your private life. Get that in order, and things will look a lot better all the way around."

"I don't see any way to get my personal life in order. I always thought Megan was mine, and Jason was the 'extra', if you know what I mean." He didn't know why he was telling Doyle any of this, but once he got started, he couldn't seem to stop the words from pouring out like water over the spillway. "Then this thing with McCree, and I'm blowing saves, and while my game is in the toilet, Jason is having one of his best seasons ever. And, get this – she's worried about him." He shook his head. "Fucking unbelievable."

"Why is she worried about Jason?"

"How would I know?"

Doyle reached for one of the baseballs in a bowl in the center of the coffee table and turned it over and over – a sure sign he didn't like what he was hearing.

"Don't worry. She's worried on a personal level. Not that I can see a damned thing wrong with him. His stats are the best they've ever been, and he has Megan. What the hell else could he want?"

Doyle dropped the ball back onto the stack and sat back again. "So, you think Megan's affections are tied to your game performance? You're blowing saves, and it looks like you're the losing horse, so she's going to hitch her wagon to the sure thing? Is that it?"

"Yeah, I guess so." It did sound pretty lame when put into words. "She's not like that, or at least I didn't think she was."

"Jeff, I can't tell you what to do, but I'd strongly advise that you talk to Megan. If this isn't going to work out, you need to make a clean break, let her go and move on with your life."

"I'll think about it, Doyle. My ass is growing moss sitting on the bench, so put me in, okay? I won't let you down, I promise."

CHAPTER FIFTEEN

Jeff recognized the sleek red sports car waiting at the gate, and the driver. Jason. Just what he needed – another inquisition. His brother unfolded from the driver's seat and came around the back of the car.

"Here, let me have one of those." Jason held out his hand and Jeff slid the strap of his duffel off his shoulder.

"Thanks for the ride."

"Least I could do. I had to hitch a ride with Tanner. Megan didn't show."

"Why not? She always picks us up."

"No clue. She wasn't at the house, either. Maybe she had to change her shift. It wouldn't be the first time."

Or, she was taking another step to distance herself from one or both of them. Shit. Jeff's already lousy mood took another dive. He climbed into the passenger seat and prepared for a NASCAR experience, without the professional driver or the safety of a closed racecourse. Jason always drove like there was a checkered flag waiting for him at the end of the road. Jeff wrapped his fingers around the handgrip on one side and clutched the center console with the other. Jason peeled out of the empty parking lot in a spray of dust and gravel.

"Slow down. The last thing I need today is to end up dead."

"So, how did it go?"

Jeff cringed as Jason swerved around one car and darted between two others to make the transition from one freeway to another. "Christ, you're a maniac. Slow the hell down!"

"Close your eyes if you can't take it."

"I'll tell you everything if you'll slow down. The only thing on my mind right now is getting home in one piece."

Jason's foot let up on the accelerator, and for every mile an hour the car slowed, Jeff eased his death grip on the sucker bar.

"Spill," Jason said as he swung the car down the exit ramp, coming to a stop inches from the bumper of another car stopped at the red light.

"There's nothing much to spill. Doyle wasn't talking trade. He just wanted to crawl up my ass about the blown saves."

"What did you tell him?" The light turned and Jeff's head hit the headrest as Jason punched the accelerator down.

"Shit. Who taught you to drive anyway? You're going to get us killed."

"Okay, okay, Grandpa." He slowed to the prevailing speed on the wide, divided road. "Talk."

"I told him I had it under control."

"Do you?"

Jeff felt his brother's gaze and turned his head. Sure enough, Jason was watching him, when he should have been watching the road. "Christ! Look where you're going!"

"Calm down. It's under control," he said, swerving into the left lane and practically taking an extra bumper with him in the process. Jason's word choice registered once the car was traveling at a safe speed.

"Just shut up, smartass, and get us home alive. Then you can butt out of my business."

"Hey, it's my business too, you know. I'd like to have a winning season and go to the playoffs too, so get this through your fucked up head. Forget about McCree. Focus on winning the games we can win, and let the rest of it go. Losing games we should have won isn't going to fix the McCree problem."

Jeff vowed never to accept a ride from his brother again as the car came to a screeching halt a split-second before they would have gone straight through the back wall of the garage. He mentally inventoried what was on the other side of that wall and decided never to eat at the breakfast table again, especially if there were a chance Jason might be coming home. He got his suitcase out of the trunk and took the duffel Jason pulled from the backseat. "Why don't you concentrate on what you're supposed to be doing, and I'll concentrate on my job. How about that?"

"I'd say that was just fine, but it must be hard for you to concentrate on your job with head so far up your ass."

⁓⧉⧉⧉⁓

Megan parked in the garage stall next to where the guys kept their see-and-be-seen car, a red Mustang convertible. Since the stall was empty, they obviously had come home and left again, probably to get something to eat. She hadn't had time to restock the kitchen while they'd been on the road, and even if she had, Jeff and Jason weren't the types to cook when a perfectly good restaurant was a short drive away.

Her feet felt like two hot bricks attached to her ankles, and tension in her neck and shoulders had her head pounding. She loved her job, but sometimes the emotional toll it took on her was worse than the hours on her feet. Today was one of those days. She desperately wanted food, and to soak away the stress of her day in the big Jacuzzi tub in her bathroom. Megan dropped her purse on the kitchen counter, toed off her shoes and went straight to the refrigerator. The wine she'd opened the night before called her name. She grabbed the bottle and a bowl of cantaloupe and watermelon leftover from breakfast that morning. Along with a hunk of cheddar cheese and some crackers, she had the makings of dinner.

She spread the feast on the center island and used the last of her energy to climb onto a barstool. She rolled her shoulders and filled her glass. It never did any good to bring her work home with her.

That road led to nothing but depression, and she couldn't afford to be anything but optimistic in front of her patients and their families. Of course, there was nothing wrong with celebrating the victories, but those were few and far between, these days. The pediatric wing was no place for the weak-hearted. Nurses didn't last long there if they didn't learn how to leave the bad at the hospital. When one of the new nurses broke down and said she couldn't do it anymore, they called Megan at the last minute to handle her shift. She didn't even have a chance to call Jeff and Jason and warn them she wouldn't be there to pick them up. An apology of Texas-sized proportions was in order, but it would have to wait until they got home.

Tilting her glass to her lips, she closed her eyes and savored the bold, fruity flavor of the wine. A faint sound or maybe it was a change in the air around her made her go still. She managed to swallow the wine in her mouth a fraction of a second before heavy hands rested on her shoulders and a hard male body pressed against her back. Her heart thudded against her ribs as she recognized Jeff's familiar scent.

"I missed you." He spoke against her ear as his hands began to knead her tight shoulders.

"You scared the life out of me," she complained even as her spine wilted and she slumped against him.

"Didn't mean to. I thought you would have heard me. I've been standing in the doorway watching you for several minutes." His hands continued to release the knots in her muscles as he spoke. Megan was putty in his hands, she always had been.

"I thought you were both gone."

"Jason went out. I don't know when he'll be home." He sounded way too happy about Jason's decampment, but Megan was too tired to care.

"I'm dead on my feet, Jeff." His hands stilled for a second, then continued to knead.

"Me too." He pushed her long hair to one side and nibbled his way from her earlobe to the neckline of her scrubs. "God, you smell good," he whispered against her neck right before his tongue swept along the pulse beating there. Megan, tired or not, couldn't help responding to the need, the desire contained in those few simple words. This was the Jeff she loved. The one who made could melt her with a touch or a few words.

"I smell like disinfectant," she said. "I need a hot bath."

"Let me run one for you," he purred against her neck. "I'll even wash your back."

Jeff," she sighed as fatigue drained away, and desire rushed in to fill all the empty spaces left behind. His hands slipped to her waist, then around to pull her tight against him. It felt so good to lean into him, to let him support her. "Bad day?"

She shrugged. "No worse than usual. Two new patients. Two new sets of anxious parents and assorted relatives." It was partially the truth. She tried to retain a professional distance between her patients and her, but sometimes one would touch her heart in ways she couldn't ignore. Christopher had been like that. He was one of the success stories, primarily because of Jeff, and he'd always have a special place in her heart. Because of Christopher, she'd met Jeff and Jason.

But, she reminded herself, there were no guarantees with the children she worked with. Letting Caroline steal her heart was probably a mistake of epic proportions, but the child was precocious and wise beyond her seven years. Her prognosis wasn't good. The doctors were doing all they could to stop the progress of her condition, but unless she received a heart transplant soon, she wouldn't live to see another birthday.

Megan shook off the melancholy. Jeff didn't need to hear about her troubles – not this late in the season when the Mustangs were in a heated race for a playoff spot. His obsession with making the playoffs was only surpassed by his obsession with striking out Martin McCree. He needed to remain focused. He didn't need the extra burden of her worries.

Jeff's hands felt so good on her, stroking her arms from wrist to shoulder. Bit by bit, she began to let the stress go. "That feels good."

"Bring the wine and I'll help you relax." How could she turn down an invitation like that? She slid off the barstool and into Jeff's arms. It had been a long time since she'd had time alone with Jeff, and no matter how awful her day had been, he always had the ability to make her forget everything but him. So what if he didn't want the kind of relationship she wanted? He wanted her, and she wanted him, and that was enough for now. Maybe she was pathetic, but she'd take whatever he was offering.

❧

She sipped wine in a tub full of perfumed bubbles while Jeff sat on the edge mostly watching the burgundy liquid swirl around in his glass. He dimmed the lights and even lit the fragrant candles she had scattered around the room. The hot water leached away the tension in her muscles, and the wine helped smooth the ragged edges of her thoughts. For the first time in days, she felt relaxed. "I don't want to talk about work tonight," she said. "Not yours, or mine."

"What do you want?"

"I want you." She placed her glass on the wide ledge next to the bottles of bath salts and bubble bath. "Join me?"

Jeff peeled his clothes off, and with the removal of each piece, Megan slipped further away from her day. The muscles in his arms bunched and lengthened as he folded each garment. His upper torso was all hard planes and valleys that made her fingertips itch to touch him. She followed the path of his jeans and boxers as he pushed them to his ankles in one smooth motion. He turned away from her, giving her a superb view of his ass. She admired the way the muscles flexed as he pulled his jeans free of one foot, then the other. There was something about the rugged strength of his legs…and then he turned around and whatever thought had been forming evaporated like water on a hot griddle.

His cock stood as ready as she'd ever seen it. He wanted her. Oh God, and how she wanted him!

He stepped into the tub and slid in behind her. She fit into the cradle of his legs like a piece of a jigsaw puzzle. His erection was a rigid support against the small of her back. Her body responded in

161

age-old invitation, going on heightened alert, and at the same time softening, inviting his attentions.

"Come on," he said. His hands gripped her shoulders and pulled her gently down against his chest. "Let me hold you."

She gave in to his coaxing and slumped boneless into his embrace. His heat enveloped her and what little tension remained from her workday dissipated, replaced by need and anticipation. Jeff stroked his hands from her shoulders to her fingertips, and back again. The worry she'd carried home with her slipped away. As his hands moved to her stomach and up to cover her breasts, her head fell to his shoulder and she closed her eyes to better concentrate on the tactile sensations.

He handled her as if she was the most delicate of creations, but it was the strength beneath his touch that excited her. Her heart thudded slow and steady as if pumping sweet molasses through her system all the while her body yearned for more. More of his touch. More of him.

"You are so beautiful," he whispered into the silence. He lifted her breasts, brushing his thumbs over her nipples. They tightened into hard little nubs surrounded by rosy puckered bunting. "So responsive." He continued to play with her nipples, now so sensitive each flick of his callused thumbs made her arch her back. "I love to touch you like this." He cupped her breasts hard and she cried out and thrust herself toward the source of the painful pleasure.

Her startled cry was quickly replaced by a groan of sheer pleasure as he trailed his hands lower, across her midriff and closer to the part of her now so eager for his attention.

"Please."

"Shh." His hands splayed across her stomach. "All in due time, sweetheart. All in due time."

Megan clamped her jaw tight against the need to beg him further. Instead, she dug her fingernails into his thighs raised on either side of her like great, forested mountains sheltering a lush valley. Where she'd been languid in the safe framework of his embrace, now her heart beat with a new, impatient rhythm.

"I want to make this last a very long time. I promise to give you what you want, but it will be so much more if you let me decide when you can have it."

Oh God. Isn't this the very thing that had kept her in Jeff and Jason's bed for so long? This promise of ecstasy they were both so skilled at delivering? Her body wept with need, but her brain understood. Surrender her body and the reward would be almost too magnificent to bear when it came. And it would come, she would come.

"Yes," she said on a desperate sigh.

"So sweet. So trusting." One hand dipped between her legs and parted her folds while the other held her firm in his grasp. The heat of his erection pressed into her back while the palm of his hand radiated warmth to her most intimate parts. "I love to feel you when you're ready for me. God, your pussy is so swollen." His fingers toyed with her engorged outer lips. "It must be the animal in me. This makes me crazy with wanting you."

Her mind registered his voice as he stoked a fire inside her that threatened to burn them both if he didn't do something quick to put it out. She ached to take him inside her, to feel his hard length invading her body, claiming her as he had so many times before.

"Ahh," he sighed as his thumb found her clit and applied pressure in a slow, circular rhythm that intensified the ache. "Your body calls to me, Megan. But I won't come inside you until I've taken you as high as you can go."

It wasn't an empty promise. Jeff knew her body, knew how to touch her, how to master her, how to make her weak, and how to make her shatter in his arms. Even when they were with Jason, it was Jeff's touch that moved her, Jeff's body that she craved more than her next breath. It had been months since she'd been alone with Jason, but she couldn't deny Jeff. When she was alone with him, she felt a soul deep connection she couldn't explain. It was as if he was made for her, and she for him.

"I've got to feel you," he whispered near her ear. "Spread for me. Let me in."

Somewhere she found the muscle control to lift her feet, draping her legs over Jeff's. He let his legs fall to the side, spreading her wide. She gasped at his blunt invasion. Two fingers, maybe three all at once. Conquering her with his first pitch. His hand pressed to her stomach kneading her tensed muscles, coaxing her to accept him. "Christ, you're tight and hot." He flexed his fingers against her inner walls and she shuddered around him.

"Not yet," he admonished as he pulled his fingers to her rim. "You know better, sweetheart." She heard the smile in his voice. He loved this, playing her like he did the weaker batters. Give them a taste of what they want with the first pitch, then take it back with the next. He toyed with her inner lips before plunging back inside up to his third knuckles. His fingers fluttered inside her like a three-headed beast, then he retreated.

Megan gasped and fought against his firm hold. The delicious torture threatened her sanity, while it drove her toward something so bright and shiny she couldn't comprehend it. All she knew was she had to reach it, and if she trusted Jeff, if she gave herself into his care, he would take her there. He always had.

He continued his assault on her senses, alternating between blunt, hard invasions, and gentle, maniacal strokes. And with each one, he pushed her one step closer to the indescribable pleasure he'd promised. He kept up his monologue long past the time she was able to discern his words. His voice reassured and coached, and as the water around them cooled, her body absorbed his heat as it succumbed to his skill.

At last, he plunged his fingers into her and set up a fast, hard rhythm. He nipped her ear lobe to get her attention before whispering in her ear. "Come for me, sweetheart. Let go."

She responded to the command in his voice and the demand from his fingers. Her body began to gather into a tight coil, ready to spring free. His fingers speared her one more time. With practiced precision, he found the soft palate of tissue on her vaginal wall and pressed her clit hard against her pubic bone. Time ground to a stop. The spring coiled inside her unwound with the force of a tornado, sweeping her up in the vortex and spinning in her head until she was lost and dizzy. Pleasure, wild and untamed, swirled through her.

Suddenly, she was flying. Her knees struck the hard marble bottom of the tub and something, someone, clamped her hands on the edge of the tub. Her knees slid apart as Jeff wedged himself between her legs. Still dazed from the strength of her orgasm, she cried out as Jeff parted her, driving hard into her pussy from behind. He rode her like a man too long denied, and when she thought she couldn't possibly come again, or come any harder, he took her up and into a storm of passion and pleasure she wasn't sure she would survive.

Clinging to the edge with white knuckles, she took all he gave, and gave all she had. His fingers dug into her hips, holding her for his assault. Tepid water sloshed against the sides of the tub as he rocked into her. Her breasts bounced with each solid thrust. Her arms burned with the strain of supporting her body. The slap of wet skin against wet skin mirrored the hammering of her heart.

This was primal. Primitive. Jeff dominated and she submitted. She'd never felt more powerful, knowing this man who rarely lost control could not contain his need for her. That she alone made him feel this way.

He'd never shown so much of himself to her. His cock grew harder, bigger inside her. His fingers dug painfully into her hips. A familiar need tightened inside her. Jeff cursed, drove hard into her, and with short, deep thrusts, poured his essence into her. With the first spurt of hot cum, Megan lost her tenuous hold on her control. Her climax slammed into her, impossibly harder than before. Her pussy milked his cock, demanding he give her everything.

She would have slipped face first into the water, had Jeff not wrapped his arm around her waist for support. He sat back on his heels, pulling her with him so she sat in his lap, her back against his front, impaled on his cock. Unable to speak, she let him hold her until his cock grew soft and he slipped from her. He helped her from the tub, wrapped her in a soft towel from the warming rack on the wall, all the while supporting her against his rock-solid body. She was putty in his hands. She always had been.

❧❧

Jeff wrapped his arm around Megan's waist and snuggled against her back. Her hair smelled like some kind of flower, and her soft skin was warm and flushed from their recent lovemaking. Once in the bathtub hadn't been enough to sate his need for her. After he dried her, he carried her to his bedroom and made love to her again. As she relaxed into slumber, he wondered if he ever would get enough. From the moment he'd first seen her, reaching out to him for his autograph, he'd felt like an invisible cord connected him to her. It had been natural to share her with Jason, but as time passed, he'd begun to think of Megan as his. Nights like this only served to reinforce the feeling. He liked being alone with her. She made him forget all about the Mustangs, and Martin McCree, and how fucked up his life was. When it was just the two of them, he could fool himself into believing she loved him, and only him. That maybe they could have a life together, as a couple.

In the distance, he heard the soft hum of the garage door opener, and then the opening and closing of the inside door. Jason was home, and with him, the reality that Megan wasn't his. She belonged to both of them. He tightened his hold on her as Jason's footsteps sounded in the sitting room that connected all their bedrooms. Would his brother look in on Megan, see she wasn't in her room and come to the obvious conclusion? Would he join them as he had every right to do? Something tightened in his chest as he strained to hear his brother's movements in the other room.

The door to Jason's room opened and closed, but Jeff continued to listen. It wouldn't be unusual for Jason to look in on his brother. They were close, and Jeff was certain Jason wouldn't go to bed without first making sure Jeff was in his room. He'd do the same. It wasn't meant to invade the other's privacy; it was something they both felt compelled to do. A twin thing, perhaps.

Jeff held his breath as a sliver of light spilled through the crack in the door and grew wider. Jason stood silhouetted in the narrow band of light. His brother took in the silent tableau, nodded his head once, and disappeared. The door closed with a soft nick, and Jeff let out his pent-up breath. For whatever reason, Jason wasn't going to join them. Megan stirred, sighing in her sleep. He relaxed his hold on her, but couldn't find it in himself to let her go. He needed her. Needed to feel her in his arms – to hold her – to imagine for this one night that she was his, and his alone.

CHAPTER SIXTEEN

"You never did tell me what was bothering you last night," Jeff said as the coffee maker beeped. Megan reached for the cup of coffee he slid across the counter for her. He put another coffee disk into the machine for himself, and she admired his broad shoulders and slim hips before he turned back to her.

"No, I didn't. It doesn't matter." There wasn't anything Jeff could do, even if she could tell him. She knew better than to get close to her patients. If she were miserable, it was her own fault. "There isn't anything you can do."

"Maybe not, but I want to be there for you."

"I know you do, but honestly, there isn't a thing you can do. You know how I am. Some of the kids get to me." Jeff covered her hand with his. It was a simple gesture, but it went straight to her heart. As she talked, his thumb stroked the back of her hand. Did he know how much his touch meant to her? "It's enough that you want to help."

"It tears me up to see you like you were last night."

Megan turned her hand in his, squeezing gently. She smiled up at him, moved by his words. "Don't worry about me. Just focus on the rest of the season. I'd love to see the Mustangs in the playoffs."

He slid his hand out of her grip and sipped his coffee. "It's going to take a miracle for that to happen."

Miracles were in short supply in her line of work, but perhaps there could be one for the Mustangs. "I'll keep my fingers crossed."

"I wish that was all it would take." He raked one hand through his hair and closed his eyes. Tension lined his face and she recognized the set of his shoulders. The stress of the season weighed heavily on him.

"You're only one player on the team, Jeff. Winning or losing is not your sole responsibility."

"I know." His breath came out on a long sigh and his shoulders relaxed a fraction. "Sometimes I wish I could do more, but I'm good at what I do."

"You're the best closer in the game, but you're also human. There's only so much you can do."

"Are you still worried about McCree?" Jason asked as he shuffled into the kitchen. He wore nothing but a pair of Elmo print boxers, and creases still marked his cheek from the bed linens. His close-cropped hair stood at odd angles making him appear rumpled, and in need of a keeper.

"Hell yeah, I'm worried about McCree, and you should be too."

Jason fumbled with the coffee maker. For a man with a million details in his brain, he had to relearn the coffee maker every time he used it. Finally, mug in hand, he braced against the counter and took his first sip. "Ahh, heaven." He took another sip before he turned to face them. "Look, I'm concerned about McCree, but he's just one player. If we keep the batters off base ahead of him, then he can only do minimal damage."

"That's not the point. If the league isn't going to end this nonsense, then we've got to find a way to shut the man down."

"Walk him. Put him on base, then get the outs so he can't score."

"You know damned well I don't walk batters. Ever." Jeff was digging his heels in. She could see it in the lines of his body and hear it in the hard tones of his voice. Jason would have to be deaf and blind not to notice, but he continued to goad his brother.

"Suit yourself. But sometimes it's better to admit defeat, and move on."

Megan stepped between the brothers. "Stop it, both of you. You need to be working together, not snapping at each other like kids." She pushed Jason toward the door. "Go get dressed. You have to leave in less than an hour." Turning to Jeff, she pointed a finger in the opposite direction. "Go. See if you can adjust the sprinkler timer. The grass is dying."

They skulked off with muttered apologies aimed at her rather than the person who needed to hear them. She didn't have time to referee between them, and she had her own worries to deal with. Having them sniping at each other didn't help one bit. As far as she was concerned, this season couldn't be over soon enough. Then maybe Jeff and Jason would remember they were friends as well as brothers.

❧

Jason followed his brother from the clubhouse to the dugout. The pre-game festivities were beginning, and as usual, he and Jeff would be signing autographs and posing for photos with the dignitaries and sponsors taking part. He just hoped his brother didn't wear the scowl that seemed to be his preferred look these days.

He thought the conversation with the team's manager would have been enough of a wake-up call for Jeff, and that didn't seem to be the case. He seemed to have given up on throwing a curve ball, but over the last few games, Jason had noted a slight increase in the velocity of Jeff's fastball. It wasn't much, but in this game, every fraction made a difference.

Jason knew he should be happy about the improvement, but that sort of gain didn't come without risk, especially if proper conditioning wasn't behind it. If Jeff weren't careful, he'd blow his arm out. Jason had tried to talk to him about it during warm-ups, but Jeff had closed him out with a stern warning to mind his own business. As if his brother, and the Mustangs, weren't Jason's business.

Jeff was acting like an ass. He wouldn't listen to reason, from anyone. His obsession with McCree was going to cost him his career if he persisted. Jason took up his place, sandwiching the representative from the insurance company sponsoring today's game between himself and Jeff. He smiled for the barrage of photographers, shook the woman's hand, and headed for the dugout to don his catching gear. He caught the first pitch, thrown by a kid who'd just made Eagle Scout. He and Jeff posed with the kid, congratulated him on his accomplishment, all without saying a word to each other.

As the team took their place along the first baseline for the National Anthem, Jason couldn't get Jeff out of his mind. They'd never been more at odds than they were right now. This closed-off scowling person wasn't his brother. They'd had their differences before – what brothers didn't? – but this was something new. Jeff rarely spoke to him off the field, and when he did, it was short, and often less than civil. Jason couldn't remember the last time they'd shared a laugh.

The McCree thing was part of it. Jason had made it clear he thought Jeff was making more of it than the situation warranted. Let McCree have his record, complete with an asterisk beside it. Once the steroid use was exposed, the record would go away. The other Mustangs pitchers had already made up their minds to issue McCree an intentional walk from now on. That was one way, the safe way, of protesting what everyone new – that Martin McCree was using, or had used, illegal steroids. Jeff's stubborn refusal to walk McCree didn't make any sense.

It was more than the McCree thing though. Jason couldn't pinpoint anything specific, but lately Jeff had seemed...restless, for want of a better word.

The last chords of the anthem echoed through the stadium. The enthusiastic crowd cheered as the players broke ranks – some headed to the dugout and bullpen, the rest to their field positions. Texas in

September could be many things, but cool wasn't usually one of them. Today was no exception. The fall sun had heated the stadium, and even though it was setting, the temperature on the playing field was somewhere close to "baking". Jason took his position behind the plate, pushing everything else from his mind – his brother, Martin McCree, illegal steroids. The Mustangs were too close to clenching the wild-card spot to let anything but this game, these batters, occupy his brain. One game at a time, one batter, one out, one win.

❦❦

Megan closed the supply room door behind her and leaned against it. God, how she hated her job sometimes. She grabbed a towel from the stack on a nearby rack and wiped the tears from her cheeks. More followed, and she wiped at them furiously. She had to get a grip. There would always be days like this – days when the sorrow would overshadow the joy. She tried not to think about how often these days occurred, but lately it seemed like they were the norm, and days of celebration would never come again.

It wasn't true, of course. Even today, if she looked close enough, she could find a reason to celebrate. There was the little girl in 303. She'd be going home soon, and chances were she would live a long, productive life. Then there was the eight-year-old boy in 320. He'd come through surgery with flying colors.

She wiped more tears away and tried to concentrate on the good things happening on the wing. Dwelling on the failures wouldn't help anyone, and the kids who still had a chance needed her to be at her best. They needed her full concentration, and most of all, they needed her to be cheerful and upbeat. Bringing her misery into their little lives wouldn't help them get well. She pushed away from the door, fidgeting with her scrubs. She dug around in her pockets for a tissue, and when she found none, she grabbed a box from the shelf. Hospital issue tissues left much to be desired, but she blew her nose anyway, and crammed a handful into her pocket – just in case. Making a mental note to pick up a supply of tissue packets – the good kind – next time she went shopping, Megan opened the door and rejoined the world.

Her first stop was the ladies room where she splashed cold water on her face and surveyed the damage. Bloodshot eyes stared back at her over a nose reddened from crying and no doubt, the attention of the rough tissues. A tear ravaged face wouldn't do. She dampened paper towels and pressed them to her eyelids for a few moments, willing the redness to go away. Her thoughts turned to the boy in 320. He'd had the same surgery Jason had undergone when he was a kid. Even though it was a routine surgery now, there was still a risk. The kid's prognosis was excellent, but like Jason, he would carry the scar for the rest of his life. The experience would be scary for an adult, but for a child? She couldn't even imagine. As she exited the restroom, she made a mental note to ask Jason if he could come by before they left on their next road trip.

Megan administered the last of the ten p.m. medications, and headed back to the nurse's station. She stopped outside the empty day room. Someone had left the television on, probably one of the siblings who'd visited earlier. They often made use of the room while their parents were occupied with the child they'd come to see. The Mustangs' game was on. Megan moved in closer to read the score box in the corner of the screen. Mustangs 2 – Miners – 1. Top of the ninth inning. Three more outs, and the Mustangs would win the game, and secure the wild-card spot in the playoffs. Lose, and hopes for a post-season were off.

The music that heralded the arrival of The Terminator began to play. The crowd surged to their feet to cheer on their closer. A surge of adrenaline brought Megan to the edge of her seat as the camera panned to the bullpen. A discreet door opened in the outfield wall, and Jeff stepped out. The announcers recited a litany of statistics and accomplishments attributed to The Terminator, but Megan barely heard them. Instead, all her attention was on the man confidently striding across the field. Jeff Holder. The camera zoomed in on his face. All concentration. Just the way he looked when he made love to her. Totally focused on the job at hand. This was the man she loved, would always love.

The station went to commercial break, and Megan snapped to her senses. She couldn't sit around mooning about Jeff Holder. She was due her last break of the night, so she crossed to the house phone and called the nurses' station to check in. Assured all was quiet, and that they knew where to find her if she was needed, Megan settled in to watch the last few minutes of the game. It wasn't anything like being there in person, but it would have to do.

Programming returned as Jeff threw his final warm-up pitch. Jason walked out to the pitching mound and dropped the ball in his brother's glove. Megan smiled. While the rest of the world could only speculate about what the brothers said to each other in these moments, she knew. Jason would hand the baseball over, raise his glove to hide his lips from the camera before delivering his parting words, "If you've got the balls, strike 'em out."

Jeff's lips curled up in acknowledgement of Jason's ribald comment, and Megan's heart squeezed. The brothers had been at each other's throats for the last week, and it was good to see that whatever was causing the rift at home didn't seem to affect them on the field. As Jason walked back to home plate, she mentally chided herself. Of course they wouldn't let it affect their work. They were professionals.

Megan silently cheered as Jeff struck out the first batter on three pitches. The team celebrated with a throw-around that ended with the ball back in Jeff's glove as The Terminator's theme song played in the background. The crowd was on their feet now, all fifty-thousand plus of them. The roar was deafening, as they whooped and waved rally towels printed with the Texas flag above their heads. Megan felt the excitement too, and scooted closer to the edge of the seat-cushion, her hands clenched in tight fists to keep them from trembling. The playoffs meant so much to her guys. It was what they worked for all season long, and now it was within their grasp.

The camera swung from the batter getting situated in the batter's box, to a close-up of Jeff's face. Megan sucked her bottom lip between her teeth and willed herself to remain calm. In contrast to her own anxiety, Jeff was the picture of confidence and composure.

If he was concerned about his opponent, he gave nothing away. He'd make an excellent poker player if he ever gave up baseball.

Jason crouched behind the plate, his legs splayed for balance. The batter settled and Jason flashed a signal to Jeff. She wished she knew what the signs meant, but they were a closely guarded secret between the pitcher and catcher. Megan wrung her hands. The announcers talked over the roar of the crowd. Jeff straightened and drew his hands together at his waist. Megan held her breath as Jeff went into his wind-up and let the ball fly.

"Strike one!" the umpire called with a flourish. Her breath whooshed past Megan's lips and she sank back in her chair, only to pop back up to resume her tense vigil. Jeff betrayed no emotion as the batter fouled the next pitch down the first base line. With two strikes on the batter, the camera cut to the on deck circle. Megan groaned. Martin McCree. If Jeff got past the current batter, he'd have to face his archrival.

The batter fouled off another pitch before he swung and missed the next one. The umpire called, "Strike three," with a dramatic gesture that fueled the crowd's enthusiasm. The Mustangs were one out away from securing a playoff berth.

Martin McCree slid the doughnut weights off his bat and dropped them to the ground, then strode toward home plate. Jason, helmet in hand, walked out to the pitching mound.

Megan forced air into her lungs. Jason's expression was one she knew well. Jeff watched his brother approach with stoic acceptance. He hoisted his pants up and shrugged his shoulders. Megan could see the tension between them, but knew most people only saw two professionals consulting on strategy. She knew better. Jason's body language and the stone cold glint in Jeff's eyes gave away the nature of their conversation. They'd worn identical expressions the other morning when she'd stepped between them to diffuse the brewing argument.

The announcers debated the wisdom of issuing an intentional walk to McCree in order to pitch to the next batter. Yes, the next batter would be an easier out, but with McCree on base, a homerun would put the Miners ahead by a run. A solo homerun by McCree would only tie the game.

Jason was arguing for the intentional walk. A chill raced up Megan's spine. Jeff wasn't going to do it. His stubborn streak was glowing bright red, and his eyes burned with determination. Seeing the brothers locking horns, the pitching coach joined them on the mound. His manner indicated he wasn't getting anywhere with Jeff either. Finally, as the umpire approached to break up the pow-wow, the coach turned and walked back to the dugout with one final glance at Jeff.

ⅇⅇ

"I won't walk the bastard."

"Look, asshole, just put him on base. Hanover is up next, and he's an easy out. All we need is one more out and we go to the playoffs," Jason argued.

"I can get McCree out."

"I know you can, but this isn't the time to prove it. The Miners are going to the playoffs. You'll have your chance to prove you're the best there."

"I can do this," Jeff argued.

Jason sighed as the pitching coach, Nate Sanderson, approached the mound. "Talk some sense into him Nate. I'm through trying."

"What's the problem, Jeff? Just put McCree on base. Don't give him the satisfaction of a challenge."

"Nate, I can do this. Let me pitch to him."

"All we need is one out, Jeff. This isn't about you. It's about the team. Do what's best for them."

"I am, Nate. We need to go to the playoffs knowing McCree is fallible. Walking him is like admitting we can't beat him."

Nate fisted his hands on his hips and looked Jeff in the eye. "I think this is a mistake, but I'm not going to talk you out of it, am I?"

"No, you aren't."

"Damn it, Jeff!" Jason shifted his weight and glared at his brother. "You damned well better throw exactly what I call, and nothing else. Do you hear me?"

176

"I hear you. Here comes the ump. Get your ass back behind the plate, and let's get this over with."

Jason kicked a clump of dirt out of his cleats and slid his helmet into place. Goddamned hardheaded dickwad. He thought of a few other colorful names to call his brother before he crouched behind the plate and waited for McCree to complete his batting ritual. If Jeff tried to throw that sorry-assed curve ball, he'd personally cut his brother's balls off and ram them down his throat.

McCree adjusted his crotch and raised the bat to his shoulder. *Time to go to work.* He wouldn't, couldn't dwell on what the outcome of the game meant to the team. Right now, it was one batter, one pitch at a time. Nothing more. Focus on the goal. Get this batter out. A mental list of everything he knew about McCree flashed into his head. Jason ran through the stats he'd committed to memory. Every pitch thrown to McCree, and the result. It seemed the man could hit anything thrown his way, and he had enough unnatural muscle to power the ball out of the park, no matter what it was. The trick was to keep the ball far enough out of McCree's reach so he couldn't get his bat on it, or if he did, he'd foul the pitch off for a strike. It was a fine line, but if Jeff was on today, he could do it.

Jason signaled a fastball, outside – just enough off the plate that McCree might be inclined to swing at it. Jeff nodded his agreement with the pitch selection. Jason concentrated on the white orb. There was no room for mistakes.

The fans took to stomping their feet like a mighty drum roll that shook the ground and drowned out everything but his inner thoughts. Crouched on the balls of his feet, the vibration shivered through his body like a low electric current. He knew Jeff felt it too. They'd talked about it before, how the sensation connected them to the fans and intensified the moment. It was impossible not to be affected by the air of expectation sizzling through the stadium. With a little luck, the invisible current would provide the energy to see this thing through.

Jeff kicked out and sent the ball hurtling toward the plate. Jason tracked its trajectory. Perfect. McCree swung, caught the ball with the tip of his bat, sending it foul toward the Mustangs dugout. *Strike one.* Jason let out a relieved breath and accepted a new ball from the home plate umpire as McCree spun out of the batter's box with a curse. Jeff was right about one thing. Advancing to the playoffs on a McCree out would make the accomplishment that much sweeter.

"Damn. That was fast." The umpire handed over the new ball with a chuckle. Jason glanced up at the center field scoreboard. Besides the pitch count, the board displayed the speed of the last pitch, registered via a radar gun behind home plate. The red display confirmed the umpire's assessment. 100mph. Shit. At that speed, McCree shouldn't have made contact at all. That he did could mean trouble. Jason called time-out and walked the ball out to the pitcher's mound.

"The bastard just fouled off a 100mph fastball," he informed his brother.

"Shit." At least his brother understood the implications of his warning. Maybe he'd listen to reason now.

"It's not too late to walk him."

"I can do this. You call the pitches, I'll throw 'em." Jeff held out his glove, palm up. Jason dropped the ball in it and headed back to his position.

"Stubborn jackass," he muttered. His helmet masked his lips from the prying eyes of the television cameras, and no one could have heard him over the roar of the crowd, even if he'd shouted.

The umpire gave the play ball signal, and Jason crouched low. Another set of signals, and he raised his glove in hopes of catching the ball for another strike. White leather spun through the haze of the stadium lights. A smudge of brown streaked past his eyes as the ball hit the palm of his glove. He reflexively closed his hand around the stinging in his palm. The roar of the crowd drowned out the umpire's call.

Strike two.

Jason glanced at the scoreboard and called time out. Without waiting to see if it was granted, he sprinted to the mound. "What the hell are you doing? That pitch was 101mph!"

"I'm getting the out we need," Jeff shouted back, his lips masked by his glove so the cameras couldn't pick up their conversation.

"We don't need it this way," Jason said. "How long can you keep this up?"

"All we need is one more strike. That's all. I can do it."

Jason slapped the ball into his brother's glove. "You're an ass."

One more strike. One ground ball. One pop-up. Any of them would do. He signaled the next pitch – high and outside. Just the kind of pitch McCree might go after. He did. The ball ricocheted off the bat, and into the stands above the first base dugout. Foul ball. Damn. The scoreboard recorded the pitch speed at 100mph.

McCree fouled off two more pitches before Jason called time-out again. Jeff wiped sweat from his brow with his shirtsleeve. Jason handed him a new ball. "I'm fresh out of advice, and ideas. You've thrown him five pitches and he's had his bat on all but one."

Jeff remained silent, his gaze focused on the ball in his hand. "We could try something way off the plate to see if he'll chase it," Jason suggested.

"No. Inside, hard. Be ready for it. He won't hit it," Jeff assured.

"What are you doing?"

"Getting the out. Just trust me, okay? He won't hit it."

They were in too deep to walk McCree now. Intentionally putting him on base would be admitting defeat, and that would be devastating to the team's morale, even if they did get the next batter out and advance to the playoffs. No. It was either let McCree hit the ball, or trust Jeff to throw some kind of miracle pitch to get the guy out. As if he had a choice. Jeff was going to throw the pitch, and he'd damn well better catch it. As Jason took his position behind the plate he flashed Jeff a series of signals, punctuated by a single finger down to let his brother know what he thought of his plan.

The one-fingered signal usually brought a smile to Jeff's lips, but today, he gave no indication he'd even seen the signal. His face was a mask of determination. Jason dismissed his worries about his brother's frame of mind. He had to concentrate on catching the damned ball, no matter what. A dropped third strike could allow McCree to make it to first base. At least he and Jeff agreed on that much. Martin McCree was not going to get on base, not if they could help it.

Jason tuned out the crowd noise. The vibration from their stomping feet, the Running Herd, they called it, had grown so strong he could feel it in his clenched teeth. He did his best to ignore it, to focus on the single spot of white, blurred with red as it hurled toward him. His eyes burned with the need to blink. He couldn't afford the luxury, not until the ball was safely in his glove.

He forced his eyes to remain open as the streak of brown brushed within an inch of his facemask. McCree danced back from the plate, the arc of the bat continued unimpeded.

A stinging pain in his palm.

His fingers clenching in reaction.

A curse.

The umpire's call. "Steeeriiiiikkkke three!"

Jason threw off his mask, ignoring the sputtering Martin McCree. He eyed the ball in his glove. Goddamn it. The thrill of victory warred with common sense. How hard had Jeff thrown that ball? His gut clenched as he looked up at the scoreboard. 104mph.*Holy. Shit.* Not a record, but damned close depending on the fractions behind that number.

It was only a second, maybe less before it hit him. Jeff. Something was wrong. A sick feeling gripped him in the stomach, and he had to swallow hard to battle the nausea. His feet carried him to the mound where the team was gathered in what should have been a celebration. Instead, the team surrounded Jeff in somber silence. Jason shoved his way to the center of the group. Jeff was on his knees, his right elbow cradled in his left hand.

Jason dropped down beside him, covering Jeff's hand with his own, willing the injury not to be what he knew it was. He'd thrown too hard, and the ligaments in his elbow had snapped. His brother wouldn't be pitching for the rest of the season, maybe never again.

"I struck the son-of-a-bitch out," he said through gritted teeth.

"Yeah, you did." What else could he say? Jason glanced up at his teammates. "Some help here? Let's get the hero off the field." Taylor, the first baseman handed his glove off to another player and stepped forward. Together, they lifted Jeff to his feet and held him until he was steady enough to stand on his own. The rest of the team had come from the dugout. Jason saw the trainer and team physician among them. They knew, but they weren't going to treat Jeff like an invalid. There wasn't anything they could do right now anyway.

Silence hung over the stadium as the fans recognized that something was wrong with their hero. The team formed two rows facing each other, an honor guard leading to the dugout.

Jason clamped a hand on his brother's shoulder. "You did it, Jeff. Go ahead. You deserve it." With each step Jeff took, the players clapped him on the back, then folded into a solid mass at his back. The crowd, still on their feet, cheered their conquering hero as he made his way to the dugout. He paused at the dugout steps, removed his cap and waved it at the fans. Jason stood alone on the pitching mound as his brother acknowledged the fans, then disappeared into the clubhouse.

⁂

"He's being an ass," Jason said minutes later. Megan held the phone with trembling hands. "How soon can you get here?"

"I don't know. Let me see if the rest of the staff can cover for me. I'll call you back."

Megan took a deep breath and let it out slowly, silently willing her nerves to calm. Talk about the day from hell. This was it. First, losing the little girl, Katelyn, who'd been with them for months. She'd desperately needed a heart transplant, but her little body couldn't wait any longer. Now this. There was no way of knowing yet what kind of damage Jeff had done to his arm, but from what she'd seen on television, it didn't look good. Jason had confirmed her worst fears. Jeff most likely wouldn't be pitching in the playoffs, or next season for that matter. What that kind of injury would do to a man like Jeff didn't bear thinking about.

Everyone knew about her friendship with the Holder brothers, but none knew the extent of her association. It was something they all agreed was their private business, so Megan put on her best face before she approached her fellow night nurses to ask them to cover the last hour of her shift. After explaining what happened, and that Jeff requested she come help him make sense of the tests, Megan was on her way.

Jason met her at the gate and escorted her to the clubhouse. A few team members lingered, still celebrating the win. Jeff sat bare-chested and barefoot on an exam table in the trainer's office - a giant icepack taped to his elbow. Her heart fluttered at the sight of him looking so vulnerable. There was still a dull shadow in his eyes. He was still hurting. How much of that was physical, and how much was worry over his career, she didn't know.

"How are you doing?"

"I'm okay. It's not as bad as they think it is." He shrugged his shoulder to emphasize his point.

"Your shoulder isn't the problem," she stated. "I was asking about the elbow."

"It's going to be fine. Ice. Rest. I'll be good to go in a few days."

She would have laughed had it not been so obvious the man was delusional. "What did the trainer say?"

"He's arranging an MRI now."

"Uh huh. That's what I thought."

"Don't look at me like that. I don't need one, but they do MRI's on everything these days."

"See? Was I right?" Jason piped in. "He's being an ass."

No. He wasn't being an ass. From where she stood he looked like a frightened little boy. She closed the distance between them until she stood between his spread legs. "It's going to be alright. We'll get the MRI, then see what we need to do." She wanted to erase the fear from his eyes, but nothing she could say would do that, so she cradled his face in her palms and lowered her lips to his. For a moment, he let her kiss him, then slowly, he relaxed and his lips began to move against hers. She forgot about everything but Jeff and the way he made her feel, like she was the most beautiful woman in the world. She forgot about her crappy day. She forgot they were in the Mustangs' clubhouse. She forgot about Jason. Forgot they had an audience.

"Uh, I hate to break this up, but this is a public place."

Megan broke the kiss and stepped back. "I'm sorry. I…I forgot."

"It's okay," Jeff said. "No one saw."

In the nearly two years she'd been with Jeff and Jason, she'd never felt like what they were doing was wrong. Not until now. Jeff might as well have hit her with a bat. This was the reality. It was only okay if no one saw. Jeff needed her, and she'd have to keep her distance so no one would find out about their dirty little secret. Her.

Her stomach twisted into a tight ball. God, she loved him so much, and she'd have to act as if he was nothing more than a casual friend – just as she'd done earlier so she could rush to be by his side tonight. "It won't happen again."

"Megan –"

"Hey, there." A tall man wearing a dress shirt and slacks, topped by a Mustangs jacket stepped into the room. "Oh. Sorry. I didn't know you had company."

Jason stepped up. "Rand, this is Megan. This is Rand Evers, the team trainer. Megan is a pediatric nurse, and a friend. I thought Jeff might listen to her."

"Good idea." Mr. Evers extended his hand. "Nice to meet you, Megan."

Megan squelched her disappointment and hurt as she shook his hand. This was about Jeff, not her. There'd be time later to think about what had just happened. "Thank you. I don't know if he'll listen to me or not, but I'll do what I can."

"Well, I have the MRI scheduled. They'll take you as soon as you can get over there. No need putting it off."

"I don't think –"

Megan reeled on him before he could finish the sentence. "You don't think? What do you know, Jeff Holder? Are you a doctor?" She didn't give him time to respond. Concern for him, coupled with her own pain of being an outsider as far as the world was concerned made her words harsher than she intended. "No, you're not. You're going to get the MRI, then we're going to listen to the doctors and you are going do what they say. Let's go. I'll drive."

"I can take him," Jason offered.

"No. You drive like an idiot. I want him to get there alive." As soon as the words left her lips, she wished she could take them back. None of this was Jason's fault anymore than it was Jeff's. She'd known what she was getting into when she agreed to move in with them. That she'd fallen in love with Jeff was her fault.

Jason backed away, his hands up in surrender. His lips curved up on the corners. "Okay, okay. I'll meet you there."

"Sorry. I didn't mean it to come out like that."

"No problem. You're right." His easy smile said all was forgiven. "I'll follow to make sure you get there alright, then I'll go on home. We still have a game tomorrow, and there isn't a thing I can do for him."

CHAPTER SEVENTEEN

Talk about hell. This was it.

Megan brushed tears from her face. She'd cried more in the last week than she had the whole rest of her life combined. They'd lost another child today. Maybe it was time for her to change to a regular hospital, to put some distance between the children and her. Once, she'd been good at separating herself from the kids. At least, she'd been able to keep a professional distance, but lately, she'd lost her heart to a desperately ill child way too often. She didn't know how much more heartbreak she could take.

Her heart still ached when she thought of the way Jason and Jeff had treated her the night Jeff injured his arm. She'd fooled herself into thinking she meant more to them than a convenient sex partner, but they'd put her in her place, and broken her heart in two.

Now, for the umpteenth time in a week, she was hiding in the linen closet, crying her eyes out. And while she was dampening yet another clean towel, Jeff was in an operating room on the other side of town, undergoing surgery on his elbow. She should be there, sitting in the waiting room with Jason. They'd scheduled the surgery in between games so Jason could be there for his brother, but in a few hours, Jason would be leaving with the team in pursuit of the regional championship – one-step closer to the World Series. Then it would be just Jeff and her for the next week, maybe more if the team won the five game series and advanced in the playoffs.

Megan dug deep for the courage she needed to go on. Another hour and she'd be off work and her vacation would begin. She'd been lucky to get time off on such short notice. If things had been different, she'd be thrilled about spending time alone with Jeff, but things weren't different. They were what they were. Jeff needed someone to take care of him, and she was it. He'd told her not to use her vacation to babysit him, but Jason had asked otherwise. Ever since his injury, Jeff had been worse than difficult. He'd argued against the surgery, convinced in his own mind that the usual orthopedic advice would do the trick – R.I.C.E., rest, ice, compression and elevation. A bevy of doctors had eventually convinced him he was wrong and he'd reluctantly agreed to have the surgery.

Named after the first pitcher to have the surgery and make a successful comeback in the major leagues, Tommy John surgery was routinely performed now on athletes at all levels of the spectrum. If Jeff followed the physical therapy regime lined out for him, there was no reason to believe he wouldn't make a full recovery and be back in the bullpen by next season's All Star break.

The hard part would be hiding her own pain from Jeff. She couldn't let him see how much his and Jason's actions had hurt her. For the next week, she'd be his private nurse, and no more. He'd made it plain that nothing had changed. He still wanted to keep their relationship out of the public eye. Her more rational self understood. The press would have a field day with the truth. Two elite athletes, twin brothers – living with the same woman. Both having a sexual relationship with that woman.

It would be a scandal that could ruin both their careers, and hers, if the media found out about it. But in the last few months the relationship had changed. Jason was no longer a part of the equation.

Somewhere along the line, she'd fallen in love with Jeff, and Jason had become little more than a friend with occasional benefits. The benefits had grown fewer and fewer until they'd completely disappeared. To say she didn't love Jason would be a lie. She did love him, but it wasn't the same kind of love she had for Jeff. Jason was her friend. What she felt for Jeff was so much more, and somehow Jason had picked up on it, probably before she had, and distanced himself from their complicated arrangement.

His reminder that they were in a public place the night Jeff injured his arm had been a sharp wakeup call, but the way Jeff practically pushed her away as if he were afraid to be seen with her was what really hurt. It was Jason who explained away her presence as a family friend, and Jeff did nothing to change that status. It was foolish, but that silent denial had cut her to the core, and made her face reality. Jeff didn't love her.

Over the last few days she'd faced the ugly truth. She'd fallen in love with Jeff and stupidly began to dream about a life as his wife and the mother of his children. Over the last week, they'd spent a lot of time together. Jeff had made love to her with such tenderness she'd begun to believe again that maybe they could make it work. It wasn't going to happen. Jeff didn't feel the same way. To him she was a friend with benefits, and for the next week, his private nurse.

❧

Jason wrapped Megan in his arms. She'd been crying again. Bloodshot eyes and a red nose gave away what she tried to hide behind her forced smile. He cradled her head in his hand and held her close in the hallway outside Jeff's room. In the last week, he'd seen the evidence of tears more times than he could count, and he was afraid he was responsible for at least some of them. He'd kicked himself a thousand times for the way he treated her after Jeff's injury. That Jeff hadn't corrected him had only made it worse. They'd hurt her, but she hadn't said a word about it. Maybe he was a coward, but he didn't know how to apologize. What could he say? "I'm sorry I treated you like a stranger?" He knew it was worse than that. He should have handled that moment in the training room differently. What would it have cost to introduce her as Jeff's girlfriend? No one had to know about her relationship with him. Introducing her as a family friend had hurt her, reducing her to someone they were embarrassed to acknowledge. Yet here she was, hurting, needing to lean on someone herself, and offering instead to be Jeff's private nurse for the next week.

He curled his fingers in her hair and tugged her face away from his shoulder. She looked up at him with liquid eyes and he didn't think about where they were, or who might see them. He wanted to wipe that lost look off her face. Her eyes fluttered shut as he dipped his head and covered her lips with his. It wasn't a passionate kiss, but much more than a casual acquaintance kiss. For a brief moment, she kissed him back, then she broke the kiss, pushing against his chest to put distance between them.

"Jeff...?"

"He's fine. The doctor said he'd be out for a while, but the surgery was a complete success." Leave it to Megan to be more worried about Jeff than herself. "What about you?"

"What about me?" She wiped tears from her cheeks with the back of her hand. "I'm fine, really. I'm sorry I didn't get here sooner."

"Come on. There's a waiting area down here where we can have some privacy." He grabbed her hand in his and tugged her down the hall. When they were settled on hard plastic chairs with cups of lukewarm coffee from the vending machine, Jason said, "What happened today? You can tell me."

"Really, Jason...I'm fine. It was a rough day, but I'm here now. Tell me everything the doctor said."

❧❦

Jeff floated in and out of consciousness. The surgery was over, and quite possibly his career now too. How he would go from this back to the Mustangs' roster, he didn't have a clue. His right arm hurt like a son-of-a-gun, and now that he thought about it, his left one did too. Memories swirled like a milkshake in a blender until they coalesced into something comprehensible. They'd taken a tendon from his left wrist and used it to replace the torn ligament in his right elbow. Now he'd have some scars too. Another way people could tell Jason and him apart.

He wiggled the fingers of his left hand and swallowed a curse as pain knifed up his arm. Not a good idea. Weren't they supposed to give him something for the pain? He lay still until the pain eased, then drifted back into sleep.

The next time he woke, he remembered to keep still and was rewarded by a much clearer picture of the world around him. Not much had changed, but he got the impression it was late. Or maybe someone had dimmed the lights in his room. Both arms still hurt, but it was manageable now. He could live with this. It was tempting to try moving them again, but the memory of the last time he tried that was still fresh. He could wait until they made him move, and they would – very soon. All the doctor's warnings came back to him now. Physical therapy would begin before he left the hospital, and it would be painful, at least at first. He wasn't looking forward to it, but if it meant getting back on the Mustangs' roster, then he'd do it.

Megan would be there for him. He'd been an ass, thinking she was in love with Jason. The last week with her had been great, better than ever. They'd spent last night together, and he'd come to some conclusions. He loved her. Had for a long time. He wanted to make a life with her. She'd stand with him, no matter what happened with his career. Hell, she was taking off work to babysit him for the next week. She never said she loved him, but she told him in other ways, like the way she let him take care of her the other night. He liked taking care of her, liked the way her body responded to his touch, liked the way she gave herself to him. She needed someone to hold her, to make her forget about her shitty day and the stress of her job. Yeah, they were good together – in and out of bed. Maybe he'd ask her to marry him. He'd be home for months with nothing to do but his physical therapy. It would be a good time to get married, maybe get started on a family. An image of Megan round with his child formed, and desire had his cock hardening. At least that part of his anatomy didn't need any repairs.

The more he thought about it, the more convinced he became that it was the right thing to do. He couldn't imagine his life without Megan. She loved kids so it wasn't a stretch to think she'd like a few of her own, and he wanted to be the one to give them to her. The thought of her with another man made him want to hit something. His fingers curled reflexively inward. The pain wasn't near as bad as before, but it was enough to snap his focus back on the task at hand. Get out of the hospital, and get back to work. He'd have plenty of time to fantasize about Megan once he got out of here.

Voices in the hallway drew his attention to the open door. Jason. Would he stand in his way when it came to Megan? He didn't think so. His brother hadn't been with Megan in a long time. He watched as Jason signed an autograph for one of the nurses and tried to remember the last time he'd seen Megan and Jason together. It seemed like months now that he thought about it. It seemed like Jason was gone more than he was at home these days. Maybe his brother had noticed something more between Megan and him and was giving them some privacy. Hell, maybe Jason was smarter than he looked. Jeff laughed to himself. Comments like that would have him in back in the hospital if Jason heard them.

Jeff closed his eyes and drifted into a light sleep only to wake again to voices outside his room. It was fully dark now, but lights in the hallway illuminated the two people embracing. Jason and Megan. His heart lurched at the sight of his brother holding the woman he loved even though he'd seen them do much more. Why the friendly embrace didn't set well with him now bothered him. Then Jason cradled Megan's head against his shoulder and Jeff wanted to shout at Jason to let his woman go, but something about the way she'd gone into Jason's arms stopped Jeff from saying anything.

He knew that body language. She looked the same way the other night after a bad day at work. She let him soothe her worries away, just as Jason was doing now. He should be grateful Jason was there for her while he was stuck in this hospital bed.

Jeff closed his eyes and concentrated on their low voices. He couldn't make out what they were saying, and then they weren't talking at all. He opened his eyes in time to see Jason kissing Megan. *The fucking bastard. I'm going to kill him.* For a moment it looked like Megan kissed him back, but then she pushed Jason away and Jeff heard her ask about him. *Well, it's about fucking time you wonder if I'm dead or alive.* His brother assured Megan that he was going to be fine, then dragged her away. Jeff had no idea where they were going, but he heard the word, privacy, and that was enough.

His temper spiked and he had to force himself to calm down. A nurse came in, checked his vitals, and asked if anything was wrong. Apparently, his elevated blood pressure had set off alarms in the nurses' station. He assured her he was fine, and after checking the equipment to make sure it was in proper working order, she gave him a drink of water and left.

What a fool he was, thinking Megan was his. If it had been anyone else, he'd have a chance, but it was Jason. How could he have been so wrong? Last week, hell, last night, she was his. She couldn't have faked the way she was with him, so what could have changed? Why was she clinging to Jason, kissing Jason as if he were the only man alive?

The nurse came back in to check the equipment again. "Get some rest, Mr. Holder," she admonished. "You'll see the physical therapist in the morning, then you'll be out of here in the afternoon."

It hit him all at once. He was what had changed. His career was on the skids, and Megan had run from his arms to his brother's. His healthy, uninjured, brother. The one still on the playoff roster. The one who still had a career. A pain that had nothing to do with the surgery knifed through him. He closed his eyes and willed it to go away. The sedative the nurse had injected into his IV worked its way through his system and he slept.

He never wanted to sleep again if he had to wake up with this kind of hangover. His head felt like a Little League team was taking batting practice inside his skull, and his mouth was as dry as the Sahara. A nurse hustled over and held a straw to his lips.

"Good morning, Mr. Holder. How are you doing this morning?"

"Like shit. How are you?" It was an unnecessary question. Her cheery attitude assured she was doing fine.

"I'm just dandy. Thanks for asking." She pulled the IV shunt from his arm with all the compassion of an axe murderer. Jeff cursed a blue streak that earned him a scolding from Nurse Perky. "Save your cursing for the physical therapist." She slapped a bandage on the puncture wound. "She'll be here in a few minutes, and I guarantee you'll want to use up your whole vocabulary on her."

Just fucking peachy. "When do I get out of here?"

"Well, let's see…after the physical therapist, there's your doctor. As soon as he sees you and signs the release papers, you can go. That should be sometime after lunch."

Jeff dropped his head back against the pillow and immediately regretted the sudden movement. "I've got a headache. Can I get some aspirin or something?"

"Oh look! Here's your breakfast." A woman slid a tray onto his bed-table and left without a word. His stomach growled as he remembered he hadn't eaten in over twenty-four hours. The nurse rolled the tray into position and raised his bed to a sitting position. It felt good to be sitting up, but the shifting of his arms reminded him how useless they were. His right arm was in a brace, and his left wrist was bandaged.

"How the hell am I supposed to eat?"

"That's what I'm here for," Megan stood in the doorway smiling at him. Well, shit.

"I can do it myself," he groused. He tried to pick up a toast point with his left hand, but only managed to drop it in his lap on the way to his mouth.

"Don't be an idiot," Megan said. She crossed the room and snagged the toast, returning it to the tray.

"I see the reinforcements are here." The nurse removed her rubber gloves and headed for the door. "Enjoy your breakfast, Mr. Holder."

"She's a lively one," Megan observed. Jeff managed a grunt before Megan continued. "And you look like hell. How are you doing?"

"I'm fucking fine. Can't you tell?" He shrugged his shoulders to emphasize his sorry state. "How the hell am I supposed to function? I can't even feed myself."

"That won't last long. You'll have full use of your left hand soon." She lifted a fork loaded with scrambled eggs to his lips as she spoke. Jeff opened his mouth and almost gagged on the cold, tasteless mess.

"No more! Christ, get me out of here before I starve."

Megan held a piece of toast to his lips. "Here. Try this."

He figured they couldn't mess toast up too bad, so he bit off a piece and chewed. It was better than nothing, so he signaled with a nod for more. Megan brought it back to his lips for another bite.

"The bacon doesn't look too bad," she coaxed. Jeff managed to grunt his acceptance, but he'd had enough of being an invalid. He reached for a slice of bacon and pinched it between his thumb and forefinger. It wasn't pretty but he got the whole thing in his mouth. His success was encouraging, so he did it again with the second slice, and followed with the toast.

"See? Better already," she said.

"Coffee."

Megan lifted the juice box to his lips instead. "Trust me. You don't want that coffee. Have some juice and when you're finished eating I'll go down to the cafeteria and get you some coffee. They serve Starbucks down there."

"I want to go home."

"I know. And you will, soon. We'll have you home in time to watch the game tonight." He turned his head away as Megan held the juice box to his lips again.

"No more."

"You have to eat, Jeff."

"Not that, I don't. Go get me some real food." He needed to get her out of his room. Feeling helpless was one thing, but having to accept help from Megan, knowing she did it out of duty rather than love was enough to make him sick.

He breathed a sigh of relief when she grabbed her purse and stomped out the door. Really? What the hell did she have to be pissed about? He was the fucking idiot who couldn't even feed himself. God help him if he had to take a piss.

His peace was short-lived as it turned out. Megan probably hadn't made it to the elevator when a woman carrying a giant tote bag entered his room. Her jeans and T-shirt said she wasn't a nurse – that meant she must be the physical therapist.

"Jeff Holder?"

"That's me."

"Hi!" She dropped the bag onto the visitor's chair and stood by his bed. "I'm Stacey – your physical therapist. I'd shake hands," she grinned a bright, all too cheery for the circumstances, grin, "but I doubt you're ready for that."

If that weren't an understatement, he didn't know what was. "No. I don't think I'm ready for that. And since I can't grip my own dick, I don't see how physical therapy is going to do me much good today." He had to give her credit. She didn't take offense at his crude language. Her next words told him why.

Stacey-the-physical-therapist shifted her stance so one hip jutted out to the side. She placed her balled fist on that hip and glared down at him. "Look, Mr. Holder. You can use all the foul language you want during our sessions, but I won't stand for it otherwise. I've heard it all before, and trust me, you'll probably make up a few new curse words before you're back on the field. I'm here to make sure you get back to work as soon as possible, but if you insist on insulting me, then your *dick* is going to need physical therapy before I'm through with you. Did I make myself perfectly clear?"

"You're tougher than you look, aren't you?"

"I'm tough enough to make you scream, Mr. Holder."

"We'll see about that."

Stacey smiled at him again, but this time it looked more like a wolf smiling at the lamb who was about to be her dinner. "So, are you ready to begin?"

Apparently, that was a rhetorical question because she turned and dug in her bag, coming up with a red ball that resembled a clown nose. "Open your palm," she stroked a finger down the length of his left forearm, stopping short of the bandage on the inside of his wrist. She was giving unnecessary orders. He could barely move his fingers without wanting to cry, much less make a fist. She dropped the ball into his palm. "Close your fingers around the ball. Lightly. You don't have to squeeze it."

"You're kidding."

"I assure you, I'm not." Her hand slipped under his and before he could jerk away, she'd pressed his fingers into a loose fist around the ball. He yelped with pain and she let his fingers relax. "Now, do that four more times, then we'll switch to your other hand."

Sweat was pouring into his eyes by the time he finished the four finger curls, and she meant for him to do it again with his right hand. Christ, she wasn't a wolf, she was the devil in disguise. He made an attempt at talking her out of a repeat performance, but she gave him no choice. One thing she was right about – he was coming up with a whole new vocabulary. Thinking up new curse words helped take his mind off the exercises, simple though they were.

When he finished five loose finger curls with his right hand, Stacey rewarded him by massaging both arms. She was packing up to leave when Megan returned with a bag from Whataburger that smelled like heaven. Jeff watched as the two women introduced themselves, sizing each other up as only women can do. It sounded as if they were going to become the best of friends, at his expense.

Stacey hoisted her bag back onto her shoulder and paused at the door. "I'll see you tomorrow Mr. Holder. I'll be at your house at ten in the morning. Be ready." She took a step out the door and turned back to him. "Oh, and I bet you can hold your dick just fine now, so go ahead and take a piss." She smiled that she-wolf smile of hers and left.

"What was that all about?" Megan asked.

Jeff tentatively tried to flex the fingers of his left hand, and was surprised at how easily they moved. He was able to make a fist, albeit, a loose one, but damned if she wasn't right. He could take a left-handed piss all by himself.

CHAPTER EIGHTEEN

Megan slammed the refrigerator door, wishing it made a more satisfactory sound than just a soft whoosh. Maybe she should strangle Jeff instead. That would certainly be satisfying. Ever since she'd driven him home from the hospital the previous afternoon, he'd been nothing but a pain in the ass. He complained about everything from the food she served him to the air temperature. He'd managed to have a shower and dress himself in sweatpants – no shirt – and now he was grousing because she hadn't fixed eggs to go with his toast and bacon.

"What am I? A short order cook?" she mumbled to herself. If she didn't know better, she'd think the surgeon had done a personality transplant, rather than an ulnar collateral ligament reconstruction. "I'll scramble his eggs if he doesn't snap out of this pretty damned quick." She broke three eggs into the pan and whisked them around while adding a dash of milk. "He might be hurting but that's no reason to treat me like shit."

She slid the cooked eggs onto a plate, grabbed a fork from the flatware drawer, and headed into the bear's den. Jeff had refused to come to the table in the kitchen, preferring to take his meal last night and this morning sitting in his favorite recliner in front of the television.

"Here." The eggs nearly jumped off the plate as she dropped it unnecessarily hard onto the TV tray. "Anything else, your Highness?"

"No."

She stood over him, trying to figure out where the reasonable man she knew and loved had gone. He ate the eggs left-handed, spilling more on the floor than he managed to get in his mouth. She was a compassionate person. Really she was. She dealt with scared kids, kids in all sorts of pain, day in and day out, so the sling holding Jeff's injured arm against his chest should have made her feel guilty for her unkind thoughts. But Jeff Holder was being an ass, and that negated every bit of her compassion for his plight.

"You're making a mess."

"So? Clean it up."

"I'm not the maid, Jeff Holder. I don't know what happened to you in that operating room, but I'm not standing for it."

"Then leave. Go back to work. I can take care of myself."

Megan stared open-mouthed at him. None of this made sense. Jeff and Jason were both the biggest babies in the world about being sick. A cold would send them into a tizzy of helplessness, and she'd indulged their misery more than once, waiting on them hand and foot. So this stubborn, ungrateful attitude when Jeff was really, truly hurting defied all logic.

He continued to eat as if she weren't there, standing two feet away, boring a hole through his skull with her anger. Megan stalked back to the kitchen. "It would serve him right if I went back to work and left him here to fend for himself," she muttered as she cleaned up the breakfast mess. Maybe Jason could talk some sense into him when he got home. The Mustangs had lost the first game in the regional series. They'd play again today; then after a day off the series would continue at the Mustangs' home stadium. That meant Jason would be home soon. "Not soon enough for me," she said to the open dishwasher as she poured soap into the dispenser.

Good God. Jeff ground his molars together and tried to imagine the pain in his elbow wasn't there. It was stupid, of course. The pain wasn't going to go away.

He flexed his fingers around the clown nose again. It was hopeless. He'd never be the same. Hell, he could barely hold a fucking clown nose without dropping it. How would he ever throw a baseball again? His career was over. Facing it now would be better than going through months of torture in hopes of changing the inevitable. Two weeks post-surgery and not a damned thing had changed, and if he had to hear Stacey's cheery voice another minute he might not be held responsible for his actions.

"That's it." He allowed the ball to roll from his weak grip. It landed with a soft bounce and rolled across the tile floor of Jeff's home gym. "I'm through."

"Okay. I guess that's enough for today. We've been pushing pretty hard." Stacey bent to pick up the ball. "We'll stop now and I can massage your arm before I go."

"You don't get it. I said I'm through. Not just for today. I'm done. Pack up your bag of torture devices and get the hell out of my house."

"Mr. Holder – "

"No. I've had it. This is going nowhere."

"It's only been two weeks. Your arm is getting stronger every day. You can't seriously want to quit now."

Oh yeah he did. Having the surgery was one of the worst decisions he'd ever made. Looking back, he couldn't even remember making the decision. One day he'd been pitching to McCree, and the next he was counting backwards from ten while the anesthesia took effect. Who had made the decision? Rand Evers, the Mustangs' trainer? Jason? Megan? It damned sure wasn't his decision. But this was.

"Maybe you didn't hear me. I said I'm done."

"Okay, okay. I'm leaving. You're making a big mistake. If you want to make it back on the roster by the All Star break, you don't have a minute to waste." Jeff breathed a sigh of relief as she headed to the door. She paused with her hand on the knob and turned. "Call me when you come to your senses."

He had come to his senses. Two weeks and one surgery too late, but he'd done it. He waited until he heard Stacey's car pull away from the house before he headed for the kitchen. Megan had gone back to work after only four days, and Jason was God-only-knew-where. Since the Mustangs crashed and burned in the Regional Championship Series, Jason had been scarce.

Jeff shoved things around in the refrigerator, cursing when his search for a beer fell short of the goal. *Fuck.* Not only was his career washed up, but his brother had stolen his woman, and the two of them had left him alone with not a single beer in the house. Life couldn't get any fucking better than this.

A search of the kitchen cabinets netted a half-empty bottle of Kentucky's finest. Judging from the looks of the curled up edges on the broken seal, the bottle was left over from some long ago gathering. So long ago, Jeff couldn't remember ever seeing it. He shrugged his shoulders and took a swig out of the bottle. Bourbon improved with age – right? He took another swig to wash down the first. He found an open bag of pretzels in the pantry and with bottle tucked under his arm and the pretzel bag in his "good" hand, headed for the den and his favorite recliner.

❧

"Thanks for stopping by today." Megan rested her elbows on the Formica tabletop in the hospital cafeteria and raised her coffee mug to her lips. "It means a lot to the kids."

"No need to thank me. You know I enjoy meeting the kids." Jason bit off a piece of the giant candy bar he purchased at the gas station on the way over. "I wish Jeff had come."

"What are we going to do about him? This isn't normal."

"I haven't got a clue. I was hoping you had some ideas."

"I've never seen anything like this." She shook her head in frustration. "The other day I suggested he see a sports psychologist and he almost bit my head off."

"He was sitting in front of the television watching the Cartoon Network when I left, and if I'm not mistaken, he had another bottle tucked in the corner of his chair." Jason washed another mouthful of chocolate and caramel down with a long draw from his soda bottle. "He can't go on like this."

"Have you tried to talk to him?"

"Yeah. He won't listen to a thing I say." He stared across the cafeteria, gathering his thoughts. "I used to know everything that went on in his head, because it was so much like what was going on in mine. But now...I don't have a clue. The doctors have told him over and over that he needs to follow the regime, and if he does, he'll be as good as new." Jason studied the remains of his candy bar. "I don't know. It's as if..."

"What? As if...what?"

"It's like he's given up. I tell you, Megan. This isn't like Jeff. Baseball...pitching...has been his entire focus since we were kids." Megan sensed Jason had more to say so she waited while he took another drink of his soda. He set the bottle down on the tabletop and spun it around slowly between his thumb and forefinger. "When I was sick, Jeff would come visit me in the hospital every day. He'd do his homework and help me with my class work. When we were done, he'd talk to me about baseball. He was learning to pitch, and he'd show me how to hold the ball, and tell me what he was learning about how to read the batters and about how he was going to be the best pitcher the Major League had ever seen. He had me convinced I was going to be okay, and that one day I'd be his catcher, and we'd be famous."

Jason paused to regain his composure. Megan slid her hand across the table to cover his, offering what comfort she could. If Jeff thought he was the only one suffering because of his injury, he had another think coming.

"He was right. He is the best, and he's so damned proud of what you've accomplished."

"That used to be true. I don't know now. He's changed."

"He's still there, Jason. We have to find a way to get to him. There's more to this than just his injury, but for the life of me, I can't figure out what it is. If we could figure it out, I'm sure we would find the solution."

"I asked Stacey what happened the day he kicked her out."

"What did she say?"

"Nothing. Nothing happened. He was doing his physical therapy, then he stopped and told her to get out and to not come back."

"It doesn't make any sense. Something had to have happened. He agreed to the surgery. The night before...well, everything was fine. We talked for a long time after...well, after. He was happy. Not about the surgery, but happy about the prospect of making it back after the All Star break next year. He knew the physical therapy was going to be rough, but he was committed to doing whatever it took to get back on the roster."

"So, everything was good between the two of you?"

Megan nodded. "As good, if not better than ever. The week before he blew out his elbow I was really beginning to think we had something special going." She sipped her now tepid coffee before continuing. "I thought we were on the brink of becoming exclusive."

"I thought the same thing. I saw it coming a long time ago. That's why I've spent so much time away from the house in the last few months. Jeff loves you. Not that I don't, but what you and Jeff have is more than you and I could ever have. I didn't want to stand between you any longer. I take it that has changed too?"

"Yes. We haven't been together since the night before his surgery. He might not be able to do much with his right arm in a brace, but..." Megan stared into her coffee cup. "I offered to...you know...help. He told me..."

"What?"

"He told me to go spread my legs for you."

"He's not going to have the opportunity to drink himself to death. I'm going to kill him myself."

"No, Jason. Don't. Don't tell him I told you. It will only make things worse."

"I'm not going to let the jackass talk to you that way."

"Really, I'm fine. I'm over it."

"You aren't over it, and you aren't fine. Jeff is being a first class asshole, and it's time for it to end."

"What are you going to do?"

"I'm going to go home and kick his sorry ass from here to kingdom come. That's what I'm going to do. He can throw away his career if he wants to, but he'll never find anyone who loves him more than you do. I'm not going to stand by and let him throw you away too."

"Don't do it, Jason. Please. Jeff is a grown man. If he wants me, he'll come around on his own."

"I'm not so sure about that. He doesn't seem to be operating on all cylinders these days."

"Enough about Jeff." She really needed to change the subject before she started crying again. Since Jeff's first day home following the surgery, she'd shed enough tears to overflow Lake Texhoma. "You're seeing someone."

"Yeah, I am."

"Well… Spill. Tell me everything. Who is she? Where did you meet her? Is she pretty?"

"She's beautiful, and smart, and sexy, and that's all I can say right now."

"Why right now? She's not married is she?"

"No. Nothing like that. It's… well, if you knew who she was, you'd want to have her over to dinner or something, and now's not a good time."

"You can't say something like that and expect me to just let it go. Tell me, Jason Holder, or I'll put starch in your underwear next time I do the laundry."

"You wouldn't do that to me." He flashed that crooked smile that always got him out of trouble with her. "I still intend to give my brother a piece of my mind. What we all had together has been over for a while, and that's mainly because of his feelings for you."

"I'm happy for you, Jason. I was afraid you'd be alone, and I don't want that, and I'm sure Jeff doesn't either. When he gets past this – whatever it is – he'll tell you so. I know it."

"You are the eternal optimist, Megan, and I love you for it. Sometimes, I wish things could have worked out between you and me, but I'm grateful for the time we had together. You know I love you, don't you?"

"I know. I love you too, but it's different with Jeff."

"I know. Look, there's something I've been meaning to say – ever since that night you came to the training room after Jeff blew out his elbow."

"You don't have to say anything. I understand."

"No, I don't think you do. We both handled the situation the wrong way. You had every right to be there, not as our friend the nurse, but as Jeff's girlfriend. If I'd had any sense, I wouldn't have said anything and the trainer would have walked in on that kiss. Maybe if he had…"

"It wouldn't have changed anything, Jason. Whatever has gotten into Jeff, it happened after that night. He was hurting then, and yes, probably taking his cues from you in order to protect me. I admit it hurt at the time, but I'm over it."

"I'm sorry. Hell, I've wanted to claim you as ours lots of times, but that wouldn't have done any of us any good. Now that Jeff has you all to himself, I don't know what the problem is. I know he loves you."

"I thought he did." Megan straightened and waved her hand as if to sweep the table clean. "Enough. How did this conversation get back to Jeff and me anyway?" She stood and crumpled her napkin into a ball and picked up her coffee mug. "I've got to get back to work, and I'm sure you have plenty to do. I'll see you at home, right?"

"I'll be there."

❦❦

Jeff was right where he was when Jason had left, only now he looked even worse than he had this morning. Jason didn't want to calculate how much his brother had drunk that day, or how little he had eaten. He promised Megan to stay out of their relationship, but he hadn't promised anything in regards to Jeff's career, and he wasn't going to sit by and watch his brother drown it in bourbon, no matter how nicely aged it was.

Jason took a deep breath and stepped between Jeff and the mock courtroom reality show on the flat screen. "How's it goin'?"

"It's fucking peachy, can't you tell?" Jeff waved his arm in a giant arc. "Move. You're in my way."

"I'm not going anywhere." Jason fished around behind the television until he found the power cord and yanked it from the socket. The screen went black.

"Son-of-a-bitch! Turn that back on." Jeff lumbered to his feet. It didn't take more than a nudge to send him sprawling back into his recliner.

"No. I've had enough of this shit, and so have you. I spent the last couple of hours sitting in the hospital with a kid who had the same kind of surgery I had. I remembered my brother spending time with me, telling me stories about how we were going to be famous baseball players. He made me believe it was possible. I hung onto those stories when I hurt so damned bad I thought dying would be easier. I hung on, and I worked my ass off to make those stories come true. And you know what?" He didn't pause for Jeff to answer. "They came true. My brother worked just as hard, and he's the best damned relief pitcher in the Major League. And I'm not going to sit by and watch him throw it all away."

"Then go somewhere else."

"What the hell is wrong with you? If you won't get out of that chair for your career, then what about Megan?" The hell with his promise. He was tired of pulling his punches. Jeff needed someone to knock some sense into him, and Jason was in the mood to do it. "She loves you, you bastard, and you're treating her like shit."

"She doesn't love me. She loved my career, and when that was gone, she didn't waste any time at all throwing herself at you. One brother is as good as another."

"Why, you slimy bastard!" Jason ground out the insult through clenched teeth. "Don't you dare throw our past relationship in my face now. And you know Megan doesn't give a shit whether you play baseball or sell shoes. She loves you."

"No she doesn't. I saw her throwing herself at you. I saw you kissing her. You want her? You can have her. Now plug the TV back in and get the hell out of my way."

"I don't know what the hell you are talking about. I haven't been with Megan in months."

"I've got eyes. She was all over you at the hospital. I saw it all. You kissed her."

An image formed in his mind. Megan looking fragile and worried. She'd come straight to the hospital to see Jeff, carrying the weight of a shitty day on her shoulders. He'd held her and offered her comfort. She'd broken the kiss almost immediately. "Shit, Jeff. You saw that?"

"Hell yes, I saw that. Don't worry. She's all yours."

"Like hell she is. Is that kiss what this is all about? Is that why you're acting like an ass? Because if it is, you've got it all wrong."

"Wrong? What part did I get wrong? The part where I fucked her that morning, and then she ran to you that afternoon? Did you fuck her in the hall? No, you'd take her some place classy like a maintenance closet. You're that kind of a guy."

Jason jerked in Jeff's direction with every intention of beating some sense into his brother. Maybe it was the alcohol talking, but all alcohol did was remove a person's filters. An angry feminine voice stopped him.

"Jason didn't fuck me," Megan said from the doorway. God, how long had she been standing there? "He held me up when I could hardly stand. Yes, he kissed me, but it was instinct, not lust." She stepped further into the room as she spoke. "I was worried sick about you, you idiot, and on top of that, we'd lost a patient earlier that day — the third one that week. I needed someone to talk to. Jason listened. That's all he did."

"Megan," Jason warned.

"Don't." She stepped between the brothers. "You're an ass, Jeff Holder. I can't believe you thought I thought more of your career than I do of you. I'd love you if you drove a trash truck, and if that's what you want to do for the rest of your life, I'm okay with that. But I'm not okay with you sitting around feeling sorry for yourself, and I'm so not okay with you doubting my feelings for you."

She picked up the almost empty liquor bottle, shaking her head. "Can you leave us alone for a few minutes?" she asked Jason.

"I don't think that's a good idea. He's a mean drunk."

"I'll be fine. He might hurt me with his words, but he'd never do anything more than that."

Jason left her alone with Jeff, but if she knew him, he wasn't far away. Her heart warmed to know he would always be there for her, like a brother. She wondered at the course of their relationship as she pulled the ottoman from the corner and sat at Jeff's feet. This close, Jason would have to have bat hearing to eavesdrop on their conversation. As much as she loved Jason, this was between her and Jeff.

She leaned in and lowered her voice. "Is this what you've been stewing over? The kiss you saw?"

"What was I supposed to think?"

"Oh, Jeff." She shook her head. "Why didn't you say something?"

"I don't know. I..." He looked like a petulant little boy, holding his injured arm against his chest, his hair a disheveled mess. Only the two days growth of beard on his jaw hinted at the full-grown man he was. As mad as she was at him for having so little faith in her love, she couldn't help but feel sorry for him.

"You should have known there was an explanation. Did you really think I would go from your bed in the morning, to Jason's that night?" She held up a hand to forestall any response. "No. Don't answer that. Not too long ago that would have been something you could have expected, but now?" She shook her head. "I don't know, Jeff. I don't know what to say that will convince you that I love you – that I want only you. Jason is a friend. He's always been a friend, and I can't change what happened between us in the past. I'm afraid it will always be between us, so I'm leaving." Megan straightened her spine, rubbing her wet palms on her pant legs as the words left her lips. She hadn't planned on saying that, but she knew it was the right thing to do.

She stood and stared down at the crumpled man in the recliner. There was no indication anything she'd said had made a difference. "I'll go to a hotel tonight, and I'll send someone for my things this weekend." Jeff remained still, his eyes focused on the blank TV screen. "I love you."

CHAPTER NINETEEN

Megan slid her arm into the sleeve of her jacket and adjusted the collar with one hand while she dug in the opposite pocket for her car keys, all the while listening to another nurse complain about working the night shift. The morning sun reflected off the polished marble entryway, nearly blinding her with its brilliance. For two weeks, ever since she'd walked out of Jeff and Jason's house, she'd lived the life of a mole – sleeping during the day and working at night. It was an exhausting schedule, but it had its merits. Especially when sleep didn't come easily. There was something about staying awake all night that made it easier to sleep. The unnatural sleep pattern was enough to allow her body to crash into a deep sleep, even on a brightly lit autumn day. Like this one. Megan stopped to pull on her gloves, saying her goodbyes as the group of nurses and staff went their separate ways.

She raised a hand to her forehead against the glare as the automatic glass doors slid open. A blast of cold, crisp air swirled around her legs, chilling her to the bone beneath the lightweight scrubs. She came up short in the shadow of the building as an all too familiar form came into view.

Jeff rose from the brick planter where he'd been waiting for her. "Hi, Megan."

"What are you doing here?" Damn. For the first week after she left she looked for Jeff everywhere she went, hoping against hope that he'd come looking for her. In the last seven days, she'd quit looking around for him, but as he smiled at her, and her name rolled off his tongue, she knew she hadn't quit hoping. Now, here he was, looking too good for words, and she didn't know if she were happy to see him or not.

"Have a cup of coffee with me?" The early November wind stirred a few errant leaves, and teased the ends of her ponytail. A few strands whipped across her face and she pushed them out of the way with gloved fingers. Her hand trembled, and it had nothing to do with the frigid temperature.

"Why?"

"I'd like to talk to you. I owe you an apology."

Megan shivered and clutched the lapels of her jacket tighter. God, he looked good. His cheeks and nose were red, but it was a result of sitting outside in the cold, rather than from drinking. His eyes were clear, and his overall complexion looked healthy.

"How's the arm?"

"Better." He held his right arm close to his body, and Megan assumed it was still in a brace by the sharp angle at his elbow. "Can we go somewhere and talk? I'll tell you everything, and answer your questions if we can get out of this damned cold."

The question was did she really want to hear anything Jeff Holder had to say. He'd hurt her. The fact remained that he hadn't believed in her love. How long had that been going on? She'd given him everything – her heart and her body, and she'd done it believing he loved her as much as she loved him. Finding out that he never understood – that he thought she was only with him because of who he was hurt the most. "Did you drive here?"

"Yeah, I did. I'm sober, I promise." He held his left hand up in a scout salute. "I can't drive the 'Vette or the Mustang, but I can manage the Escalade with my left hand."

She called herself every kind of idiot for agreeing to meet him at the coffee shop a few miles away. It was morning rush hour, and as she searched for a parking place, she realized the place would be filled with people desperate for their morning jolt of caffeine. They'd have very little privacy, even if they could find a table. Maybe that was a good thing.

She circled the parking lot twice before she found a parking place. As she gathered her purse, she saw Jeff's car in her rearview mirror as he cruised the lot too. She clutched her coat tight and sprinted for the door. A familiar deep voice told her Jeff had caught up with her. "Damn, it's cold out there."

The line moved quickly, and it wasn't long before they sat across from each other at a small table. Megan pried the lid off her cup and blew across the steaming liquid before taking a tentative sip. Jeff sat silent, spinning his cup on the tabletop. "You're using your right hand," she said.

"Yeah. It's getting better every day. I'm back in physical therapy."

"That's good."

"Look, Megan...I owe you an apology. I said some things that were wrong, and I'm sorry."

"You accused Jason and me of things that weren't true."

"I know that. I knew it then too, but I was so messed up I couldn't stop the words from coming out of my mouth."

"Jeff – "

"No. Please. Let me say what I came to say. I don't expect you to forgive me, but I owe you an explanation."

"Okay. Go ahead. I'm listening." She fisted her trembling hands in her lap.

"I want you to know that I love you. I have for a long time, but somehow I got it in my head that you were in love with Jason. I know it doesn't make any sense, but none of this really makes any sense. Anyway, I thought I'd lost you, and then there was Martin McCree, and I focused on him, obsessing about striking him out instead of focusing on what was really important – you. I pushed too hard, trying to figure out a way to best McCree – a new pitch, a variation on another, anything that would get him out. Jason tried to make me see reason, but I wouldn't, couldn't, back down. I don't know what got into me. I'm competitive by nature, but this went way beyond normal competition. I was obsessed. I couldn't see it then. Doyle even called me into his office to talk about it. Shit, Megan. I thought he was going to tell me I was on the trading block. As scared as I was, thinking how close I'd come to getting my ass traded, I still kept on pushing myself. It was stupid.

"Jason had quit joining us by then, but I was too deep into my obsession with McCree to notice. I don't know what I thought, how I imagined he was spending time with you. Looking back, I can see he wasn't home much.

"Then you and I had that amazing night together, and I began to hope again. I thought we had something special. I thought everything I'd believed about Jason and you was wrong. I was sure you loved me, and I was planning to ask you to marry me when the season was over."

Megan's heart did a somersault in her ribcage. Two weeks ago, she would have given anything to hear him say those words, but now they scared the hell out of her. Was he going to ask her to come back? And if he did, would she go? She forced herself to remain calm. "So what went wrong? What happened, Jeff, to make you say those things?"

"Insanity?" The way he delivered the remark told her he didn't intend it as a joke. "I don't know, Megan. I don't have an excuse. All I have is the truth. I was scared. Scared of losing you, then I dug myself in too deep with the McCree thing. I went into that last game thinking about you, but when it got down to the end, and the last man standing between the Mustangs and the playoffs was McCree, I couldn't back down. Lord knows, Jason tried to talk me out of it, but I was too stubborn to listen. Anyway, I did this to myself. That much I do know. I pushed my arm to the limit with the extra pitching sessions, and trying to learn a curve ball. I never could hit the broad side of a barn with a curve ball. I don't know why I thought it would be different now. Anyway, it all took its toll. When it got down to that one moment and it was just me and Martin…I don't know. It was like the O.K. Corral or something. I didn't have anything but the one gun, and I made up my mind to go after him with everything I had in me. My average pitch is usually ninety-seven, ninety-eight miles an hour. Martin had been sending those into orbit all season, so I knew I had to do better than that. I threw him six pitches, Megan. Not a one was less than a hundred miles per hour. Jason said the one that blew out my elbow was a hundred and four. It's not a league record, but it's damned close."

"You sent the Mustangs to the playoffs."

"Fat lot of good it did. They lost in the first round, which makes my actions that much more insane."

"It's not your fault the team didn't do better. You gave them a chance, that's all you could do."

"Maybe. But that's another discussion. Most of those two days after I blew out my elbow are a blur. One minute I was pitching to McCree, and the next I was waking up in the hospital. Or so it seems. It happened fast. I remember kissing you after the game. My arm hurt like a son-of-a-gun, I remember that too. I also remember the look on your face when Jason introduced you to Rand as our friend. I'm sorry, Megan. I wanted to tell the world right then that you were my fiancée, but I hadn't asked you, and that wasn't the time to spring something like that on you. Everything happened so fast after that. I don't know who made the decision to have the surgery. I guess I agreed to it, but I don't remember doing it. My career was in the toilet, and my arm hurt, and shit...." He waved his hand in a sweeping motion. "That's neither here nor there. I woke up in the hospital after the surgery and I heard your voice. You sounded like an angel and all I wanted was for you to come take me out of that place. I looked around and found you out in the hall with Jason. Christ, Megan. He was kissing you. That image was burned onto my brain, and something snapped. I don't know if it was the drugs, the anesthesia, or what, but I couldn't get out of there fast enough. All I could think about was that I'd lost you and my career in one fell, fucked up swoop."

"Why didn't you say something?"

"I don't know." The pain in his voice almost had her feeling sorry for him, but she wasn't ready to let him off the hook for what he'd said.

"I stand by what I said. You're an ass, Jeff Holder."

His crooked smile was sincere and disarming. "Yeah, I know. Responsibility for everything that happened lands squarely on my shoulders. I made the choices, and I've got to live with the consequences. I can't tell you how sorry I am. The day you left, I said some particularly nasty things. I had no right to think them, much less say them. I was drinking too much, and feeling sorry for myself. It's not an excuse; it's just the truth. After you left, Jason sobered me up. At first I thought he was being a good brother, but I found out he had another motive. He said he wanted to make sure I heard and understood every word he said. Trust me, my brother knows quite a few choice ones."

"You fought with Jason?"

"No. Not exactly. He called me a bunch of names, all ugly, and they all fit. He also set me straight about you and him. I had no reason to believe the things I did. It seems my imagination is better than I ever knew."

"What do you want from me?"

"I don't have any right to ask anything from you, but I'd like for you to give me, give us, another chance."

"I don't know, Jeff. I…" Megan clenched her fists tight to keep her hands from shaking.

"Please. Don't answer yet. Think about it. I'll give you all the time you need. I'm trying to get my life back together. I started the physical therapy. I'm behind, but Stacey thinks I can make up for the time I lost. We had a meeting – Doyle, Stacey and me. He said he'd put me on the roster after the All Star break if I could prove to him I'm ready. I'll be ready."

"You aren't pushing too hard, are you?"

"No. I've learned my lesson in that regard. Stacey is working me hard, but she says it won't take too long to catch up to where I should be." He flexed the fingers of his right hand. "It's a lot better already. I can dress myself now, zippers and all." He smiled at that. "No more sweat pants."

"That's good. I wish you all the luck. I know how much baseball means to you."

"I used to think it was my life, but that was before you walked away. That was a real wake-up call for me. I realized the game doesn't mean as much to me as I once thought. You're all that matters, Megan. I want a life with you. I want the whole thing. A home. Kids."

Megan didn't know what to say. This was her dream, but it was two weeks too late, the two longest weeks of her life.

"Just promise me you'll think about it."

"I…I will." Like she'd be able to think of anything else. "I can't promise you anything, Jeff. The things you said about Jason and me…" she shook her head, "they got me to thinking. As much as I love you, I don't know if we can get past what happened between the three of us."

"I want to try, Megan. I don't think you ever had the same kind of feelings for Jason that you did for me. Am I wrong about that?"

"No. I love Jason, but it's a different kind of love. I never would have done the things we did if I hadn't had strong feelings for him, but it was always just a physical thing between him and me. I'm not sure how you could ever get those times out of your head. I'd always be worried that you'd misinterpret something else, and I'd be caught in the middle again. I can't live like that."

"I wouldn't ask you to." He glanced at his watch. "I've got to go. Stacey is a tyrant, and she punishes me if I'm late for my sessions." He rose and moved to stand beside her chair. "Thanks for meeting me." Megan turned her face up, and Jeff bent. He cupped her cheek in his good hand, bent and placed a gentle kiss on her forehead. "I love you. Call me."

She ran her conversation with Jeff over and over in her mind as she drove to her friend Karen's house where she'd been crashing in her spare bedroom for the last two weeks. A part of her wanted to grab the phone and call him right then, or better yet, turn the car around and go to him, but mostly that was her body talking. She still wanted him, craved his touch, but her rational side argued for caution. He said he would give her time, and she would be wise to take it.

Megan slipped between the sheets. She'd never been more exhausted in her life. Not even the extra coffee she'd had on the drive home, or the sunlight peeking through the blinds could keep her awake.

⅋⅋

Two days later, a familiar figure waited for her as she left the hospital. "I thought you said you would give me time."

"I did say that. I was hoping you would let me buy you breakfast. I think we need to get to know each other. I know we've lived together for a while, but things have changed. I want to see if we can build a new relationship – just you and me."

"And breakfast will do that?"

"It's a place to start."

For the next few months,she never knew when Jeff would be waiting for her. He managed to drop by several times a week. He never asked for more than to spend time with her, and she was grateful because she was terribly afraid all he had to do was crook his finger and she'd fall into his arms.

Jeff was working hard to get back into playing form. He'd gained full mobility in his elbow, even though he still wore a brace. Training the transplanted tendon to act as a ligament took time, and persistence. He complained about the way Stacey pushed him, but beneath the complaints was a grudging respect for her professional abilities.

The holidays came and went. Jeff and Jason invited their family to visit so Jeff wouldn't have to miss his physical therapy. Megan declined an invitation to join them, opting to work extra shifts so the other nurses could spend time with their families. It was a glimpse into her future – if she couldn't find her way to accept what Jeff was offering. She knew in her heart that there would never be anyone else for her.

CHAPTER TWENTY

Jason left for the Mustangs' Spring Training facility in Arizona, and Jeff was alone. Nearly five months post-op and his arm was healed, but he was still a long way from being ready to pitch. He was still doing the plyometric exercises, but now Stacey had added weight training to strengthen his arm in hopes of preventing a recurrence of the injury. It was tedious and frustrating. He'd recently been given the go-ahead to start throwing again. It wasn't pitching, but it involved holding a baseball, and that fueled his ambition to keep going.

Used to being part of the team, he missed the camaraderie of his teammates. He missed Jason. And most of all, he missed Megan. As each day passed, he regretted more and more his promise to let her have all the time she needed. He hadn't pushed for a physical relationship, transferring his physical needs into countless hours in the gym, and running. He'd run more miles in the last few months than he'd driven, and that was about the saddest statement of fact he'd ever heard. It was time to at least let Megan know how he felt. With a little luck, she'd have similar feelings.

He chose his time wisely. Megan had two days off in a row. He called the day before and told her he was too tired to come into town, but maybe she could come out to the house the next day. He'd throw some steaks on the grill and they could spend some time in the pool. She hesitated, but eventually agreed to his plan. It would be the first time she'd been back to his house since the day she left, and if he played his cards right, she might stay both days. His hands itched to touch her again.

✎✐✎

Megan took a deep breath and steered her car under the portico only visitors used. Jeff waited for her on the doorstep, looking as good as ever. He no longer wore the protective brace on his elbow, and the surgical scars were nothing more than thin pink lines that would eventually fade completely. From the smile on his face, no one would guess what he'd been through, or sense the anxiety she knew he still harbored about getting back into the game.

He opened the car door before she'd cut the engine off. "God, I'm glad to see you." She went into his open arms. "I've missed you."

"It's only been a few days, Jeff."

"Maybe, but it's been forever since you were here. It's good to have you home."

Megan stiffened and he let her go. She grabbed her purse and followed him into the house. "This isn't my home anymore."

"It could be."

Megan accepted the bottled water Jeff took from the fridge. "I don't know if I'm ready for that, and I don't know if you are either. Jason still lives here."

"Why don't we sit down?" She followed him into the den. Nothing had changed. It was still a man-cave, and tidier than she expected.

"You must have hired a housekeeper," she said as she settled into Jason's favorite recliner.

"We did. That's one of the things I wanted to talk to you about. Until you left, we didn't comprehend all the things you did for us. I want to apologize for that. We took advantage of you, in more ways than one." Megan didn't miss the veiled reference to their sexual relationship. They hadn't spoken about it in months. Perhaps it was time.

"No you didn't. Everything I did, I did because I wanted to. That includes having sex with Jason – alone, and with you."

"I understand that now. I know we can't go back and change things, but I would like to make a fresh start – to give it – to give *us* another chance."

"I won't lie to you, Jeff. Jason is more to me than just someone I once slept with. He always will be, but I don't want a repeat. From the first moment I met you, I wanted to be with you. I never would have slept with Jason if you hadn't initiated it. I'm not going to say I didn't enjoy the things we did together. I did. Very much. But it was always you that I felt a connection with, not Jason."

"I think I can live with that. I didn't know what it was to love someone the way I love you. Jason and I have always shared a connection, but as you well know, we're different people. More so as we get older. It's time for us to grow up, and I think we are."

"Growing up doesn't mean you have to grow apart. I'd hate to think I came between you."

"It's not you, Megan. It's us. We're alike, but we need different things. I need you."

"And Jason doesn't."

"No, Jason doesn't. If he did, he'd fight for you, but he's not. He loves you, but he doesn't need you to make his life complete. I can't imagine being with anyone else, Megan. I don't want to be with anyone else."

The wall she'd spent so long building around her heart began to weaken. She was hopelessly in love with Jeff, and the sincerity in his voice told her how far he'd come in understanding his relationship with his brother, and more importantly, the relationship between the three of them.

"I know I told you I'd give you all the time you needed, that I wouldn't pressure you for more than you're willing to give, but…I'm dying here, Megan. I need you so bad it hurts."

Desire and need made a powerful aphrodisiac, but a lingering doubt made Megan hesitate long enough to alert Jeff. He jumped to his feet and paced away from her. When he turned to her, the devastation etched on his face shattered all her doubts. "Megan…" he raked his fingers through his hair like he always did when he was frustrated.

"Jeff…Don't." In a second, Megan was in his arms. "I'm sorry. I didn't mean for you to think I don't want you. I do. More than anything." His erection rode against her stomach, and she thought she might die if he wasn't inside her soon. It had been way too long since she'd felt that connection, and suddenly, she couldn't think of a single reason to deny her needs. "Take me to bed, Jeff."

His kiss weakened every ligament in her body. It was tender, yet a sense of urgency under laid it. Megan threaded her arms around his neck and pressed as much of herself against his hard body as she could. He coaxed her lips apart and his tongue plunged inside, heating her blood to the boiling point and igniting a hunger she'd thought safely banked. Desperate now to feel his skin on hers, she slipped her hands to his waist and tugged his crisp button-down shirt free of his jeans. As soon as her fingers touched Jeff's heated flesh, he broke the kiss and pushed her away.

Stunned, Megan protested the sudden halt, then Jeff grabbed his shirt by the back and yanked it over his head. She thought she heard a button or two pop, but couldn't muster a care for the state of his shirt when he stood before her bare-chested. As he worked the button on his jeans Megan placed a hand on his breastbone. His heart beat steady beneath her hand and all that warm satin skin.

"Clothes." Jeff's voice broke into her lust coma. "Off. Now."

It was an order she was all too willing to comply with. She was grateful for the oversized sweater and leggings she'd chosen to wear. No buttons. No zippers. In a flash of need, she stood naked except for a scrap of lace covering her mound, and a soft but serviceable bra. Jeff's appreciative smile and heated gaze, not to mention his rampant erection, would have banished any doubts, if she could have found one.

"Jesus, Megan."

"Protection?" she asked in a brief moment of sanity.

"Don't need it. Haven't been with anyone else. You?"

She was absurdly happy to hear his admission of fidelity. In the months since they'd been apart, she'd wondered if he had found release in someone else's arms. Knowing he hadn't cemented her decision. "No."

Before the syllable left her lips, Jeff's arms banded around her, binding her to him, surrounding her with his strength. Her breasts flattened against his chest. Barefoot, the top of her head barely cleared his shoulder. She placed a soft kiss to his pectoral, and he tightened his hold.

"I don't know if I can make this last."

"We have all day," she said. *Forever*. Megan refused to think about the possibility. Now was enough. Wasn't it?

They came together on the plush rug in the center of the room like a summer storm in the dead of winter. Hot. Fast. Furious. Jeff parted her thighs, sinking his shaft into her with enough strength to force a gasp from her lips. He braced himself above her to keep from crushing her into the rug and set a frenzied pace. Megan arched her hips to meet his, stroke for stroke. It felt so good to have him inside her again, filling her, completing her. He was magnificent above her. The powerful muscles in his shoulders flexed with each thrust. Megan trailed her hands over his shoulders, and down. When her fingers found the scar on the inside of his right elbow, she tensed.

"Oh God, Jeff. Your elbow."

"No problem." He collapsed to the side and pulled her with him. Megan found herself staring down into Jeff's eyes. "You ride for a while."

It took a few tries to find her rhythm, but with Jeff's hands guiding her hips, she soon picked up a smooth, easy pace. This was so much better. She could take all of him this way, and Jeff's hands were free to roam. He took advantage of the position, caressing and teasing every inch of skin he could reach, and he could reach all of them. She ground her clit against his pelvic bone, and he hissed a curse.

"You're killing me," he complained in a gruff voice that conveyed his willingness to die this way.

Her body screamed for her to end it, but her brain, drugged on endorphins, urged her to take it easy, to make it last as long as possible. Ultimately, Jeff took the decision from her, grabbing her hips to steady her as he bucked beneath her. One thumb slid between them to find her magic button, and she flew. Jeff gripped her hips hard, and thrust into her one more time before he joined her. His cock pulsed deep inside her, like a second heart that beat in tandem with her own.

Megan crumpled in a boneless, gasping heap. Jeff's body felt like a buoy in a storm. She closed her eyes and clung to him, unwilling to lose the connection again so soon. How had she ever thought she could live without this, without him?

The room was silent but for their breathing and in the distance, the faint ticking of the grandfather clock in the entryway. Megan drifted on the edge of sleep.

"They're sending me to Oklahoma City next week."

What? Megan shifted and the connection broke as Jeff's softened penis slipped from her. "What did you say?" She rolled to her side and rose up on one elbow to look at his face.

"I have to go to Oklahoma City next week. I need to start throwing, but I can't take anyone away from the Mustangs to throw with me, so they're sending me there. There's a triple A team there. I'll work with them until I'm ready to come back to the Mustangs."

Megan' s heart dropped like a stone. She rolled to her back and stared at the ceiling. He was leaving. She felt numb all over. By her calculations, he'd be gone five, maybe six months.

"Come with me, Megan."

"I can't…"

"Take vacation…a leave of absence…quit."

Could she? "Why? Why should I, Jeff?"

His hand found hers and he threaded their fingers together. "Because I'll be there. And because I don't think I can do this without you. Come with me. Please."

"You don't need me." She almost choked on the words. Had he asked her here today to seduce her into going with him? Was he that lost without Jason?

"You're wrong. I do need you, but more than that, I want you to be there. We'll have time to be together, just you and me. No hiding. I'll get you your own apartment if you want, but I'd rather have you live with me, as my girlfriend."

Hope began a slow build. What would it be like to live with Jeff – all alone – away from everything and everyone? It would give them a chance to see if what they had was real, if they could put their relationship with Jason behind them, if they could build something on their own. "Where do you think it this would go? I mean, I guess I want to know what would happen when you come back to the Mustangs? What would happen to us then? What if you can't come back?"

Jeff rolled and stretched out half over her. She had no choice but to look at him as he spoke. "I'll come back." Conviction laced his voice. "Rehab is going fine, better than fine. I'm ahead of schedule." His tone grew lighter. "We may have to get creative with our positions for a while yet," his grin told her he didn't have a problem with that. "What will happen to us? I don't know. I don't want to hide you. Not ever again." His hand stroked along her ribcage, past the indentation at her waist and over the swell of her hip. "I'll tell you what I'd like to happen though. I'd like to for you to agree to be my wife. We could give this a try, and if you think we can make it work, we could get married over the All Star break – right before I come back."

"Jeff…" tears blocked her throat, making it impossible to say more.

"I love you, Megan. Say you'll come with me, that you'll give us a chance, that you'll marry me." His lips brushed hers in a soft caress that went straight to her heart. "You don't have to answer the marriage part yet. I'll wait for you to make up your mind."

Oh God! Megan tried to speak, but her throat was clogged with emotion, and Jeff's hand was moving again, exploring places that took her breath away. Maybe if he stopped touching her she could answer him. Her mind screamed 'yes', over and over, but the word wouldn't pass her lips.

"I'll worship your body every day." His lips grazed her breast, giving expert testimony as to his ability to fulfill the promise.

"I'll claim you as mine, every day." His fingers slipped between her swollen folds, then claimed her. Promise fulfilled.

"I'll give you my heart, every day." He settled between her legs and gave her his heart in one slow, deep stroke. Promise fulfilled.

"Ah, Christ, Megan." He stilled, buried to the hilt inside her. "The only inside heat I need, is yours. Say yes."

"Yes."

ABOUT THE AUTHOR

Award winning author Roz Lee has penned over a dozen erotic romances. The first, The Lust Boat, was born of an idea acquired while on a Caribbean cruise with her family, and soon blossomed into a five book series published by Red Sage. Following her love of baseball, she turned her attention to sexy athletes in tight pants, writing the critically acclaimed Mustangs Baseball series.

Roz has been married to her best friend, and high school sweetheart, for over three decades. Roz and her husband have two grown daughters (and a new Son-in-law) they couldn't be more proud of. They are currently raising a thirteen-year-old Labrador Retriever, Betty Boop, who isn't aware of her canine heritage.

Even though Roz has lived on both coasts, her heart lies in between, in Texas. A Texan by birth, she can trace her family back to the Republic of Texas. With roots that deep, she says, "You can't ever really leave."

When Roz isn't writing, she's reading, or traipsing around the country on one adventure or another. No trip is too small, no tourist trap too cheesy, and no road unworthy of travel.

www.RozLee.net

OTHER TITLES BY ROZ LEE

Mustangs Baseball Series
Going Deep
Bases Loaded
Switch Hitter
Free Agent
Seasoned Veteran

Lothario Series
The Lust Boat
Show Me the Ropes
Love Me Twice
Four of Hearts
Under the Covers

Also:
Sweet Carolina
Still Taking Chances
Making It on Broadway
The Middlethorpe Chronicles

Made in the USA
Charleston, SC
29 June 2014